FIVE POTATOES

One Potato
Two Potato
Three Potato
Four
Five Potato
Six Potato
Seven Potato
More
Eight Potato
Nine Potato
Ten Potato
Eleven
Twelve Potato
Thirteen Potato
Fourteen Potato
Heaven

FIVE POTATOES

THINGS ARE AS CLEAR AS VICHYSSOISE.

HUMOR, HUBRIS, HUMILITY AND ONE HUMAN'S
HUGE HALLUCINATIONS FROM UN HOMME DE TERRE!

WILLISTON LAMAR

Copyright © 2005 by Williston Lamar.

Library of Congress Number: 2005902048
ISBN: Hardcover   1-4134-8922-2
           Softcover   1-4134-8921-4

All rights reserved. No part of this book may be reproduced or transmitted in any form or by any means, electronic or mechanical, including photocopying, recording, or by any information storage and retrieval system, without permission in writing from the copyright owner.

This book was printed in the United States of America.

To order additional copies of this book, contact:
Xlibris Corporation
1-888-795-4274
www.Xlibris.com
Orders@Xlibris.com
28379

CONTENTS

INTRODUCTION 15

ONE POTATO: THE BEDROOM

THE 22-YEAR-OLD GUY! 19
MY WIFE THINKS MY IDEA OF FOREPLAY IS
   TO TELL HER I TOOK A VIAGRA AN HOUR
   AGO! OF COURSE, SHE'S RIGHT! 22
SURVEY SAYS! "LIE!" 24
THE DESIRE PILL 26
JEWELRY SUCKS! 27
SWING! (DANCING) 29
FOUR-DAY LIMIT! 30
SO WHAT DID THE DOCTOR SAY? HE SAID I
   SHOULD HAVE SEX FOUR TIMES A DAY! 31
WHAT IS VICTORIA'S SECRET? 33
SAT SCORES 34
CAUGHT ME! DAMN IT! OF COURSE I WAS
   LOOKING AT HER ASS AND HER BOOBS! 35
GREAT SEX IN GREAT HOTELS! 36
EVEN MY FEMALE DOG WHINES! 40
DAYS OF WINE AND CONDOMS! 41
RIP VAN WINKLE WAS NO DUMMY! 43
THE GERMANS WORE GRAY,
   YOU WORE BUTT FLOSS! 45
BACKRUBS! 46

TWO POTATO: THE KITCHEN, DINING AND EATING OUT

SEVENTY-THREE YEARS OF NOT EATING WHAT YOU WANT!..................... 49
FRIES AND A COKE 51
THE PURSE 52
THE GOURMET HEADACHE 54
DISHES 56
DANGER: HIGH VOLTAGE! 60
CULINARY HAPPINESS 62
THE KIDS ARE FINE, BUT DID I TELL YOU ABOUT THE SCALLOPS? 63
GET THE WAITER! 65
FROU-FROU FOOD 67
WHERE'S THE BEEF? 69
OUR "WORLD FAMOUS" BUFFALO WINGS! 71
PAYING FOR THE EXPERIENCE 72
THE NEW DELHI DELI 75
MEN MUST DROP ICE CUBES! 77
CORPORAL PEPPER 78
I'M NOT GOING TO STOP LIVING BECAUSE I'M ON A DIET! SO SHUT UP, EVERYONE! 80

THREE POTATO: THE DEN

REMOTE-CONTROLLED CHEETOS 85
HIDDEN TALENTS 88
I HEAR AND OBEY 89
IT'S ONE THING! 91
LISTENING TO MOVIES 93
P.N.B.F.H. 95
I DIDN'T DO ANYTHING ALL DAY! 96
PART OF A MOVIE 100

WHAT ELSE DON'T YOU NEED THAT
   I CAN'T DO FOR YOU?............... 101
MOVIES ALL GUYS SHOULD WATCH
   (ACCORDING TO ME!)............... 103
STAIR MASTER............... 105
WHAT ELSE CAN BE SAID?
   ENOUGH ALREADY!............... 106
POST-FRAT HOUSE STYLE............... 108
GIVE ME COLLEGE FOOTBALL OR
   GIVE ME DEATH!............... 110
CLEANING FRENZY!
   EVERYBODY RUN FOR YOUR LIVES!............... 112

FOUR: THE WORKPLACE

HE'S THE GARDENER, NOT A HARVARD MBA!....... 117
SHE IS A GOOD PERSON, BUT 119
DON'T TELL ANYBODY, BUT 121
SPREADSHEETS............... 123
THE ANTI-INTELLECT............... 125
IF YOU PUT A BANANA IN YOUR BRIEFCASE,
   USE IT WISELY!............... 127
"YOU PEOPLE MAKE MY
   ASS TWITCH!"............... 128
WHY DON'T YOU CALL?............... 130
THE LEISURE SUIT............... 131
LET'S TALK RIGHT OVER THE
   MOST IMPORTANT POINT!............... 132
IT'S THE RESTROOM, STUPID!............... 135
REPLAY YOUR WHOLE DAY FOR ME, DEAR!........ 137
SOME WHO ARE NOT PAID WHAT THEY
   ARE WORTH OUGHT TO BE GLAD!............ 138
DADDY, WHERE DO INTERIOR
   DECORATORS COME FROM?............... 140
WORK SHOULD BE LIKE SCHOOL!............... 141

FIVE POTATO: GUESTS

MAKING FACES 145
STOP! DON'T TELL ME ANYTHING ABOUT
   OUR GUESTS! 147
THANK MY WIFE! SHE CALLED
   THE CATERER! 149
"THANK YOU FOR DOING THIS—ELLEN" 151
HAVE IT YOUR WAY! 152
MY WIFE LIKES TO GIVE ME THE FINGER! 155
FIVE POTATOES 157

SIX POTATO: TRAVEL

PARIS ON $10,000 A DAY! 161
"EVER RIDE THE WAVES IN OKLAHOMA?"
   A TRIBUTE TO ROUTE 66 162
STRAP ME IN! TAKE ME TO 35,000 FEET! 164
THE INTERNATIONAL SUPERSTUD OR
   I SHOULD HAVE BEEN A POLYGLOT! 167
CLUB DEAD 170
MENTAL MORONS MOVING ON PLANES! OR
   PLANE STUPID! 171
PRADA, PRADA, PRADA 175
SURVIVAL 178
A ROOM WITH A VIEW 179
HOTEL ROOMS YOU SHOULD KNOW! 180
OH SHENANDOAH! 181

SEVEN POTATO: THE CAR

TEMPERATURE CONTROL 185
ROAD TRIP! 187
SHE CAN'T SEE BEYOND THE HOOD OF HER
   CAR! OR, I WAS RIGHT IN FRONT OF HER
   BUT SHE STILL COULDN'T SEE ME! 189

THE SHAGUAR 191
IF SHE LOVES YOU FOR YOUR CAR, YOU
    PROBABLY DON'T WANT TO MARRY HER! 192
LIKE A ROCK! 194
PASSENGER SEAT DRIVING! 196
CRUISING THE GAP 197
OIL AND WOMEN DON'T MIX! 199
SELF-SERVICE 200
WHITE ASPHALT 201
DRIVING MR. LAMAR! 203
WHILE MY OLD CAR GENTLY WEEPS 205

MORE . . . SPUDS

DIE LAUGHING 213
ALL DRESSED UP! AS NUNS! 216
I WONDER WHAT THE POOR PEOPLE ARE
    DOING TODAY? 218
"WHEN ARE THEY GOING TO
    PLAY BASEBALL?" 220
I CAN'T REMEMBER THE BRILLIANT
    THOUGHT I HAD TWO SECONDS AGO! 222
DON'T CRY FOR ME BETHESDA 225
LATE-NIGHT RADIO 227
SHE LOVES THE DOGS MORE THAN ME! 229
"THE LAST TIME I SAW HIM, HE WAS
    HAVING A GOOD TIME!" (AL WARD) 231
THE OTHER SIDE OF THE AQUEDUCT 233

EIGHT POTATO: THE FAMILY

I WANT TO GO HOME! OR
    THERE'S NO PLACE LIKE HOME! 237
THINGS MY FATHER LOVED, LIKED, DISLIKED
    AND HATED: MAYBE YOURS DID TOO! 240
CONDESCENDING CELEBRITIES! 246

I'M ABLE TO SIT UP AND TAKE LIQUID
 NOURISHMENT!... 247
YOU'RE NOT GOING TO WEAR THAT,
 ARE YOU?... 250
WORLDS COLLIDE!... 252
MOM 254
TO MY DAUGHTER:
NO BOYS UNTIL YOU'RE 45!
TO MY MOTHER:
NO BOYS UNTIL YOU'RE 85!........................... 255
SWAN LAKE 256
WHAT!... 259

NINE POTATO: KIDS

GOD AND MAN, COGNAC AND CIGARETTES 263
POPSICLE STICKS 265
SUNDAY SYNDROME 266
SON OF A . . . GOLFER!.. 270
WOULD I LIKE HER? A STORY OF
 FATHER AND SON 273
SITTIN' IN THE RITZ!... 274
THIS IS YOUR DAY!.. 277
HEY MOM, I'VE GOT A BONE IN MY
 ICE CREAM! 279
MIDDAY IN THE SCULPTURE GARDEN OF
 GOOD KIDS AND EVIL HUMOR OR
 LEARNING FROM ART 281

TEN POTATO: JUST FOR GUYS

KILTS 287
ONE BERATING IS NOT ENOUGH! HURT ME!
 HURT ME! BEAT ME! BEAT ME! 288
TRIBUTE TO TOP GUN 289
SUNKEN GRAY HULLS OF STEEL 292

OF COURSE I WASN'T LISTENING! 294
THE MARTIANS ARE COMING! 295
THE MOST ROMANTIC SCENES IN THE MOVIES—
    MADE ESPECIALLY FOR YOU, DEAR! 296
DON'T GET MARRIED 'TIL YOU'VE SEEN
    THE TAJ MAHAL! 300
DEFINITION OF A NOUN 301
KEEP BREATHING! 303
I DON'T KNOW! 304

ELEVEN: JUST FOR WOMEN

THE FRECKLE PILL 309
JOHN HENRY NEWMAN—THE GENTLEMAN 310
SEVENTY-FIVE PERCENT OF ALL MEN LIVE
    THEIR LIVES BETWEEN THEIR LEGS! 311
SYLVIA PLATH AND THE SILVER BULLET
    MARTINI 313
BERMAN & BERMAN 316
BABY, YOU CAN RIDE MY BIKE! 317
NO MAN IS AN ISLAND 319
IN PRAISE OF GLASSES! 320
WOMEN I'D LIKE TO HAVE
    COCKTAILS WITH! 321

TWELVE POTATO: MONEY

THE LESS MONEY I HAVE, THE MORE
    CREATIVE I GET! 325
IF YOU DROPPED A BOWLING BALL INTO
    THE OCEAN, HOW LONG WOULD IT
    TAKE TO HIT THE BOTTOM? 328
NINETY-FIVE CENTS NOW VERSUS A
    DOLLAR LATER 329
EXACT CHANGE ONLY! 331
DEEP THROAT 333

THE $1 PURCHASE VALUE REDUCTION THEORY
  OF HOME ECONOMICS (PURVRT) 334
LESS IS MORE, MORE OR LESS! 336

THIRTEEN POTATO: POLITICS

MIDDLE-OF-THE-ROAD EXTREMIST OR
  RADICAL FENCE-SITTER: I'M NOT SURE! 341
WOMEN OF MASS DESTRUCTION 344
DIVORCE—THE OTHER REGIME CHANGE! 346
MUD BALLS 347
JUST SMILE! 349
SOCIALLY FISCAL 351
EVERYONE IN AMERICA HAS MULTIPLE
  COMMENTS AND COMEBACKS FOR
  WHATEVER YOU SAY! 352
IRONICALLY ENOUGH, I ONCE COOKED
  HOT DOGS FOR SPIRO AGNEW! 354

FOURTEEN POTATO: JUSTICE

SMART PEOPLE DON'T GO TO COURT 359
THE BAD GUYS DO WIN! GET OVER IT! 361
WHY ISN'T GONE WITH THE WIND GONE
  WITH THE WIND? 363
IT'S ALL BULLSHIT! (QUID DE UTILITATE
  LOQUAR STERCORANDI?) CICERO,
  DE SENECTUTE, XV, 54 364
THE JUSTICE OF JUSTIFICATION 366
THERE IS NO JUSTICE; THERE IS ONLY
  THE LAW! 368
I WAS MISINFORMED! 369

HEAVEN

I'VE ONLY SAVED ONE PERSON'S LIFE, BUT HE'S DONE WELL EVER SINCE!	373
WHO WERE THOSE DEAD GUYS?	375
THELMA & MEL	377
JUST SPREAD MY ASHES IN THE END ZONE NEXT TO THE STUDENT SECTION!	379
TO DIE IN AN ATTEMPT TO SWIM THE HELLESPONT!	381
I'VE NEVER WON A TROPHY!	383
PENNY'S IN HEAVEN	385
ARLINGTON	389
INSIDE THE COFFIN! WHAT ARE YOU GOING TO TAKE WITH YOU?	391

Introduction

We've observed and occasionally been reminded that things tend to come in threes. The Father, Son and Holy Ghost, plane crashes, hat tricks, book shelves, combo meals, tennis balls, Ocean Liners that sink (Titanic, Olympic, Britannic), six packs shared with a friend and cocktails before dinner. We are never reminded that things come in fives. It's an odd sort of number, isn't it? As complex and sometimes overwhelming as life has become, three just can't be enough of anything. It takes at least five points of view to begin to comprehend our environment, our relationships and the very nature of our fairly insignificant lives, and even then things are only as clear as vichyssoise.

This book is about many things. It's about family, travel, money, dining, working, living, politics, romance, driving, movies, books, sports, art, guy stuff and a whole bunch of other stuff. There are humorous accounts and serious thoughts, none of it meant to be any more than something my kids can read when I'm dead so at least they will know what I was thinking at one point in my life. Some of the focus is on men and women and their relationships. It is not another man vs. women book. In some instances, I'm just calling attention to the things we men usually keep to ourselves. But roles can just as easily be reversed.

I want to emphasize that this is not a biography of any kind! These are stories, not factual representations of my life. I would also like to make clear that the stories about husbands and wives are intended to be humorous exaggerations—not snapshots of my relationship with my own wife, for whom I have the deepest love, admiration, and respect.

This book is also a narrow view based on the limited experience of one person. It is not about you and your relationships. Nor does it dictate to you how to conduct your life or what you should do to "get better." This is not a book that should be found in the Self Help section of the bookstore, although there could be observations in which you see yourself, your partner, your friends or your family. Therein lies one of the secrets I have found to understanding and coping with life. Common observations by some people produce uncommon results in others. It's a kind of acknowledgement that the observation was wise enough to cause some action or at least laugh at! The exposure to these observations compels us to think and talk and reveal to each other our mostly irreversible idiosyncrasies, which hopefully leads to greater mutual appreciation. That's my hope for this book.

It should be noted that no focus groups participated in the research for this book. There was no research for this book! No surveys were conducted. No chat rooms were contacted. Only one website is quoted. No polls or network news stories are quoted. This book is written through observation, memory and opinion only. There are, however, quite a few references to movies and books. I like movies and books for stories they try to convey to us. We picture the situations in our minds and try to figure out what we might do within the circumstances they depict. *Five Potatoes* is like lots of movie shorts put together on one video. It is a story within a story. It has no beginning or end. Picture yourself or your family and friends in these situations. This is just fun stuff. Add to it in your own way. Discuss your variations. Let the conversation lead you to a greater richness of life. Think a whole lot and laugh a whole lot! Find joy!

Williston Lamar

ONE POTATO:
THE BEDROOM

THE 22-YEAR-OLD GUY!

Double standards are funny. But also really annoying!

My wife makes appointments and goes to special Pilates sessions. I guess that's ok. She wears a tight-fitting bikini-like exercise outfit underneath sweats or a warm-up outfit. She goes alone to a small storefront on a side street. The person behind the counter sends her down a hallway to a door. She goes in. A 22-year-old guy awaits her. He's built like a rock and is wearing tiny gym shorts and a tank top. There is one of those half-bed, half-table things in the middle of the room.

For the next hour this guy is going to touch almost every inch of my wife's body as he stretches, pulls, twists, tugs and massages her. He contorts her into all kinds of unusual shapes and positions. They are alone and the door is closed. As she puts her sweats back on over her tight spandex bikini-like exercise outfit, she slips him some cash, opens the door, and gives the person at the desk some more money; then she returns home.

"How was your massage, dear?" I ask as she comes in the door. "I told you, it's not a massage, it's Pilates," she answers. "Yeah, right!" I say under my breath. "How do you feel?" I ask. "Oh, I feel great! Relaxed and refreshed. God, that was good!" she expounds.

"Here's a glass of your favorite Merlot," I offer. She reaches for the glass and I ask, "So, since you are so relaxed, why don't we drink this wine and go upstairs and get naked?" "Oh no! I'm way too sore for that! I can hardly move. But the wine is nice. Thanks," she responds while not making eye contact.

I just walk away quietly, thinking about the 22-year-old guy, the little room, my wife and the 15 more sessions she is determined to complete. I'm determined to stay cool and ask no questions. Although I do wonder whether this guy is gay or straight. Maybe I'll save that question for after the 14th session. How much can this guy know at 22? He can't possibly carry on a decent conversation. He can't be well-traveled. What can he know about life? Well, maybe he's not talking in there!

Later that week I'm headed out the door in my sweats as my wife is coming in. "Where are you going?" she asks. "I'm going over to Helga's," I respond sheepishly. "What's that?" she inquires. "Oh, didn't I tell you? It's a new Swedish massage place for men." "You're doing what?" she asks incredulously. "You know, it's like your Pilates thing only for men. Well, gotta go, ya, ya, ya!"

Later that evening the wife asks, "How was your massage, dear?" "Oh, that wasn't just a massage, honey. They call it the Smorgasbord! It was the first in a long series of treatments. They put you in a little room and a beautiful Swedish girl comes in and does everything to your body! Well, you know what I mean. I feel great! I should do that more often! I think I'll continue the treatments."

Silence overtakes the room.

I start making a martini.

A few moments later my wife asks, "Hey, since you're feeling so good, why don't we go upstairs and get naked? You can show me what she did to you!"

"Uh, well, uh, OK!"

(Shhhh, there is no Helga's. But now I'm going every week to Home Depot!)

My Wife Thinks My Idea Of Foreplay Is To Tell Her I Took A Viagra An Hour Ago! Of Course, She's Right!

This story is all about the title. Could you tell? Actually, you could make up your own story to go with the title. It's really about how controlled substances control you. And Viagra is a great example.

Ok—you take the pill. The directions say 30 minutes to an hour and a half before it kicks in. Once it kicks in you think you have to use it. This thinking modifies your behavior. Gotta get going now if you know what I mean. Oops. A phone call interrupts. You forgot to get the cleaning and tomorrow is Sunday; the place will be closed. The mental clock is ticking. "Damn, I hate to waste this thing! These things are expensive," you think to yourself. "If we don't get around to it, I'll get one of those horrible headaches and that will ruin the rest of the evening." "Damn, I forgot to put the cars in the driveway." "Where is she?"

She's finishing some household stuff and looks a mess. She's going to want a shower and some wine and some tenderness. She's going to want to make it part of settling in for the evening. You'd like to have a drink and relax, but the alcohol might diminish the pill's effects and will slow you down and maybe put you out

Five Potatoes

for the evening. You know that afterwards you want to get back to your work in the garage.

Settle in? Cuddle? I don't think so! But your face is now flushed. It's time to get it on. If not, it might wear off! Geez, why can't we just wham bam thank you ma'am like we did years ago?

Alas, it's now or never. Waiting patiently for her to get out of the shower, you realize there is nothing much to do but lay there and hope she senses your urgency.

I guess just blurting out, "Hey dear, I took a Viagra an hour ago" really doesn't set the mood. On the other hand she's getting used to the idea that it's only gonna be 60 seconds' worth anyway and you've endured an hour of a controlling substance. So, get going. Get it over with and she can watch reruns of *Sex and the City* and dream about new shoes and you can finish up in the garage!

Survey Says! "Lie!"

Sex surveys are worthless! Think about it. Have you ever read a *Playboy* sex survey or any other magazine sex survey? Is anyone going to tell the truth in a sex survey? Of course not! Picture some 18-year-old college freshman guy on the phone with the survey-taker. "Have you had sex with two women at once?" the interviewer asks. "Uh, well, uh, yeah, I mean, yeah, uh sure, a couple of times!" he responds sheepishly. He can't possibly disappoint the interviewer. "How many partners have you had?" the interviewer asks. He can't say "none." He can't say "one." Even if it's true, he can't admit that. "Uh, gosh, uh, let me think about that." As if there are just enough he can't quite remember them all and he'll have to mentally sort of count them. "Uh, hmm, uh, let's see, uh, seven, no eight, uh well, just say nine." Think about the 18-year-old college freshman girl who did the whole football team in high school and is now after the basketball team at the University. What is she going to say in response to questions about her sex life? She's not going to say, "Gee, I'm a total slut and I go down for tree frogs!" But she might adjust her response to please the interviewer and say, "Well, uh, yes, uh, I've had some experience. But not that much, you know." Lies, exaggerations, false pride, phony bravado, shyness and fear of sounding too innocent or too guilty all play into our answers.

There is no truth when it comes to answering questions about sex! Therefore, there can be no accuracy in sex surveys. So why do we put so much stock in them? Sex surveys are all over every men's and every women's magazine. We can't escape them! The results are part of news programs, documentaries and reality TV shows. We just get bombarded and brainwashed with this stuff and the inaccuracy of it all makes life that much more complicated.

"Hey honey, it says here that the average couple over forty has sex three point five times a week! Wow, I guess we must be way above average!"

The Desire Pill

The pharmaceutical companies have blown it! They've wasted years. Oh sure, we have Viagra and soon there will be female Viagra. But these drugs are of no real value. These medications would not even be necessary if we had "the desire pill." Guys, so what if you can get it up? If she's not interested, she's not interested. Women, who cares if blood rushes to your crotch? If he's watching the game, he's watching the game. But what if you both took "the desire pill"? In a mind-expanding way the desire pill would change the appearance of the other person! He would suddenly have hair and appear slender as a rail. She would have a tight ass and no cellulite. Nothing could stop you, not the game, not the headache. It would be like college.

Just make sure that you both take the pill at the same time and that there are no animals around! Well, unless you're into that kind of thing!

Jewelry Sucks!

Ok, let's get right to the point. Jewelry sucks! It's meaningless, overpriced, pagan, usually fraudulent and just plain wasteful. Yet we guys are told over and over again that women love jewelry. When I ask my wife what she wants for her birthday or for Christmas she always says, "Jewelry." For a while, purchasing jewelry results in a little romance. You know, the diamond earrings, the bracelet, the artsy ring, the gold necklace, the gold necklace with the diamond pendant, the pearls, the jade, the turquoise, the emeralds and the sapphires, women want all of them. I can't understand why.

First of all, men don't notice jewelry and don't care. Only women notice jewelry and other women always have a bigger one! I guess that would be jewelry envy! Second, did you see *20/20* when Diane Sawyer did that segment on how corrupt the jewelry industry can be? Her husband spent $5,000 on a necklace that turned out to be a fake! It was worth about $50. Who can tell? In order to tell what is real you need to be a geologist or a gemologist and have an electron microscope!

Maybe you have a friend in the jewelry business or a favorite jeweler in town. It's still a rip off! I've bought everything imaginable, yet my wife visits New York and spends $10 on crap jewelry from a street vendor and wears it more than the real stuff!

And why aren't the environmentalists all over this stuff? Imagine, digging rare stones out of precious Mother Earth! Not to mention the slave labor it takes to dig those stones out of the ground! Splitting open poor, defenseless oysters and ripping out their pearls! Disgusting! What's the difference between beating a harmless, rare stone into a geometric shape and beating a baby seal to death? Greenpeace, get on this!

Marilyn Monroe and Jane Russell never explain why *Diamonds Are a Girl's Best Friend.* I guess women like diamond jewelry because it doesn't talk back! My dentist's assistant just told me she thinks it's because they sparkle, and that "makes me sparkle," she explains. Other than that, she couldn't articulate the phenomenon. Hell, there are lots of things that sparkle, like metallic paint on a Jaguar! I suppose it could be said that jewelry doesn't mess up the house, doesn't watch football, doesn't belch and, as the song says, doesn't lose its shape! Oh yeah, and one other thing. Jewelry has cash value when the relationship ends!

Thank goodness dogs are a man's best friend!

Swing! (Dancing)

Once when I was on a trip out of town a couple I was meeting with asked me if I wanted to go swing dancing. I said I didn't know how to swing dance, but I'd be happy to go along and watch.

They were great at swing. They had been taking lessons for a long time. I even got out on the floor to learn a few basic steps, but I quickly figured out that, like anything you want to do well, swing dancing takes a lot of work and practice. A few basics weren't going to cut it! So I just watched. The outfits, the music and the movement were awesome.

Afterward, over a drink, they told me how hard it had been for them to learn. In fact, the woman said that they simply could not learn swing dancing while dancing with each other. So they got new partners as the lessons went on. After only a few lessons with the new partners she said that they improved by quantum leaps. "Really!" I said. "That's amazing. I would think that you would have a more difficult time learning something so intricate with a stranger." "Not at all," she said. "It's the only way to get better."

I knew I was never going to be a swing dancer, but I was certainly wondering how the "stranger/partner theory" worked with sex!

Four-day Limit!

I have a friend who has never been married. He is now sixty years old. Actually, he's only had one relationship with a woman in his life that has lasted more than four days. One day I asked him why he could not deal with a woman for more than four days. He answered quickly. He said in an exasperated voice, "Because on the third or fourth day they start saying, 'You ought to—fill in the blank.' That does it. That's the end of the relationship!"

So What Did The Doctor Say? He Said I Should Have Sex Four Times A Day!

One of the best "drunk" comedies ever is the movie *Arthur* starring the late Dudley Moore. As his character, Arthur, is dining with his anal, soon-to-be fiancée he holds up his Scotch and tells the waiter, "My doctor has ordered that I have ten of these an hour!" Anyway, we all know that men hate to go to the doctor. When we do go it's usually for a checkup or something like a bad cold or cough or stitches from some home improvement accident. Men always know that they have to go through the kabuki dance and make up answers to the doctor's questions. Like, "Oh yeah, doc, I'm keeping up the jogging! Nearly every day!" Then we pay the outrageous bill, which screws up our insurance, and end up waiting an hour for a prescription. All this only to be told to rest a day or two, lose weight and get more exercise. But that's only the beginning. After returning from the doctor we have to answer even more questions from the spouse. "What did the doctor say? What medication did he prescribe? Did he say anything about exercise? You're not going to work tomorrow, are you? What about your cholesterol? When do the blood test results come back? Did he say anything about your drinking? Did he say you should have a body scan? He said to stop eating so much red meat, didn't he?" she quizzes in the Socratic method. Then the orders go out. "Don't go near the kids with that cough! Don't go outside in this chill! Did you take your pills? Well, take them now! You're not drinking enough water! Keep that blanket on! Don't use my cup in the bathroom!" "Ok, ok, I might as well be at work!" I think to myself.

If only doctors would prescribe sex, none of this would be such a hassle. Just think. You walk in the door. She asks, "What did the doctor say?" You respond, "He prescribed that we have sex four times a day and that I would be fine in a couple of years!" This going to the doctor stuff might not be so bad after all! How about, "Take two women three times a week and get plenty of rest!" Is there anything that won't cure?

What Is Victoria's Secret?

Oh, isn't that clever. Let's name a women's lingerie store with a name that summons up the mystery of the female sex. Like we guys just have to rush out and figure out the mystery. What a crock! But what is Victoria's secret, really? Is it an extra body part? Is something missing down there? Is she bi? Is she tattooed? Has she read the kama sutra and yet knows even more? No! No! No! It's none of these most thought-provoking, sexually inspiring things. It is not some ménage à trois. It's not even any of the really twisted things your sick mind is constantly fantasizing about. Victoria's Secret is simple. She's going to get you, yes you, bub, to buy her all this crap. Yes, it will stimulate your appetite for the sex and therefore you will pester her constantly for sex. But she knows this and she knows that she outfoxed you into buying all this stuff. She's never going to have sex with you and if she does the underwear isn't going to make you perform any better. Basically, you're just paying for it so you can brag to the boys that your wife has all that crap and you make her feel good for a few hours so she won't talk to you during the game!

Don't worry, though, it's like buying a gravesite. You pay for it, you might see it once, you're never going to see it again, but you feel secure knowing it's there!

SAT Scores

Wouldn't it be funny if after all these years of boys achieving higher math scores on the SAT than girls that the person back in Princeton, N.J. doing all the calculating and statistical analysis was a woman! Of course, if that is the case then maybe a man is grading all the verbal scores! This could lead one to the conclusion that the scores have actually been reversed all these years.

Nah! I don't think so! My wife still calculates that when we have sex once a week that she can round up to 10! But then again, I can't verbally convince her otherwise!

Caught Me! Damn It! Of Course I Was Looking at Her Ass And Her Boobs!

Come on! Do I really need to write a story about this? You get it from the title, right? So why do women get so mad when you look at other women? There's the classic answer you can give, which is, "I might be married, but I'm not dead!" But that just isn't a satisfactory response. And your wife doesn't think it's funny. The truth is any woman worth taking a long look at or getting distracted by is a woman you can only fantasize about. It's not going to happen! You know that. She's young and beautiful and shapely. What are you going to do? Walk away from your wife and go ask her for a drink? Or you could say, "Hey baby, my wife is standing over there, but let's go behind that bush and do it!" Yeah, right. No, you just want to look and imagine! It's kind of like Johnny Carson once said to Dolly Parton: "I'd give a week's pay to see those!" Think about how much you make in a week and then look at her again and see if she's worth a week's pay just to see "those."

My answer to myself is always yes! But she'd have to dance around naked for about five minutes!

Great Sex In Great Hotels!

I'm going to write another book. It's going to be called *Great Sex in Great Hotels*. It should be a huge bestseller and maybe even made into a movie. You see, this book is not pornography or a murder mystery or a legal thriller or a techno novel. This book is about individuals: real or fictional, single or married, straight or gay, young or old, rich or poor, experiencing a very special part of life with another person in a memorable environment. It is a series of stories that are but fleeting moments in anyone's lifetime, yet are gilded by the architectural magic created in a great hotel, a very real hotel, in a city, town or resort destination. Some hotels will be historic with iconic features. Some will be recent monuments to the hospitality industry. Others will be insignificant, but all will be classic in their sheer presence and sense of place. The stories will be more romantic than sexually explicit, against a backdrop of both natural beauty and the built environment. The scenarios will be moments in time among romantic monuments large and small, reachable and touchable by anyone with a desire to do so.

This will be great for our sagging hotel industry. It will be kind of like Sylvester Stallone in *Rocky* running up the steps of the Art Institute in Philadelphia. People want to run up those steps and have their picture taken at the top with arms raised high! People will want to go to these hotels after reading the book or seeing the movie. People will remember the place behind the statue, next to the fountain in the Raffles Hotel in Singapore where Scott and Cindy first kissed and fell over backward into the pond!

Five Potatoes

Tourists will come in just to have their picture taken right at that spot. Not to mention trying to make love on the balcony of their room overlooking the lights of Singapore. A guy and a girl will see each other for the first time since high school while having tea at the Dorchester in London. They will spend a splendid afternoon lying in the grass of Hyde Park! I see Warren Beatty and Natalie Wood types in this one! A couple will celebrate falling in love by making love high upon the balcony of the St. Regis in New York. A hardworking truck driver and a pharmaceutical saleswoman meet in the pool of the Best Western in Fort Stockton, Texas and chase each other through the scrub of West Texas, laughing with joy as they fall wrapped around each other into the dust at dusk. The Best Western sign lit starkly in the background spelling out "Be t We tern."

Each episode or scene will have an architectural look. You know, a kind of edgy, geometric, polarized view, emphasizing the place and its significance of detail, identifiable characteristics and originality. The architecture of the hotels becomes the leading actor and at the same time the actors become the overlay of ornamentation within the scenes.

Ah, but this sounds too artsy for me, you say. Hold on! This is not an art movie or philosophical narrative. Although it will work for the artistic and non-artistic in each of us, the stories of love, romance, and sex will be so personal, touching, fun and adventurous that you'll want to run up the steps and raise your arms in exaltation and say to your partner, "Come laugh with me, let's make love!" You'll sort of know these people. You'll say to your spouse, "Next vacation, let's go to that hotel and drink champagne right in that spot and ask for the same waiter and get room 601 with the balcony with the view of the Eiffel Tower!" (Hotel Balzac, Paris).

The book or the movie or both will be educational, providing potentially historic or whimsical knowledge along with a sense of place. You will learn little things through the story, like where the best people-watching seat is in the lobby of the Pierre in New York. The reader or viewer will come away with a sense of place and time and an appreciation of architecture and hospitality that will feel good! And as dessert, a large helping of romance! All of it combining to be completely memorable!

Did you ever see Alan Alda and Ellen Burstyn in *Same Time Next Year*? It was filmed at a lovely hotel on California's Mendocino coast. You probably know the story and the movie is a bit dated now, but it's kind of what I'm talking about. Anyway, rent it if you haven't seen it. The point is, the cottage where Alan Alda and Ellen Burstyn filmed the movie is still there and it's booked years in advance. The hotel has a sign in front that tells passers-by on the Pacific Coast Highway that this is "the" place where *Same Time Next Year* was filmed. They've had a great business ever since, proving that the hotel industry has got to love this kind of recognition. Hell, I think when hotels get wind of this they will probably invite me to stay for free so I will consider them for the book!

About twelve little vignettes ought to do it for the first book and the first installment of the movie. All plots lines for the vignettes will be different with different actors in each one. Think about the buzz. "Well, which one did you like?" "I liked the one in Buenos Aires because I've been to that hotel! I want to go back! Wasn't he hot! And did you see the neckline on her dress? No wonder he spotted her across the ballroom!" "Well, I liked the one at the Homestead in Virginia. Playing backgammon in the lobby and then sneaking up to the roof! How about that scene where they chase each other on horseback? What gorgeous scenery! I've never been there. But now I really want to go! Geez, was she funny, and her silhouette behind the curtains! Man, that made my teeth sweat!"

So, it's going to be a great book! I hope you enjoy it. The movie will be awesome and of course filmed on location inside and outside of great hotels around the world! Great hotels always lead to great sex! I think that's mostly why we go to them. Sex sells and so will this book and movie. Don't misunderstand; as I said earlier, this is not a porn film. There may be some minor nudity when appropriate. Mostly it is romantic, cute, sexy, fun, smart, loving with enough sex to be sexy and tantalizing without being blatant. The circumstances will be clever. The writing will be refreshingly realistic. It will be a great date film. Women will live the romance. Guys will love the material things, i.e. cars, buildings, etc. But, mostly the guys will get an education in history, architecture, etiquette, manners, style, hospitality and good living! Then after the movie everyone will want to go home and have a romantic, sex-filled evening!

And somehow, civilization will continue to move forward.

Oh yeah, I want Steven Spielberg and Kathleen Kennedy to produce the movie. I want Robert Zemeckis to direct. I want John Williams for the score. I want all unknowns for the parts. I'd like a cameo. Oh, yeah, my wife would, too!

If any of you buttheads in Hollywood think you are going to steal this idea, I'm hiring Alan Dershowitz to sue you. Jeffrey, don't even think about it! Harvey, lose some weight!

But, hey I gotta go now. Gotta catch a plane to Thailand to try out the Amanpuri Hotel in Phuket! You know, meet my wife there. Do some research for the book!

Do you think the IRS is going to go for the travel expenses?

I guess I'll need some of those creative Hollywood accountants!

Even My Female Dog Whines!

Bitch, bitch, bitch! Did you ever hear the Jewish American Princess joke: "What is a Jewish American Princess's favorite wine?" Answer: "Buy me something!"

My beautiful female golden retriever has the same traits. She approaches me; she looks at me with those big brown eyes, puts her nose up under my hand and makes little whining sounds. When my wife and my dog get together, they whine in unison! My dog is telling me she wants me to pet her, get her a treat, take her for a walk and buy her a new toy. "Pet me! Pet me!"

She gets what she wants every time. She is irresistible. All I get in return is her unconditional love every single day. And she sleeps with me whenever I let her up on the bed!

If only, if only, it worked this way with wives!

DAYS OF WINE AND CONDOMS!

If the fifties and sixties were days of wine and roses than surely the eighties and nineties were days of wine and condoms!

Remember when we heard about condoms nonstop? Remember when you used condoms nonstop? What happened? It's like they vanished. Sure, they're all still there in the drug stores but no one even mentions them anymore. They are not funny anymore. They don't make kids laugh and giggle anymore. I don't even know of any kids that use them for water balloons! I haven't heard the word condom mentioned at a cocktail or dinner party in ages. Remember when you gave condoms as birthday gifts? I once gave my brother-in-law stealth condoms. The joke was that they'd never see you coming! Ha, ha. Not funny anymore. Have we just plain rolled up the idea? When is *Wall Street Week* going to analyze the performance of condom companies over the last ten years? Where are Maria Bartiromo and Lou Dobbs when you need them? I haven't seen any reports on that, but I bet the performance charts of those companies go from upper left to bottom right! I bet sales have been limp, putting condom companies in a slump! That's not hard to figure out!

Frankly, I don't really know and don't really care. Maybe everybody is using the pill. Maybe everybody is using something else. Maybe everybody is getting old. Maybe there is not as much sex going on as we are led to believe.

Williston Lamar

Well, at least the wine industry is going strong! And wine is getting less expensive. As I get older, I'm inclined to think about days of wine and more wine!

And you! Of course!

Rip Van Winkle Was No Dummy!

Life getting you down? Work not going well? The wife bitching again? Your boss is an illiterate ass? The kids driving you crazy? Your team loses in the finals? Get dumped by your girlfriend? Can't sleep? No money? Take the hibernation pill!

It's new from the Winkle Company! Just take one pill and let it Rip! You've earned it!

Wake up twenty years from now!

Think of all the bitching you'll miss! Plus all the wars, heartache, pain and suffering! Think of the changes you'll encounter twenty years from now! By then we'll probably have a pill that makes you young again and one that cures any disease! It won't matter that you were never any good on the computer. We'll be way beyond computers!

Think of the peace! The rest! Most of the people you can't stand will be long gone or retired to their doublewide in the Nevada desert with the above-ground pool from Sears!

The wife will have moved on to the software salesman while you were sleeping. Huh! No more bitching from her!

No more small worries! There will be new things to learn and discover. Old sports scores to catch up on and alternative fuels!

Shit! I'd miss the next episode of *West Wing*! Never mind!

The Germans Wore Gray, You Wore Butt Floss!

God, I love this trend in recent years toward butt floss panties for women. Looking at those butts makes my teeth sweat!

If only the French had developed butt floss panties just before the war. The Germans would not be wearing gray. They would be wearing nothing at all! Their weapons would have been up— I mean down. The efficient German war machine would have been blitzed by the German love machine! Think how much more interesting the History Channel would be today.

World history would have been twisted! Or at least bent over! The French would have won! Imagine that! My teeth are sweating!

"Honey, what are you wearing?"

BACKRUBS!

My last two wives think I give them backrubs in order to lead them into sex. This is NOT true. I give them backrubs so that they would give me a backrub that would lead to sex!

Just in case it doesn't lead to sex, at least I get a backrub!

TWO POTATO: THE KITCHEN, DINING AND EATING OUT

SEVENTY-THREE YEARS OF NOT EATING WHAT YOU WANT!

Guys, remember in college when it was five or six o'clock and you and your buddies would leave the dorm and head for the dining hall? Do you remember how you would go through the cafeteria line and get anything you wanted? Do you recall what it was like before you started getting told what to eat? Was that great or what? Picture John Belushi in *Animal House*. Why is it that now—fifteen, twenty, thirty years later—we can't eat what we want? Obviously, for some of us there are health reasons. But let's face it: if we weren't getting told what to eat, we would never eat any healthy stuff! Right? Now all we hear is, "Don't order that, get something good. Try the house salad." We are constantly reminded to stop putting salt on that or butter on this. Who reminds us of these things? Our spousal units! It was bad enough that our mothers told us what to eat for the first 17 or 18 years. Then we only get a 4-8 year break for college, grad school and bachelorhood, and then for another 55 years we are told what to order, what to cook and how fast or slow to eat it! Imagine on your deathbed having lived 80 years and told what to eat for 73 of them.

What's up with that? Why do women insist on telling us what to eat? Are they really trying to help us live longer? All that does is extend the misery. Aren't life and the food required to nurture it meant to be enjoyed? Or is it possible that they are really trying to kill us for the life insurance? After all, they know we're not going to listen and the moment we get away we are going to pour salt on everything and eat buckets of french fries and fried chicken. The more they nag us the more of the other stuff we are going to try and eat. So that deadly heart attack is coming earlier—and they know it! Once that happens, it's cruises to Alaska with the new boyfriend. Condos and golf club memberships in Florida and more frequent visits with the children!

Fries And A Coke

How many times have you pulled up to the drive-up window at a fast food restaurant and turned to your wife/significant other and asked politely if she would like anything? Of course, she says no (she's trying to stay in shape or at least maintain that girlish figure she used to have before having children!). So you merrily order the 10 piece chicken nuggets, large fries and a Coke. You're really hungry. You need to go to the drive-up window because if you go home you know what waits in the refrigerator; you hate all the screaming kids inside the restaurant so you can't go inside; and you know by going to the drive-up you can get home fast to catch the fourth quarter. But what happens the moment you pull away from the drive-up window? You know it's coming! "Can I have some of your fries? Why did you get the sweet and sour sauce? I like the barbeque. And you know regular Cokes are so heavy; you should have ordered a Diet Coke!" "Damn it woman, if you had wanted something why didn't you say so when I asked you?" "Oh, but they smell so good!"

You really wanted all of the fries for yourself; now they are half gone and you still have to go home and face the refrigerator!

The Purse

We've all discussed the contents of a woman's purse on many occasions. Even women make fun of the stuff in their purses. It's amazing that they require a suitcase when traveling. You would think everything they ever needed was in their purse. But that's not what this is about. This is about the accidentally-forgotten purse. Accidentally on purpose, that is!

You are a two-income family. You both do pretty well. Either of you can pay for things. But just after getting in the car to go out to dinner it happens. "Dear, are you going to pick up the check tonight?" he asks naively. "Oh dear, I didn't bring my purse," she proclaims. You are already strapped in and headed down the driveway. Too late! She's done it again. She's avoided the check by "forgetting her purse!" Or the check arrives and she exclaims, "Oh dear, I didn't bring my purse and I have to go to the ladies' room."

I doubt any woman has ever forgotten her purse when leaving the house for a shopping trip. Have you ever seen her come back after a half hour at the mall saying, "Sorry to interrupt you, dear, but I forgot my purse"? Never!

The purse is just a container for all the things she also forgets when you need them: the house keys, the extra set of car keys, tissues, her checkbook, ChapStick and change for parking meters. Why is it when you need something from that vast warehouse of utilitarian stuff, she never has it? If we did random checks on women's purses like the kind of searches we are now doing at airports, we would find that everything is in there. Everything we ever asked for that she never has when we're around. We would have to catch these women alone without their husbands or boyfriends. But that won't be hard, since they left him at home!

The Gourmet Headache

"I'm hungry!" she exclaims from the passenger seat. You've both been running errands all Saturday. It's getting on toward 1:30-2:00 pm. You haven't stopped for anything to eat and the morning coffee and toast has worn off. A few of your errands were failures. The blouse she wanted from the dry cleaners still had the wine stain on it and had to be sent back. They were out of cream for her coffee at the grocery store and you stayed too long in the hardware store and bought a few things no one will ever need. On an empty stomach the grouch factor for both of you begins to build. While getting stuck at every stoplight in the Saturday afternoon traffic she finally orders, "I want to go home. I'm tired of driving around. We're wasting a beautiful day." "Fine with me—let's forget the video store. I'll take the movie back tomorrow." By saying this, I hope to make her happy and communicate to her that I'm ready to point the car back home. Then it comes. She makes a statement that contradicts all logic. "I'm hungry; let's get something to eat quickly." "Ok," I say to myself, "she's hungry and wants to get home quickly to enjoy the day, but to do that she must get something quick to eat. How can both happen to make her happy?"

So, applying some logic, I conclude that on the way home we can stop at the drive-up window at a fast food place. Once again trying to please her every wish, I blurt out, "Let's stop at the drive-up." Then it comes, the double contradiction. "Oh, gross, I don't want any fast food. I want a salad or something decent!" Ok, how can any man on Earth figure out what to do in this

Five Potatoes

situation? There is no such thing as a drive-up fast salad place or quick-order gourmet restaurant. She wants to be home in ten minutes and she's got to eat something other than at a drive-up window. Plus, we've got the grouch factor working against us, and a beautiful day is slipping away. The pressure is on! How can I keep her happy?

I've got it! I'll ask her where she wants to go and what she wants to eat and when she wants to be home. She can make the decision. That way if it's not what she wants it's her fault! What a stroke of genius! Hey, I'm a flexible kind of guy. So I ask her. God, I'm dumb. What a response I get. "Oh, let's just go home. I'll eat the leftover pizza from last night. God, I'm getting a headache from not eating and now the day is cloudy." Silence accompanies us all the way home. But you know what has happened. It's your fault. The weekend is ruined.

She's hungry, tired, pissed and has been able to work the word headache into the conversation. We all know that the headache will get worse—and any heterosexual, married man knows what the word headache means!

Dishes

Men are so bad at doing the dishes it's ridiculous. The first time I had to live off campus and actually do the dishes, I didn't know how! Of course, neither did my housemates. None of us had ever done the dishes at home! The thought of having to do them never occurred to us until that first night in the house. The idea was that we would take turns. Two of us would cook the dinner and the other two had to clean up. We got some really neat yellow dishes at the Salvation Army. My friend and I had to do the dishes that first night. We would pick up one dish at a time and pour a ton of liquid dish soap on it then scrub it under the tap. The house was too old to have a dishwasher, so at least we didn't have to figure that out. Then one of our housemates walked into the kitchen and started laughing his ass off at us. We had used half the bottle of liquid dish soap for about six dishes and four glasses! Ok, so we were momma's boys from old-fashioned families in which the men never did the dishes! And, like everybody else, we eventually learned about soaking, scrubbing, rinsing and drying. We even learned what an advantage a two-compartment sink could be!

Now, thirty years later, after bachelorhood and our own apartments and a few accidents with dishwasher technology, like putting dish liquid in the dishwasher instead of detergent and turning the kitchen into a bubble bath, we have learned the art and science of dishwashing.

Well . . . not really!

Five Potatoes

You see, in marriage, dishwashing requires a degree in metallurgy, organizational theory and time management. I never suspected dishwashing was so complicated and that it required such knowledge. Gee, mom, you really knew some stuff! Of course, your wife knows all this stuff, too. Over time, she seems to have acquired an expertise in this field that is worthy of All American Dishwasher status. You are her student and you can do nothing right! You are a grunt, a maggot when it comes to dishwashing. Here are just a few of the things this maggot has learned in dishwashing boot camp.

NO DISH IS EVER TRULY CLEAN! You can scrub it first, then run it through the dishwasher, but in the end it still has to be cleaned off by hand before being put away. Then when it's pulled out it has to be inspected and cleaned again before using. Can you imagine doing this in the frat house?

THERE IS NOT A DISHWASHER MADE BY ANYONE ON THIS PLANET THAT CAN WASH A DISH ALL BY ITSELF! All dishes must be washed and rinsed in the sink, then inspected, then put in the dishwasher. So what is the dishwasher for, anyway?

CAST IRON PANS CAN ONLY BE WASHED BY HAND! I can't believe this one! Did anyone ever point out that cast iron pans are made of CAST IRON! Hello? Yes, of course you did but if you put them in the dishwasher they lose their "seasoning" and start to rust!

HOLIDAY DISHES AND THE "GOOD CHINA" CAN ONLY BE WASHED BY HAND! This one just kills me. They are dishes, ok? China, plastic, ceramic, whatever—I don't understand how the dishwasher hurts them. I suppose the rationale is that you wouldn't take your Porsche to the car wash, so why would you put your expensive dishes in the dishwasher? But therein lays the fallacy of this argument. If you pay that much money for quality dishes, shouldn't they be able to handle a dishwasher? What's going to happen? Are the little flowers on the plates going to come off in the dishwasher? What a crock! It seems to me that by hand washing them you are more likely to drop one or rub off some pattern or gold plating or something. Hasn't technology come far enough that we can deal with this with a machine and not waste our time?

ALL DISHES MUST BE WASHED AND PUT AWAY OR AT THE VERY LEAST BE PUT IN THE DISHWASHER BEFORE GOING TO BED! Oh please, get over it! Scrape the dishes and put them in the sink if you must, but relax and enjoy your family or your guests. The dishes can wait until tomorrow. You've had a great meal and good company. You've probably had too much wine. Just let the dishes go till morning. In your exhaustion you might drop a piece of the "good china" and get crucified for it, so just wait until tomorrow. I promise the little flowers won't come off.

EVEN IF YOU HAVEN'T FINISHED EATING, THAT'S NO EXCUSE FOR NOT GETTING THE DISHES TO THE SINK SO THE MRS. CAN GET GOING AND FINISH WASHING THEM BEFORE DESSERT! What is with this? Women want to get those dishes away from you as soon as possible. They say, "Oh, I'm just going to get a few of these out of the way." Yeah, right! An hour later all the dishes are done, the guests are ready to leave, and they haven't seen your wife since the main course! "Come and say goodnight to the Andersons, honey."

NEVER ATTEMPT TO LOAD THE DISHWASHER WITHOUT YOUR SPOUSE'S ADVICE! All those little compartments and stalagmites have a specific role to play in loading the dishwasher. In addition, unusual items have to go into certain places just so. Hard to believe, but there is even a way to put the detergent into its little compartment just so it can magically do its thing. You can try, but inevitably she will walk up and say, "No, no, it goes in this way, over here. Oh, here, let me do it!" She can fill that dishwasher with more stuff than you ever imagined (like her purse). When she's got it all in there, take a look at it. Squint your eyes and you will see a magnificent piece of modern art! I can't believe Kandinsky never painted this subject!

In conclusion:

You've got to ask yourself, "What went on with the school cafeteria dishes all those years?" Yuck!!

So what can we do about overcoming our male dishwashing disability? How can we overcome poor training? What can we do to improve our organizational skills? How can we master technique and technical knowledge about this daily activity? Listen to our better half? Nah! HIRE A CATERER EVERY NIGHT!

Danger: High Voltage!

I suppose one of the reasons that Walter Mitty was such a weak individual had something to do with electrical shocks that consumed his body and mind when his wife ordered him around. After a while his muscle mass must have been pure Jell-O. Have you ever felt one of those shocks? Men yell. They do. But you know it's coming, like you might expect from a drill instructor. When women snap it's so quick it's like sticking your finger in a socket when you thought the power was off. She can shake you to your soul, paralyzing your entire body.

I once reported to a woman at work who blasted me so quickly, without warning, that afterward I sat there staring at the wall for ten minutes. It's the quick knife that gets to men. Slow criticism by women doesn't work; we guys are usually not listening or we just don't get it! Outbursts of this nature always provide an electrical shock to the body and mind. I don't think this has anything to do with hormones or time of life or breaking the glass ceiling; it seems to be built into the female chromosomes as a tool for controlling the behavior of males.

These encounters manifest themselves in many ways. You can see it on your buddy's face when he's on the phone with his wife. You can see your brother-in-law jump when your sister bursts out. You can feel the terror in the room when a woman does this in front of others. There is no warning, no introduction. Everything is going along just fine. Afterward there is no explanation and certainly no apology. It's like an

Five Potatoes

earthquake, a thunderbolt and lightning hitting at the same time.

I was once standing in a room with four others when George (the husband) gently asked his wife if he could make her a sandwich for lunch. She said, "No, not right now, dear." The conversation in the room went on. It was a peaceful, quiet summer afternoon. The windows were open and a nice breeze was flowing through the room. Everyone was in a good mood. Then, without warning, the poor husband was struck by the high voltage! ZAP! "George, get me that sandwich NOW!!" she screamed. The others in the room involuntarily jumped back a step. Heads turned to look at the woman as if she might be possessed or about to vomit split pea soup like in *The Exorcist*. I kept thinking to myself, "She just said two minutes ago she didn't want a sandwich. What happened here?"

No one in the room knew what to do or say next. Two people in the room didn't even know this woman very well. They looked on in horror, wondering if they should leave. George's body was still smoking from the high voltage contact. His shoes were burning into the carpet. But George took it like a man. After a ten second pause for shock recovery he said, "Yes, dear, would you like mayonnaise on that?" And then he put what was left of his tail between his legs and hobbled off to the kitchen.

There was no apology for the loud outburst. There was no change in the tone of the rest of the conversation. Not even one ounce of recognition from the woman that she had interrupted the tranquility of the afternoon and scared the hell out of her guests. Pleasantries were exchanged and the afternoon visit came to an end. As I left by the side door I couldn't help but notice a small sign above the fuse box. "Danger: High Voltage!" No kidding!

They say that lightning hits 600 people a year. I bet it hits millions of Walter Mittys every day.

61

Culinary Happiness

It's seven thirty in the morning. "What do you want for dinner?" she yells from the bathroom. Why are women obsessed with what's for dinner? My mom, sisters, spouse, and daughter are obsessed with what's for dinner. They are profoundly obsessed with going out to dinner. "We'll be at Mom's house next week. Where do you want to go for dinner? You know Dad doesn't like that Japanese place. My mom wants to know what you want her to buy for dinner. She wants to know if you still like carrots. Do you? Well if not, what do you eat now?" I really love that all these people are concerned for my well-being and culinary happiness. It's heartwarming. But get over it!

Do you remember coming home from work when you were single? I'd strip down to my boxers. Read the paper. Make a gin and tonic. Turn on the news. Grab a bag of barbeque Fritos. Plop down in my leftover frat house chair. Watch the news. Get another gin and tonic. Watch *Jeopardy*. Get another gin and tonic. Watch *Happy Days* and fall asleep in the chair! Ironically, I never worried about what was for dinner and I was never in better shape!

That's culinary happiness!

The Kids Are Fine, But Did I Tell You About The Scallops?

My sister is a compulsive culinary conversationalist. She and her husband and various friends dine out often. They try different restaurants and go back to their favorites. I call her frequently in order to keep in touch since we live at opposite ends of the country—and, since she's on the East Coast, she gets TV shows three hours before I do. I like to find out what she and her family have been doing. I try to ask her for her opinions on world events, the country's economic situation and the latest news stories. I try to find out what is happening with her kids. You know, stuff like major developments in their lives. Jobs, school, boyfriends, girlfriends, new cars, problems, whatever—I want to hear about what their lives are like. We never get much past the weather when she insists on telling me about her latest restaurant adventure.

"We went out with the Snosreans last night," she gushes. I have no idea who these people are, though I would actually be more interested in hearing about them than what comes next.

"We went to this old place down by the water. Oh! They had this fabulous menu. Paul had the sweet corn Rizzoli with blackened shrimp. We split a huge Caesar salad with balsamic vinaigrette dressing that was the best I've ever had. The Snosreans had baked, herb-crusted halibut in a white wine, butter, lemon and garlic sauce with braised baby carrots. Oh, and for dessert they had maple gelato with raspberry sauce with thin chocolate wafers on top. The place has been around a long time, but for some reason we had never been there. It wasn't that fancy inside, but what a meal! Did I tell you about the bacon-wrapped scallops? They were amazing and were served in a terrine with a touch of spicy, hot butter! I could have eaten the scallops for my appetizer and my main course!"

Unless I'm your dietician, I really don't care who ate what and whether it was good or not. I'll probably never go to this restaurant in my life and we could spend my five cents a minute talking about more meaningful things.

But now I have a new approach. Whenever I'm out to dinner, particularly with family, I take along my cell phone. I call my sister as we're dining and start telling her what everyone is eating. It's hysterical. Right in the middle of a bite I'll hand one of my kids the cell phone and instruct them, "Say hi to your Aunt and tell her all about your veal osso buco and your fettuccine carbonara!" This seems to satisfy her appetite for culinary conversation.

Finally, when the conversation ends and we're about to hang up, she says, "Wait, I haven't told you the answer to the final question on *Jeopardy* yet!"

Now that's a world event!

GET THE WAITER!

It happened again just last night. We're at a restaurant. My wife wants a glass of water. She glances about for the waiter. There's no one in sight. So she looks at me and says, "Get the waiter, I need some water." I usually have my back to the rest of the room, because I'm polite and give my wife the view. So, I put down what I'm eating and turn around and notice that there is still no waiter in the room. So I say, "There's no one around at the moment. Here, have some of my water." Somehow, this isn't good enough. "Well, go get someone," she pleads. "What do I look like, your waiter?" I'm thinking. She can't eat anything while she looks around the room. This makes me feel bad, because I want to keep eating. I offer her my water again. But no! She can't take a sip of that. "How about taking a sip of your wine?" I suggest. "I want water!" she exclaims. I've got my already-sore neck twisted like a cinnamon roll so I can try and get a glimpse of someone even if it's the maitre d'. Finally someone comes out of the kitchen. He doesn't see my wave and goes to another table. Now she proclaims, "I'm never coming to this place again!"

What am I going to do? It's so embarrassing to everyone if I stand up and chase down the waiter. Finally, a busboy arrives and I ask him to bring us some water. He just stares at me because of course he doesn't speak English. But a waiter across the room sees me talking to the busboy and thinks something must be wrong, so he finally approaches and I ask for water. By the look on his face you'd think it was too much to ask. My wife notices this look and makes several more comments about his service and manhood.

Alas, the water arrives. But the conversation has changed, the light mood is gone and there is no chance of ordering dessert.

The next morning, reading the paper in bed, my wife asks me to get her another cup of coffee. Snuggled in our warm bed, I think cautiously for a moment and suggest to her that she "get the waiter!"

Frou-frou Food

My son and I were in Chicago recently. We were at one of the finest hotels in Chicago, the Four Seasons. After dinner we retired to the bar. I asked the waitress to bring me a cognac, but first, I asked her for some ice cream. I told her that I only wanted vanilla. I knew that this was the Four Seasons and that the chef would make a big deal out of a scoop of ice cream. So, I made sure to tell the waitress that I just wanted a scoop of plain vanilla ice cream. No frou-frou stuff. No little pieces of fruit. No little green twigs. No little waffle cup. No cream sauce in a rich, Corinthian design underneath the scoop. Just bring me a scoop of vanilla ice cream! Please!

It didn't happen. The chef just couldn't do it! The waitress couldn't make it happen. The sous-chef couldn't make it happen. I got my scoop of vanilla ice cream in a waffle cup with three different kinds of little berries and a green twig! Unbelievable! This is the Four fricking Seasons! What happened to hospitality? What happened to catering to the needs of the guest? What happened to just plain service? What is with it with the frou-frou food!?

The frou-frou phenomenon has been going on way too long. Yeah, I know that chefs need a creative outlet. I know that expensive places have to justify charging twelve dollars for a scoop of ice cream. And yes, it is a competition to be cool and get good reviews. Not to mention that a restaurant must add to its menu a touch of the cuisine of every other country on Earth so they can be more diverse and worldly. But so what? I don't want Vietnamese Italian burritos!

Frou-frou food is like a Jackson Pollock painting on a plate! It's abstract expressionism that no one understands. The food critics speak of culinary context, texture, color, presentation and design. I bet the populations of India and Central Africa really don't care about those things! How about just giving us some food? Ever seen a Wolfgang Puck's at the Rwanda airport?

Women seem to like frou-frou food more than men. It must have something to do with the big plates and small portions! All the guys really care about is that frou-frou restaurants usually have alcohol and valet parking. The alcohol makes the food palatable and the valets will leave the Mercedes, Jag or BMW right up front. The frou-frou food will be consumed and forgotten, but the car will be right there when you come out!

Don't forget to tip the Vietnamese, Italian or Mexican valet parker!

Hmmm! So that's where they got the recipes!

WHERE'S THE BEEF?

I have two nieces and a sister-in-law who are vegetarians. I admire them tremendously. I really don't want to eat a cow or a chicken. I really don't. I just couldn't bear to be one of those people that zaps cows or pigs and then cuts them up. How barbaric! I like cows and pigs. They're really interesting animals. Chickens are kind of stupid, but hey—so are some of my friends! What about the poor lambs? Who could kill those gentle little creatures? I don't even want to eat eggs. Um, yum, scrambled chicken embryos! Whenever I see Tom Hanks cooking "ground cow flesh" in the movie *Bachelor Party*, it really makes me worry about my eating habits.

My nieces and my sister-in-law eat pizza, pasta, rice, potatoes, fruit and vegetables. They seem healthy to me. Why can't I do that? I guess it would help if I actually liked fruit and vegetables! Maybe as the human race evolves we will change our habits, probably over many centuries.

But for now, as long as I occasionally hear Jimmy Buffett's *Cheeseburger in Paradise*, I'm not going to be credited with helping to advance the human race. However, I don't think the animal world is going to be giving out the "Veggie Awards" any time soon.

I don't know of anyone who says, "I want to kill cows and cut them up when I grow up!" Animal death squad—your job will be ending sooner than you think!

Where's the beef?

The beef will be found grazing in the field under a shady tree!

Our "World Famous" Buffalo Wings!

When will restaurants stop putting the phrase "world famous" in front of some dumb, remarkably average appetizer or entrée? It's so stupid! Just the other day I was in Bangkok talking with a local when he said to me, "Hey, have you ever had those buffalo wings at Sandy's Bar and Grill back in South Bend, Indiana? Wow, they are the best in the world!"

Yeah, sure—like the gross exaggeration that they are "world famous" is going to make me order them! Like anyone outside of a one-mile radius has ever heard of Sandy's Bar and Grill! What are these people thinking? I've seen this on menus from Boone, North Carolina to Eureka, California. Why, just the other day my wife said, "Let's go get some of those world famous hash browns over at the sports bar." Oh, please! Give me a break! Hey, restaurant people—stop it! Just say something on the menu like, "Our customers tell us these are among the best buffalo wings they've had anywhere!" Now that's an endorsement!

Otherwise, I'm going to walk in to your restaurant and say, "Hi, I'm a "world famous" customer! I'd like a complimentary order of your "world famous" buffalo wings so I can assure the "world" that your buffalo wings are still "world famous!"

Paying For The Experience

Presumably, most people consider dining out a pleasure and part of what should be among the good experiences of life. We should be grateful we are able to eat well and pay for the experience. We enjoy romantic dinners for two, large family dinners and dinners with colleagues. Sometimes we're alone. Sometimes it's that special place you always visit. Sometimes we are trying new things and new, hot restaurants that are presented as the latest cool place to go. Sometimes it's planned. Sometimes it's extemporaneous. There might be a new chef in town or an old favorite. Restaurants can serve specialty foods, ethnic foods, regional cuisine, pizza, or burgers and fries. Some dining experiences can create some of life's best memories. Nothing is new here. We all know this. So what's this about?

It's about how many meals have been ruined or at least aggravated by the woman at the table who just loses it when the check is late or the food is not what she expected or the college kid waiting the table has not been seen in a while.

Now, these things should aggravate most people. We take our time and pay good money for these meals. We expect good food and good service, sometimes even great food and great service for our money. No problem with that. But there is an art form to not ruining a meal for others when your particular problem with the food or the wait staff spills over to ruin the evening for everyone else at the table. Women have mastered this behavior. "If I'm going to have something go wrong for me, then the rest of you will have to suffer my wrath! And I'm going to say something to the manager on the way out. He should know how I feel. I'm never coming back here again!" Men don't seem to have this problem. In fact, when our steak is not cooked enough, we don't announce it to the whole table. We try not to interrupt the others at the table. We just quietly whisper to the waiter to take it back and cook it some more. In the process we try and make as minimal a disturbance as possible. Of course, your wife/girlfriend observes that you are sending the steak back and makes a huge deal of it in front of the whole table anyway. "I just hate that about this place! They never get it right! This has happened to us before at this restaurant. We're never coming back! I'll be finished with my meal before they even come back with your steak!" she exclaims so loudly the next table can hear. You suddenly feel totally guilty for having sent it back in the first place. Now that everyone is good and uncomfortable, there is a silence creeping over the guests at the table because they really want another glass of wine and now they're afraid it will take too long and another diatribe will spew forth from the mouth of the host's wife.

Of course, Murphy's Law kicks in, and the waiter is nowhere in sight in order to attract his attention and get the check and get out. When you've repeated a few more conversation topics with your guests, the check finally arrives. Now you know what is going to happen.

After the requisite, "I'll get it. No, you paid last time," crap, you are determined to get the check because you are the host and your meal was sent back and your wife/girlfriend has already announced that the glass of water she asked for never came. You wouldn't want your guests to pay for your bad experience so you welcome the chance to just take care of it and get the hell out of there. But the moment the check hits the table and while the waiter is still within earshot, she shouts out, "Don't you dare give him/her a big tip! The service was lousy!" This makes the whole process even more uncomfortable. Your mental math suddenly processes faster than your home computer. You give the guy/gal the normal tip anyway and get up as quickly as possible, being careful to get the check away from your wife so she can't do the math and get even more upset that you gave a reasonable tip to some starving college student working his/her way through school. You hand the check to the head waiter on the way out, placing yourself between him and your wife, all the while hoping she'll be distracted by your guests on the way out the door.

Presumably, most people consider dining out a pleasure and part of what should be among the good experiences of life. We should be grateful that we are able to eat well and pay for the experience!

The New Delhi Deli

Somewhere in New York City there must be a place called the New Delhi Deli. I've looked, but I've never found it. If you find it, don't ask for a roast beef sandwich or a cheeseburger!

Anyway, one of my son's friends came up with this idea and it's a good one. You see, one of the reasons that America is continually bashed by most of the rest of the world is that we don't disguise any of the stuff that we force on their countries. McDonald's is the cliché of worldwide American corporate dominance and those poor bastards take a beating in the press, in movies, in intellectual society, in acts of terrorism—it's endless. They should take a lesson from Disney. It's the name, stupid! Change the name! If Disney wants to make an R-rated movie they can't call it a Disney film—because the brand is synonymous with family-friendly entertainment, not blood and guts—so they release it under Touchstone, Buena Vista, Hollywood Pictures or Miramax and they invade the movie world!

So, suppose McDonald's in India changed its name to the New Delhi Deli? And in France they might change the name to Monsieur Jambon or Le Grand Boeuf. In Italy it could be Bono Geopetto's! In Japan, how about Sumo-san! In Mexico, how about McJesus! In Scotland, uh, how about McDonald's! Then in each country throw in some regional cuisine, take out the religious no-noes, keep a few old standbys for branding and control, and voila! Everybody gets something to eat quickly and at a reasonable cost. The design of the facilities should use regional materials and architectural styling that is just consistent enough to be cost-effective to build. The patrons think they are eating in an original restaurant with clear ties to their country or region. No one is offended. No more America-bashing! Each restaurant becomes a local success story, not an international monopoly. Nobody gets torched and Americans might actually learn something about food from other countries. The executives at McDonald's get disgustingly rich. The stock goes up. The shareholders are happy. One day, the appointed CEO turns out to be from France! What a concept! Imagine, a Frenchman in charge of global fast food!

It's the name, stupid!

Changing the name is the quickest, smartest way I can think of to achieve non-violent civil disobedience. Then what a wonderful world this would be! I wonder if Gandhi would eat at the New Delhi Deli. Hmmm?

Hi! I'm Mahatma Gandhi. I'd like a number 3!

Men Must Drop Ice Cubes!

What is it with men and ice cubes? We reach into the freezer, pull out the ice compartment, reach in to get a handful and drop most of them on the floor! I've watched all my male friends do this. The wife never drops any! I hate that! I drop one or two every time. Then I have to look for the nearly invisible ice cubes on the floor and when I find them I toss them on into the sink, but it doesn't end there. The ice cube hits the empty martini glass with just enough speed to knock it over and break it. Damn, another trip to Crate and Barrel! Nope! It's still not over. The one ice cube I couldn't find on the floor melts. Who do you think is going to step in it with her bare feet?

"Hey, did you make this wet spot? Why don't you ever clean up your mess?" she screams. "I guess that would be me!" I say. "I'm the man!"

Corporal Pepper

My brother-in-law and I used to repair things ourselves. We worked on things like Volkswagen engines and assorted car stuff. We would take things apart and not be able to put them back together. He would always tell me, when all else fails, "Beat the shit out of it with a hammer!" That was twenty years ago today.

Every restaurant on Earth seems to have the same style of pepper shakers. None of them work! We pepper lovers can't get any out. The particles of pepper are too big for the little holes in the shaker. You can hit it and still nothing comes out. You can unscrew the cap and end up dumping a pile of pepper on your food that looks like the latrine at a fly convention. You can ask the waiter for another one, but that won't help because they're all the same design. They just don't work. Maybe they will when I 'm sixty-four.

Chefs spend years developing their skills in the kitchen and they think their food is perfect; therefore, pepper is not required. But hey, they put it on the table, right? Can't they just take a minute to realize the shakers don't work? It's poor service when things don't work. Maybe the manager could have some custom-made or something with a little help from his friends.

My wife doesn't use any pepper. This is irritating because, if she did, restaurants would never hear the end of it. She'd have a recall petition on pepper shakers going across the land. She'd have them fixing the holes!

I don't have the patience for that. So, next time, I'm just taking a hammer along to the restaurant! We hope you will enjoy the show!

I'm Not Going To Stop Living Because I'm On A Diet! So Shut Up, Everyone!

Don't ever tell anybody you're on a diet. Realistically, most of us are going to be on some sort of diet on and off for the rest of our lives. But if you tell people about it they give you endless shit. My wife tells me I need to lose weight. So I finally decide now is the time. I get mentally and physically ready for the pain. I have enough projects to do to keep my mind off food and drink. So I begin. Within a day or two, my wife is griping that I'm in a lousy mood. Of course I am in a lousy mood! I haven't had my usual vodka tonics and cheeseburgers. I'm hungry! I know that alcohol plays a huge role. So I eliminate it completely. But then she tells me if I'd have a cocktail I would be in a much better mood. I want to say, "Take your pick, fat and drunk or slimmer and in a bad mood!" But I don't. I just try harder. Then after a dinner of skinless, boneless chicken breast and six tiny carrots she starts cooking brownies! God Almighty! How can I make any diet last when I can smell the brownies cooking?

Then word starts to spread to my family and friends that I am on a diet. With the news only a day old, everybody is on my case. "Try this! Try that! Well, on my last diet I could only eat xyz. My doctor told me those aren't good for you. Try this herbal stuff!" my friend says. "Have you started jogging again? We got a Bowflex! You should get one!" someone advises. It never ends!

Five Potatoes

Then after a week or so I begin to feel like I might be able to keep going. Like, ok, I can do this. So, I'm feeling good and decide to treat myself. Maybe it's just a regular Coke or something, but whatever it is it's not on the diet! And of course, I get caught! "Dad, you can't have that Coke!" my son shouts. "Since when is barbeque sauce on your diet?" my wife asks.

Sitting around the table watching everyone eat as they please makes me sick! If I could just have a baked potato with butter and bacon bits! Potatoes are vegetables, right? After two weeks my sense of humor is gone and I'm snapping at everyone. I get headaches and I hate myself for being so short with people. In the third week, true enjoyment of the day is gone. Everything is about drinking water and running enough errands to avoid stopping at fast food places. My morning Cheerios are shared with the dog, because I no longer have a taste for them. Exercise is getting harder and harder. I stare at the pantry door. This sucks. I've stopped living.

Bad idea! I don't want to stop living! I want to start eating! My wife says, "It's ok, dear, everything in moderation."

Unless you've known the extremes you can't know moderation! I guess I've got some more extremes to learn about.

Oh, the hell with clever sayings! We need a magic diet pill!

THREE POTATO: THE DEN

Remote-controlled Cheetos

Think back to the days of manual television, if you are old enough to remember them. Remember how someone in the family would have to get up, walk a few feet, change the channel and sit back down? Usually the kids got ordered to do this because Dad didn't feel like getting up and Mom was always busy somewhere else and really never wanted to watch anything her husband wanted to watch anyway. Then within a few seconds or at most a few minutes, another order went out. "I don't want to watch this. Johnny, go change it to *Bonanza*."

With the advent of remote controls for everything, this whole situation has changed dramatically. Remote controls are responsible for a whole new category of aggravation between man and women. We've all heard about "channel surfing" as a male-dominated finger sport. And we've all heard about how women just want to watch something, anything, for more than 10 seconds. This thesis is well documented in pop culture. However, what has not been documented by print media or television is how the remote control has sped up the ability of women to "control" the environment of the room and aggravate her husband/boyfriend in a relentless hail storm of orders and cruel comments about his ability to even push the right button. She knows he doesn't push her buttons anymore in any part of their lives. But she views the remote as the ultimate tool to push his anger button.

As a separate thesis, I think it's evident that more women have joined the military in recent years as a direct result of learning at an early age how to give orders via the remote control! And they are very, very good at it. Over the next decade it's possible that the American woman will become the new "drill instructor" of the American home and possibly take over the Pentagon. All because of the remote control! By the way, female command of the Pentagon would probably bring about world peace. You think AlQaeda is scared now! Watch out, you bastards!

Anyway, back to the den. You are doing some channel surfing but mostly going back to the movie or sporting event and staying on the channel for five to ten minutes rather than the usual five to ten seconds. So you are sort of proud of yourself. Through her yell therapy you're actually cutting back on channel surfing and demonstrating to her that you are nearly cured. But then it happens. A commercial comes on which has a loud obnoxious sound track, even louder than the program. Of course, the networks deny commercials are louder, but whom are they trying to kid? You know it's loud; despite holding a drink, reading *Sports Illustrated*, eating Cheetos and petting the dog, all while watching the TV, you reach as quickly as possible for the remote to attempt to turn the volume down when the blast comes. "Turn that down! That's horrible! I can't hear myself think!" she shrieks. You know it's too loud. You knew it before she did, but in the half second it took to reach the remote the shrill of her voice combined with the musically challenged commercial have rattled your cage. With Cheetos falling and your drink about to go over you manage to throw off your glasses (because you're nearsighted and can't see the buttons on the remote). You lose the page you were reading in *Sports Illustrated*. Then—within three quarters of a second and the verbal barrage behind—you do the worst thing possible. You hit the wrong button on the remote! Oh God! Now everything has fallen, you're spinning the remote to try and get back to the original station at lower decibels. And here it comes!

"What are you doing? Jesus dear, I was watching that show! What have you done? Turn it down for God's sake! Oh, just give me the remote. I'll do it. What's wrong with you? Can't you work a remote?" she says in a loud, exasperated voice. What else is there to do but hand her the remote, sink deeper into total failure and respond silently, "Yes, drill sergeant! The private is a maggot!"

Not to mention that once again you will miss the fourth quarter—but hey, those Meg Ryan romantic comedies are a good background for cleaning up Cheetos!

Hidden Talents

Isn't it amazing how talented your wife is? When you're away she can do anything! She is strong! She is invincible! She is woman! Ah, but when you're home—that's a different story! She can't change a light bulb. She can't lift the bottled water out of the car. She can't reach the wooden salad bowl. She can't pull down the attic steps. She can't turn on the surround sound. She can't get the cork out of the wine bottle. She can't get the top off the jar. She can't find the checkbook. She can't call the cable company. You get the idea. "Honey, come fix this dryer exhaust!"

So, next time you go away, stay away. Everything will get done! It's amazing. The groceries get carried inside. The car gets washed. The movies get returned to the video place. The ladder gets put away. The batteries get changed in the flashlights. The picture gets hung in the den. The touch-up on the accent wall gets fresh paint. The azaleas get planted.

You didn't know your wife had these hidden talents, because they only get used when you're away.

Better stop and think next time you're going away. What other talents does she have?

Leave a few things undone and you'll find out!

No wonder Martha Stewart's husband left her! He knew Martha would do everything if he left!

I Hear And Obey

Why is talking on the phone so difficult? It rings. You pick it up. You say hello. You listen. The conversation begins. It's not too hard, right? Wrong! You see, it's never a call between you and the party on the other end. It's really a three-person call with only two phones. No one mentioned this in the marriage vows. The minister/priest/rabbi/J.o.P. should have added the to the vows the words, "I shall obey the facial expressions, background comments both whispered and shouted, written messages, pantomime acts and all other methods of communication by my spouse, while I am politely trying to listen to the person at the other end of the phone!"

This behavior is, of course, very distracting. I can't really pay respectful attention to the caller while my wife is sticking her finger in her mouth and gyrating across the floor signaling like an umpire signals strike three. My only hope is to try and interpret that she doesn't want to go to dinner with these people if they're the last people on Earth and then think of an honest-sounding excuse as she listens in to make sure it sounds ok. Usually, this happens when you really do want to accept the invitation.

After hanging up, even though she's listened in on everything I've said and given me most of what to say, she still asks me to replay the entire conversation. "What did he say?" she asks. "Oh, they wanted us to go to that new hip restaurant on the West Side that was written up in *Los Angeles Magazine* last month. They got a break on a reservation and thought we might like to join

89

them. That's all." "What!" she cries. "I'd love to go there." "Well, when you made the vomiting signal followed by the throat cutting signal, I thought you meant no way!" I expound. "Call them back, I want to go!" she pleads. "Oh! Yeah! Great! What would you like me to tell them now? Oh, I've just checked with my wife and even though she would rather swallow spiders, we'd love to join you for dinner!"

When I'm on an important call with my sister, brother, or kids it's ok for her to talk up a storm. She tells me from the background what to say, what to do and even includes editorial comments. I can't hear a thing over the phone with her talking in the background. I can't concentrate. So what else can I do but be obnoxious and hold up the phone to her face and say, "Here—you talk to them!"

Role reversal just doesn't work with the phone. She's on a half-hour call with one of her family members. About twenty minutes into it I really need to jump in and say that it's time to go somewhere. But this only gets you the frown and the sweeping, horizontal, full arm wave, meaning, "Go away! I can't be interrupted!" Having received the sweeping, horizontal, full arm wave so many times, I am prepared the next time. I get results by announcing, "We have to go somewhere," and pointing at my watch. But this time I do it only ten minutes into her phone call. I suffer through the sweeping, horizontal, full arm wave and the obligatory sneer that comes with it and realize I have made a preemptive strike. Now she will be thinking about this and feel pressured to get off the phone. It might only get me an additional five minutes, but hey, that's five more minutes she can bitch about the temperature inside the car.

It's One Thing!

In the beginning of the movie *City Slickers*, Jack Palance holds up one finger and tells Billy Crystal that the value of life can be summed up in "one thing." Billy Crystal takes the rest of the movie to figure out what that one thing could be. My experience tells me that Jack Palance was right. The "one thing" that defines life is the "one thing" out of two or three hundred things you do in a day that your wife notices you didn't do! It is as if she has a video camera following you around. She and her girl friends are sitting around watching the monitor all day, taking bets on which of the several hundred things you will forget. Then that "one thing" moves up to the top of the list of the most immediate things to bitch about the moment she walks in the door. This way she can be upset enough about the "one thing" to rage at you. That means there will definitely be no sex that night. In addition, you will have to be sucking up all night to make sure she's not too mad about the "one thing." You will have to make up for it the next day by doing the two or three hundred things that are on your list anyway, but also by doing the thing that you missed the day before plus doing it better than anyone under any circumstances in the history of marriage.

The example that comes to mind is the time my wife left for a three-day weekend to visit her parents, who, fortunately, live fifteen hundred miles away. I could have chased women, flown to Vegas, had a party, hired hookers, watched ESPN all weekend or just plain chilled. But did I do any of these things? No! I spent the entire three days doing things I thought would please her!

I cleaned and waxed the kitchen floor. I watered all the plants. I did the laundry, vacuumed every room, cut the grass, dusted all the furniture, put everything away, bought fresh flowers for each room, bought groceries, put them away, polished some silver, took old things (of mine) to the Salvation Army, fixed the leaking faucet, scrubbed the tub, bought her a book, cleaned the windows and blinds, reorganized the front hall closet, washed the car, put our photos in an album and dozens of other little projects too numerous to remember or mention.

All was in order. All she had to do was walk in and throw her arms around me and let me take her on a tour of all the good things I had done by sacrificing my weekend to help make her happier. Hell, I would have unpacked her suitcase if she wanted me to.

But, no!

You see, the moment she gets out of her sister's car in front of the house, before she says hello, before saying or doing anything other than walking up the sidewalk, she has spotted it! The "one thing"! Oh, God, I can see it on her face! She's found it! What could it be? Damn, she's not even in the house yet! This is amazing! I should have sat there watching ESPN all weekend! My body actually aches from all the work! This can't be. No sex for months! What is it? What in the hell is it?

"The flower under the boxwood we planted last week—it's dying! Why didn't you water it? It's dead! That flower was beautiful. That was the flower that my cousin gave us on July 4th! It's dead. Well, have you done anything since I've been away?" she shouts!

"Yeah," I respond. "I did 'one thing'!"

LISTENING TO MOVIES

Women are always slamming men for not listening. I admit it. They are right. We don't listen. It's true.

Just to be fair, it is equally true that women don't listen to movies. Hence, they don't usually appreciate the story, the talent of the writers or the message of the movie. Oh, they think they get it, but they don't. They never hear the really funny lines and they always interrupt when an important scene is unfolding. Then they ask you to rewind it for them but just continue brushing the dog without looking at the movie. Not to mention that women can't quote any lines from movies.

What's the matter, ladies? You can't handle the truth?

Why can't I?

Because we're not in Kansas anymore.

Yeah, but I'll be back.

I'll make you an offer you can't refuse. I'll listen to you for two and a half hours without interruption, if you will sit down, sit still, shut up and pay attention to the movie in its entirety. (If she can take it, so can I.)

I don't buy or sell human beings!

Williston Lamar

Show me the money!

I'll never let go, Jack.

Here's listening to you, kid!

Road trip!

P.N.B.F.H.

There have been so many TV shows and movies with acronyms for titles. Who can keep track? *CSI, JAG, SVU, T2, NYPD, ESPN, NCIS, The Man from U.N.C.L.E.*, etc. I get them all mixed up with SUV, MSNBC, MTV, BET and VH1. I don't really mind all of them and I have to admit it kind of adds an air of mystery to whatever the show may be about. Shows and movies with acronyms for titles seem to be popular and get good ratings.

There is one show that has never been done. There are plenty of real life and fictional characters to draw from. The story possibilities are endless. It could be the longest-running series ever! It would run longer than *M.A.S.H.*!

I call it *P.N.B.F.H.!*

PYSCHO NAZI BITCH FROM HELL!

Y.K.W.Y.A.

YOU KNOW WHO YOU ARE!

I Didn't Do Anything All Day!

As my wife leaves for work, I'm sitting on the couch watching the *Today Show*, still in my sweats that I wore to bed. I'm drinking my morning Coke. As she goes out the door, I shout, "Have a good day, dear! Call me sometime! Bye."

I'm unemployed.

It's 8:00 am. I get off the couch. I use the bathroom to its fullest potential. I'm feeling a little rushed and therefore skip the shower. I remain in my sweats.

Then:

- I change three light bulbs. All require a ladder.
- I clean the barbeque grill.
- I urinate.
- I put away the CDs and videos.
- I install a timer on a lamp.
- I pay the bills.
- I urinate.
- I brush the dogs.
- I throw some chlorine in the pool.
- I empty the little recycling bin into the big recycling can.
- I call the airline and make some reservations.
- I urinate.
- I get another Coke from the refrigerator.
- I put the papers, book and shoes away that are on the stairs.

Five Potatoes

- I call my mother.
- I pick up the dog crap in the backyard.
- I sweep off the porch.
- I water the plants.
- I cut off the dead leaves from the houseplants.
- I gather the dead tree limbs from the yard and fit them into the yard bin.
- I urinate.
- I cut some roses and put them in vases.
- I make and eat a turkey sandwich.
- I write a thank you note.
- I check the Internet for possible jobs.
- I hop in the car and go to the post office.
- I wait in line a half hour at the post office.
- I stop by the liquor store and get two new Cabernets.
- I get the oil changed in the car.
- I urinate at Jiffy Lube.
- I drop off the dry cleaning.
- I fill the car with gas.
- I pick up the dog medicine at the vet.
- I get cash at the ATM.
- I check out the sale at the bike shop.
- I urinate in the restroom at the bike shop.
- I go to the grocery store and pick up something nice for dinner.
- I stop at the hardware store and pick up batteries, light bulbs, and extension cords.
- I stop at the office store and get ink refills for the printer.
- I get fries and a Coke at McDonald's.
- I get home and put the groceries away.
- I put all new batteries in all seven flashlights.
- I urinate.
- I clean off the workbench and put the new light bulbs away.
- I go through the mail.
- I throw out the junk mail and leave the bills and magazines in order.
- I urinate. (It was the third Coke from the drive-through!)

- I put together a bookcase I bought last week and put books on it.
- I urinate.
- I toss tennis balls to the dogs.
- I refill the 5-gallon water jug for the dogs.
- I clean the glass coffee table with glass cleaner.
- I go back on the Internet.
- I send my resume to two headhunters.
- I urinate.
- I start getting the table set for dinner.
- I take the trash bag out of the trash compactor and put in a new one.
- I take the trash out one more time.
- I get all the food prep done.
- I urinate.
- I make a vodka tonic.
- I turn on the news.
- I sit on the couch.

I hear the garage door opening. I tell the dogs that Mommy is home.

She walks in and sees me drinking and watching TV on the couch in my sweats!

"Did you leave the couch all day?"

"Are you going to be unemployed for the rest of your life?"

"Paybacks are hell, buddy! Wait until you get a job! I'm going to quit and sit around like you!"

"What did you do all day? Did you even move off the couch?"

She says all these things in a fairly serious tone that scares me a little.

"Have a glass of this new Cabernet, dear," I say, as I avoid answering all of her questions.

"As you sip this glass of wine and make yourself comfortable you can read from this status report the things I've done today! As you can see by the length of the list, I didn't do anything all day! Mostly, I just pissed the day away!"

Epilogue:

God Bless June Cleaver. She and millions like her did all this and managed to shower, dress up, and make the kids' lunches, pick them up at school, take them to Cub Scouts and Brownies and wear pearls while doing it! Maybe that was your mother, too! Thanks!

Part Of A Movie

Guys can watch a movie on television regardless of how much of the movie has already aired. Even with only ten minutes left in the movie guys can watch it. Who wouldn't watch the last ten minutes of *Animal House* or *Butch Cassidy and the Sundance Kid* or *The Patriot* or the last half of *Patton* or *True Lies* or *Rocky*? So, it's 8:30 p.m. and you both have decided to watch a movie. Surfing over a couple hundred stations on your satellite TV, you keep making suggestions of movies to watch. But it's an infuriating process. Why? Because she can't watch any portion of a movie. Most of the movies on TV started at 8:00 p.m., so you're thirty minutes into whatever movie you both want to watch. It's too late. "That movie has already started! I can't watch that!" she cries out from the kitchen.

So what else can you do? Just watch old episodes of *Seinfeld* and *M.A.S.H.*! They start a new episode every half hour!

WHAT ELSE DON'T YOU NEED THAT I CAN'T DO FOR YOU?

You know how it is. She has asked you repeatedly to fix the curtains in the living room. The curtains look great. They are just a little tilted by 1/2 an inch to one side. So finally, one Sunday, I decide it's time to fix the curtains. I set out to do it.

She goes shopping!

I get out all the tools and the stepstool. I think it's an easy fix. But alas! While taking the first screw out of the wall the plaster breaks off. This leaves no room for the screw to go back in at the new height. Plus the wall is really unsightly now that a big chunk of it is missing. This means I have to take the whole curtain set down and get out the Spackle and somehow find matching paint for the wall. And that means getting out brushes and drop cloths and clean-up materials. "Good grief, Charlie Brown!" I whisper to myself along with a barrage of four-letter words. You know what happens now! I lose patience. I've got to see the fourth quarter! So obviously a drop cloth isn't necessary and there is no need to wait for the Spackle to dry. So on I go. Little drops of paint splatter on the table and carpet below. "That's ok—I'll clean those up later," I'm thinking. The curtain rod won't go back up in the same place and you realize it's too short to screw into a different part of the wall. As I realize this one end of the curtain dips into the paint can. "Well, maybe she won't see it. That won't show behind the couch!" Then it happens. I fall from the stepstool while holding up all the curtains. I feel a pain in my back and then realize the cordless drill is underneath me! More four-letter words spew forth. But now the curtain rod has bent and there's more paint on the curtains. "Damn it!" I shout. There is only one way out of this. The rods, the curtains—all go in the trash. Quickly I patch and paint the hole in the wall and clean up all the tools and get the paint back to the basement.

Here's the plan. Get on the couch to watch the fourth quarter. When she arrives home from shopping she realizes the curtains are gone. In dismay she calls out, "Where are the curtains?" Here's the good part. "Oh dear, I got up there and started to fix them but they were really dirty and the rod was not in good shape so I just took them down. You can get new ones sometime this week."

This temporarily satisfies her until I hear, "What's this paint on my table?" Damn, forgot to clean that up!

Movies All Guys Should Watch (According To Me!)

Ok, this is mostly addressed to younger guys, but you older guys should see these movies again. Here's my list:

The Day of the Jackal
Chariots of Fire
Heaven Can Wait
The Caine Mutiny
The Right Stuff
Breaking Away
Apollo 13
Boys Town
Dances with Wolves
Rudy
True Lies
Braveheart
The Enemy Below
Patton
The Bridge on the River Kwai
The Magnificent Seven or Seven Samurai
The Good, the Bad, and the Ugly
Arthur
Jesus Christ Superstar
Castaway

The Hunt for Red October
Black Hawk Down
The Flight of the Phoenix
Crimson Tide

That's a start!

Why should you watch these or watch them again? What else are you going to talk about with the guys when you don't have a date? Are you going to read a book? I doubt it! What are you going to do when your wife leaves you? What are you going to do if she doesn't leave you?

"Houston, we have a problem."

Stair Master

I often leave things around the house. Yes, it's a leftover habit from bachelorhood. I admit it! However, I am organized about where I leave things around the house. For example, I like to put things on the stairway that belong upstairs. I place them neatly to the side of the stairs. Then, later on, I pick up two or three things as I go upstairs and put them away. This leaves three or four things to take up the stairs the next time. These things are not just my things. They might be her things. Her shoes, her watch, her bath things or things for the medicine cabinet in the upstairs bathroom are possibilities. Among these things is usually a book or two and some paperwork or photos to be put away. She will make a dozen trips up and down the stairs this day and never take anything up to be put away. What's with that? She can spot anything else anywhere in the house that needs cleaning up, but she can't see things on the stairs! Nothing ever goes up the stairs! Indeed, this seems to be the "invisible zone." So next time you want to buy new golf clubs, just bring them home and put them on the stairs! Yesterday, I brought home a new mini flat screen TV and sat the box on the stairs. She never saw it!

Indeed, I am the Stair Master!

What Else Can Be Said? Enough Already!

What else is there to be said about sharks? What more can be written or televised on the Titanic? Gosh, let's do a few hundred more shows on the pyramids! Oh, but what about dinosaurs? Gee, we haven't heard enough about them! UFOs, enough already! How about reincarnation? The redundancy of these programs is redundant! How can people continue to watch this stuff over and over? We get it! Stop it!

Anyone out there need to see any more documentaries on Hitler? Hey, I think we get it now! Geez, why don't we just create the Hitler Channel? There is so much stuff on Hitler, sometimes I think the big gold "H" History Channel logo on the bottom right of the screen really does stand for Hitler!

Let's ask the networks and cable companies to take a programming hiatus. I need a sabbatical! Just for one year. That's all I ask. One year without a single show about sharks, pyramids, dinosaurs, UFOs, reincarnation and Hitler! Please give us a chance to regenerate brain tissue. Give us a chance to forget. Please!

One year should be enough time to give someone a chance to produce some new material. I was thinking maybe it could be something like this: Hitler arrives on Earth in a pyramid-shaped

Five Potatoes

UFO from the planet Titanic and kills off all the dinosaurs. Tired and old from killing all the dinosaurs, Hitler dies and is reincarnated as a great white shark!

Post-frat House Style

The last generation has fought hard to avoid creating a Levittown environment. We've avoided look-alike houses, look-alike dens, look-alike living rooms and look-alike dining rooms. We wanted to be unique and artistic and define our lives and our excellent taste (which of course is better than any colleague, friend, neighbor or classmate) by restoring a house, refinishing the floors, selecting special furniture and meaningful artwork, refinishing this and repainting that. We immerse ourselves in the "Five P's"of home design. These are paint, plants, pictures, photons and people.

We've failed miserably! Everyone's house still looks the same—only now, the interiors all look like the "Pottery Barn" or "Crate and Barrel"! The new housing developments are just the next generation of Levittown, only with Corian counters and tiled foyers. "We got to pick the colors!" you rationalize. By the time you've renovated an old house you've been caught up in credit card debt, lost weekends, missed fourth quarters, blood, sweat and tears. Plus you can't invite anyone over for four or five years because the place is renovation hell!

Oh, how we've lived up to what Dennis Miller calls, "The reduced expectations of an off the shelf culture." I guess it's not so bad. If we guys lived alone and didn't have anyone to impress or compete with we'd still be living in something that looked like "Early Frat House Style." And after all, don't all frat houses look alike? Now with our wives and some girlfriends still along for the ride we've just been forced to elevate ourselves to "Post-Frat House Style" and maybe some Michael Graves-designed teapots from Target!

The beer-soaked, vomit-stained, bugger-filled couch in the old frat house was still more comfortable than the "Pottery Barn's" newest creation, even if my wife did pay for it!

Give Me College Football Or Give Me Death!

I've never done drugs. I don't have a gambling problem. I drink vodka tonics with some regularity. I've never been in jail. I never got kicked out of school. I never failed a single subject! I don't fight with people. I've never hit anyone or physically harmed anyone in any way. I don't chase skirts. I vote. I like my family. I rescued two dogs. I was a Big Brother. I help people and support various organizations. I enjoy traveling, reading, cycling, tennis and organizing the garage. I write thank you notes. I have no problems to share on daytime talk shows.

Just let me have college football! I want to sit alone in front of the TV on fall Saturdays and scream and cuss! I want to throw things. I want to jump up and down and shout, "Go, go, go!" I want to be upset when my team loses. I want to mope for a while. I use the "f" word constantly and plenty of other four-letter words. I want to run around shaking my fist in the air and shouting, "Yes, yes, yes!" when my team makes the last-second touchdown. I want to flip the bird at the TV screen and the opposing coach! I want to feel the vibration in my chest from the drums of the marching band. I want to bask in the glow of reading about my team's victory in the Sunday morning paper. I want to think about all the people that I know who went to the losing school and say "Gotcha!" I want to feel the sweat on my palms before a big game. I have a good-luck chair to sit in. My

Five Potatoes

school flag hangs above the garage on football Saturdays! This is important stuff!

My mother thinks something is wrong with me. She thinks I have some sort of Jekyll and Hyde personality disorder. I ask her just to allow me this one vice. "It could be a lot worse!" I explain. "Think about all the problems I don't have!"

She wants to help. So, I ask her to say her rosary before each game to help out the team!
I'm a tortured soul. I do need help. My mother is looking into a Betty Ford rehab program for me! She told me there is a twelve-step program—every Saturday in the fall!

Cleaning Frenzy! Everybody Run For Your Lives!

I know a woman who goes into such convulsive cleaning frenzies that she actually wears her bike helmet while cleaning so she won't hurt her head!

I hate it when women go into cleaning frenzies. We all have them sometimes, but women make you feel particularly guilty when you don't share in their frenzy on that particular day. There's no warning. She just starts on a Saturday morning. First she gathers the laundry and one thing leads to another. Before you know it she's tripping over your outstretched legs, rolling her eyes and huffing and puffing at your laziness. She's got five or six things going at once. The laundry, the dishes, the vacuum, the reorganization of the pantry, the scrubbing of the shower stall and the disposal of the stack of magazines, not to mention the rearrangement of the linen closet—and this is just the beginning phase of the cleaning frenzy.

A heavy cloud of guilt is beginning to circle over your head. Your fat ass is just sitting there in her view every time she comes through the den. Any moment now she's going to ask you to get up and help her with something. Although you'll give it your best effort to clean up the one thing she's asked you to do, you know that your methodology will be unacceptable and that sooner or later she'll have to show you how she wants it done. My favorite is when I get to make the beds. I've never made them to her standards in twelve years! So I avoid the bed-making now. She makes the beds and I just sleep on top of the bedspread so I don't have to make it in the morning!

Men go into whacko cleaning frenzies as well. We just don't want any help and don't expect anyone else to help. This is because during the cleaning process we know we don't want anyone to see the really stupid things we are going to do or the big mess we are going to make that requires triple the time and effort to clean up. We don't want anyone to make fun of us when we do these stupid things and we don't want to be interrupted when we find the twenty-year-old copy of *Penthouse* in a box in the garage! Most importantly, we never make anyone feel guilty when they would rather do something else!

"I can clean this garage myself! Please—go shopping!"

FOUR:
THE WORKPLACE

He's The Gardener, Not A Harvard MBA!

My gardener is as successful as they come. He's probably going to heaven when he dies. He is a fine man. He is humble, honest and gracious. He asks for nothing other than to be my gardener and come every week to do what he does to keep my place neat. He is not a landscape architect or a botanist. He doesn't know a single Latin name for a plant. I suppose he doesn't know many English names of plants. But he comes every week without fail. When his day to come falls on Christmas or the Fourth of July he comes the next day without fail. He never sends me a bill. He just waits for me to remember to pay him if and when I see him. If I ask him to do something out of his normal routine, he just does it without asking for more money. He has some equipment, but not much and everything is old. My yard is just one of eight or so he does every day, six days a week. On many days, I leave him some cold drinks on the back porch. He rarely takes any. Sometimes he fixes things that I don't even know are broken. Sometimes his young nephew comes to help him. When it's time to fertilize or cut the roses he does so without saying a word. His old pickup truck is battered and beaten. When loaded with lawn equipment it looks like a small scrap metal yard. Through his work he accomplishes something every day. Few people can say that in the business world. His work makes forty-eight families happier once a week by making their environment just a little nicer. He is such a good man. He is a successful man.

I didn't understand all this when I hired him years ago on a recommendation from a friend. I thought he was a businessman. I thought he was doing a job for money, trying to get more work and trying to please his customers. I thought he would be trying to earn a little more to save for a new truck. I thought I was going to be receiving invoices in the mail and lots of additional billings for the extras I asked him to do. I thought if a holiday came up he would skip that week and still bill me for the whole month.

In the first month of our association, I called the number on his card several times to tell him about things I wanted done. No one ever answered. There was no answering machine. Once I did get someone who just told me he wasn't there. But, he never returned the call. In the second month I started leaving him notes taped to the fence. Still no response on the note though it appeared the work had been done by the time I got home. The second month came and went. I thought I must be running up a hell of a bill.

Growing impatient, I went to my friend who had provided the original recommendation. I said, "What's up with this guy? I can't get a hold of him. He has no answering machine. He doesn't return phone calls. He never leaves me any notes in the mailbox. I can't wait around at home for him to show up. I've gotta be at work. He never sends me a bill. I thought you said this guy was good. And I thought you said he was reliable. What's the deal?"

My friend just put his hand on my shoulder and said, "Relax. He's the gardener, not a Harvard MBA."

After another month went by, I figured that out for myself.

Seven years later, I'm thrilled to say he's the gardener, not a Harvard MBA! Thank God!

My gardener knows success!

SHE IS A GOOD PERSON, BUT . . .

Conversations about people at work are so lame. Our litigious, politically correct society, compounded by our own selfish desire to be perceived as a thoughtful and decent person, has forced everyone to place restrictions on what they say. So much for free speech and the First Amendment! This is not about things like verbal abuse or sexual harassment in the workplace. It's really about how we talk about others when they are not around. No one ever says what he really wants to say. Gee, some feelings might get hurt or word might make it back to that person. As well, no one wants to be perceived as mean, because mean people suck in the new millennium. So what are we to do?

We always start the conversation about the person by saying, "She's a really good person, but . . ." Now, what this little preamble has done is given notice that you think this person you are about to talk about is probably a church-going, charitable, family type, with good intentions and a dog at home. You don't actually know any of these things because you rarely talk to her and if you did it wasn't about her church or dog! Actually, you're just giving her the benefit of the doubt with the old "good person" line. It also eliminates any possibility that the receiver of the upcoming information will be put off by what you are about to say, since you are, of course, the most fair, reasonable, non-judgmental, sincere and ethical person in the company. Then you go on to say, "But I think she's way out of line here. Why can't she get her report in on time? Doesn't she understand grade-school math? And what about that outfit? Jesus, she looked like she was going fishing! What is she thinking? You know those guys in I.S. hate her! I can see why! Did you hear what she said to the boss in that status meeting the other day? Boy, her husband's not getting any! Can you imagine having to deal with that twenty-four hours a day?"

So that's the bulk of the conversation. The person you're telling this to is agreeing and nodding and pointing out some other obvious shortcomings and behavioral problems. Then eventually other people get talked about.

But think of the shareholders' money that just went down the drain. You've wasted fifteen minutes of company time trashing somebody for the sport of it. What's the point? All of you will be laid off when the company runs out of work and you'll never have to see these people again. But the conversations never stop and shareholder money just flows away into your undeserved paycheck.

My suggestion is to get it all over with in thirty seconds and save the company fourteen and a half minutes. Here's what you do. The moment her name comes up, forget the pleasantries. Just get to the point. "I know I speak for everyone here when I say she's a psycho Nazi bitch from hell. Screw her and the horse she rode in on! What's next on the agenda?"

Don't Tell Anybody, But....

I hate it when people at work use the phrase, "Don't tell anybody, but...." This phrase is a license to tell everybody everything. Ninety-nine percent of the time it's bad news, bad gossip, cynical thinking or something to do with sex! Everybody knows this so why bother to say it? Just say, "Hey, I'm going to tell you something and you should tell everybody!"

"Hey, did you hear George is getting laid off?"

"Jennifer told me that Bob is hot for Lynne!"

"Can you believe they're going to hire a new V.P. to study the organization?"

"He's an ass!"

"Boy, has he gained weight! He looks like a pig!"

"The budget is going to be arbitrarily reduced! Can you believe it?"

"He's in big trouble with the boss!"

"I heard she's not sick! She had to visit her mother!"

"I hear we're not getting increases this year!"

If you are going to use the phrase, "Don't tell anybody but . . .," say something like this:

"Don't tell anybody, but . . . I finished the project a week early and $30,000 under budget! The boss said it's state-of-the-art and that it will make huge money for the company! And, he said I'm going to get the credit! I worked sixty hours a week and didn't charge any overtime! I'll probably get a promotion! Oh yeah, and my girlfriend, you know the model, says that I'm the best she's ever had! But don't tell anybody!"

Spreadsheets

What a joke! I was just in a meeting with a CEO of a major U.S. corporation. People had spent days writing and rewriting reports, estimates, organization charts and plans. There were spreadsheets and stacks of paper everywhere. There were lots of people trying to examine them as if they could actually make a decision from some minute piece of data buried on page 37. Oh please! Get a life. This meeting was costing the company a fortune in executive time. The CEO actually didn't have to suck up to anybody so he got right to the point. "Ok," he said. "I understand we need some resources. What do we need?" "Well sir," the senior person spoke up. "If you will go to page 37 and note that project X and project Y have schedules that overlap with project C and project D which shows up on page 59 and that the revised organization chart on page 22 will change the location of one of our offices shown on page 18, therefore involving the facilities group and the . . ." "Stop right there!" the CEO said. "Does someone have one sheet of paper that tells me who we need to hire and at what positions?" Silence filled the room. There was no sheet of paper with just that information. There were MBAs and CPAs and a lawyer or two and a bunch of project types, program directors and managers, but no one could provide the one piece of paper with the answer! "Ok then, let's reschedule when you are ready," the CEO responded. More hours and profits down the drain. Days were spent reworking the spreadsheets. What a waste!

But who cares? We're all getting paid! Let's take another week to figure out what we already know! We'll just have to use bolder graphics to make sure it says what we want it to say! But this time let's make sure we have even more spreadsheets and charts and graphs! "Yeah," I said. "But who's going to do that?" "Well, isn't it obvious?" my friend retorted. "We make a bunch of red marks and give it to the secretary! She'll do it! She doesn't want to get laid off! She doesn't look at anything she types anyway!"

More spreadsheets!

THE ANTI-INTELLECT

I always like the people I work with who actually think about stuff and then formulate their thoughts into words and share them with their colleagues. Too many of us don't do this.

It doesn't matter if your thoughts are profound or profane. It doesn't matter if you think about something stupid or something important as long as you put some intellect behind your thoughts. And, most importantly, it certainly doesn't matter if it's about work. We learn much more about our colleagues and their humanity when we are capable of talking about something other than work. Those are conversations that truly add to our appreciation of others.

To stimulate or advance one's intellect, one must have an intellect to begin with. Sadly, in my opinion, most American workplaces by their very design tend to discourage the advancement of intellect. People wander down the hallways bemoaning the fact that "we" are so dysfunctional. "Oh, woe is me! We have no organization and no communication. The right hand doesn't know what the left hand is doing! Do the guys with the windows have any clue what we do here? Does anything ever change, other than Vice Presidents?"

Come on, people! Is that the most thought and intellectual power you can put into some of these work situations? Scott Adams did it and he's kicking butt with *Dilbert*! Are you such vegetables that you can't put a little thinking behind the standard workplace clichés that come out of your mouths? You're not doing your job anyway, so you might as well think up some interesting stuff! Why sit there like a turd?

Come on! Put the "fun" back in dysfunctional! Think! It may be a new experience!

If You Put A Banana In Your Briefcase, Use it Wisely!

An architect, a contractor and the client were having an intense, combative, all-day meeting to resolve some money issues on a large project. As the meeting reached the late afternoon the screaming and blaming got out of control. Trying to prove his point the architect grabbed his briefcase to pull out a document. Still yelling at the contractor, the architect didn't even glance at his briefcase before reaching in and pulling out the banana he had planned to have at the lunch break.

Without a moment's hesitation the architect said to the startled contractor and client, "And don't ever think that I won't use this in court if I have to! Take that!" And he took his banana and his briefcase and stormed out of the room!

Perplexed, the contractor and the client didn't know what to do next. After some silence the client said to the contractor, "Well I guess he's got us! I've heard about the banana defense. It's worked in court before." The client then got up and left the room. Left alone to ponder what had just taken place the contractor just sat there expressionless. That was the end of the meeting!

Not funny! But a true story! I was there!

"You People Make My Ass Twitch!"*

Have you ever sat in a business meeting where you had nothing to contribute because you thought everyone in the room was an ass and that they were wasting the company's money by talking in circles, making no decisions and dwelling on the absurd? Each person thought his or her job was so important that they had to say something whether it was of any substance or not. Millions and millions of shareholder dollars go down the drain every day in corporate business. The company bottom line would be way up if everyone would just shut up!

Everyone who manages someone just has to have a staff meeting to ensure that everyone knows who sits at the head of the table. No one listens. No one wants to listen. They just want to know if you're going to have lunch brought in! This is why most bosses fail. They won't leave their office unless there is a meeting. Instead of taking an hour to meet with twelve people in one room, a good leader should meet with one person in that person's office for five minutes. Hey it's the same amount of time and both individuals get eye-to-eye contact, personal attention, a visit from the boss, clear one-on-one supervision and instructions. Maybe some work would actually get done.

If leaders of a company want to get something done, they should announce "No Talking Days," or, even better, "No Talking

Five Potatoes

Weeks." Then everyone would have to communicate through actions, not words. Forget e-mails, memos, and telephone calls.

When Strother Martin says to Paul Newman in *Cool Hand Luke*, "What we have here is a failure to communicate," he wasn't talking about talking more; he was talking about failure to take the action he wanted. Everyone is afraid to take action because that would mean some sort of work product would be produced and no matter what work you do you are bound to be criticized for it. Criticism is the disincentive to everything. So if we all just sit around talking about stuff there will be no time to actually get anything done and that becomes your excuse. "Well, gee, I was in the meeting all day. There was no time to do the project! Now I guess we'll have to call a meeting to discuss the project all over again!"

So next time you're sitting in one of those meetings and nothing of substance is being said, and certainly nothing is going to be accomplished, get up as if you're going to the bathroom and don't come back. Otherwise, your ass will begin twitching and leave an embarrassing yet appropriate mark on the chair!

* Meg Ryan in the movie *French Kiss*.

Why Don't You Call?

When you were dating, women were always upset because, "You don't call." Basically, it's not because you weren't going to call her or because there's another women you want to call. It's just that you don't want to end up spending the entire fourth quarter talking about your relationship! One really needs to set aside a lot of time to do that because you know all conversations lead to "the dreaded relationship." So you don't call much. This goes on for years.

Later in life, you're married. Each of you works. You love her, so you call her at work. Actually you call her a couple of times a day. What's this? She goes crazy! "Don't call me at work! What do you want? My secretary thinks you're insecure!" she cries. You ask yourself, "How did this happen?" All those hours I gave up yakking about her hair, her skin, her brother, her mother, her roommate and of course "the dreaded relationship." Hey, it's not like she's curing cancer at work.

She always wanted you to call. Now you're calling her three times a day. So what gives? She never calls you anymore. So to solve this problem, next time you call her and she picks up, say, "Hello, hello," and then hang up quickly. Then don't ever call her again. She'll be calling you in about a week saying, "Why don't you call?" But you can always say, "Hey, last I time I called you, you hung up on me!"

THE LEISURE SUIT

My wife once spent the entire day at Saks Fifth Avenue. She was shopping for one thing. She needed a business suit for an important job interview. I was at work. She called me a couple of times to say she was trying on many things. She never left the store. At 6:00 p.m. she called to say she thought she had found the perfect outfit. Could I please come over to Saks and take a look? "Sure," I said.

A half-hour later I found her at Saks. "Ok," she said. "Let me go try this on." Waiting patiently for her, I couldn't wait to see what had taken eight and a half hours to pick out.

Suddenly she was there, standing in front of me with some kind of bizarre, pinkish, retro 70's leisure suit strapped to her body! It was really hard not to laugh. I had to bite my cheeks. After all, she had been there for eight and a half hours! Therefore, there must be some rationale behind this. While she was trying to explain it to me, I stood up, walked about six feet over to the Versace area, pulled out a sharp suit in her size and said, "Here, try this." All of two minutes had passed. The suit fit perfectly. It was classic yet stylish; sophisticated and sexy, yet conservative.

She got the job after interviewing in the suit I selected!

Who says men don't have an eye for fashion? We know what we want to see in the interview!

Is that sexual harassment?

Let's Talk Right Over The Most Important Point!

Rearranging the deck chairs on the Titanic is an art form! Some people can do it. Some people have to jump or they're forced to get off. Just remember, only those who got off the Titanic actually survived! This is true in business and family life.

Rearranging the deck chairs on the Titanic: is there any more appropriate analogy to a doomed relationship or business? Avoidance of the thing that's really gone wrong—all humans seem to have mastered this behavior. It happens to us every day in the workplace. It happens to us every day at home and at social functions. It happens with your kids and with your in-laws. It happens with your neighbors, friends and colleagues.

No one wants to be bold. It hurts too much. Maybe things will get better. Maybe someone will plug the leak. Wishful thinking. It's more difficult to say what you really want to say for fear of retaliation.

In your personal life you might want to say things like, "I hate you! I want to leave the room! I want to leave the house! I want to leave the marriage!" But you can't bring yourself to do it. In the business world you might want to say, "We have no work and no money coming in. Our industry is dead. Our attempts to revitalize it have failed. We've let down our client base. We're in

Five Potatoes

the wrong location." But, saying things like that would be perceived as defeatist and pessimistic. Your guts are screaming out to you, "Stop! Look, I just want to get off this voyage and get in a lifeboat! You can swim for it if you want or stay on the ship, but I'm outta here!

"Why? Because the goddamn SHIP IS SINKING!"

How do we miss the point so often? We talk around it and over it and under it, but no one will say it. Maybe it's because we are all wimps now. We don't want to hurt anyone's feelings. They might be traumatized. Worse, they might file a lawsuit.

So the ship has hit the iceberg. It's going down. Few will live. And there is your old buddy placing the deck chairs in symmetrical double rows with little tables in between and folded blankets on top. You want to help. But he's a sensitive guy. You pause just long enough to roll your eyes and think of the right thing to say. Upon your approach you shout out, "Nice arrangement! Oh, the blankets look really nice that way! Have you thought of placing the deck chairs around the shuffleboard court? I'm impressed with your attention to detail and the timeliness of your effort! Remind me to put something about this in your next performance review!"

"Thanks," he states calmly. "Finding a new arrangement for the deck chairs was one of my goals for this year!"

I want to scream out, "Save yourself, you ignorant fool! What the hell are you doing, you stupid shit? The SHIP IS SINKING! You'll probably die!"

But, with a moment's hesitation, I look at the futile situation and say, "Nice job; while you're doing that, may I borrow your life jacket?"

Epilogue: Cruising With The In-Laws

(My in-laws wanted to go on a cruise to Alaska. I told them I'd be happy to go. No problem. I'd love that! But I gave them one condition. If the ship hit an iceberg and started to go down, I would be dressing as a woman and getting in a lifeboat!)

It's The Restroom, Stupid!

Does everyone in your office hate work? Are your profits down? Have some good people resigned? Are people coming in later and later in the morning? Are they leaving earlier and earlier? Are they taking longer lunch breaks?

It's the restroom, stupid!

Clean up your office restrooms! Renovate them if you have to! Get the dirty old broom, mop and vacuum cleaner out of there. Remove the stuff that's stored in the restroom. Change out the old fixtures for the latest environmentally sound ones. Put in new partitions or renovate the old ones. Make sure the latches work. Increase the number of air changes in the mechanical system. Make sure your restroom is clean and well lit. Make sure you have coat hooks and a table or folding shelf for purses and briefcases. Definitely make sure your restrooms meet ADA standards for accessible design. Create private and somewhat separate entrances to the men's and women's rooms. Place a stylish cabinet in each restroom with little travel samples of items from toothpaste to mouthwash to disposable shaving materials. Think of visitors that have flown halfway across the country to visit your office and need freshening up. Come to think of it, how about that garlic chicken you had for lunch? Make sure your restrooms are well stocked with tissues and toilet tissues. Provide air fresheners. Create privacy. Build in soundproofing.

Employees who aren't comfortable in the restrooms they have to use several times a day will end up going down the hall or down the elevator to someone else's restroom. This will be a source of great embarrassment and lost time. Few things make an employee more content than knowing they will have some privacy and cleanliness in the company restrooms! When you think about it, the restroom is the only refuge for privacy in most offices with lots of open space and cubicles.

Additionally, no one wants the cubicle right outside the restroom door! Move the cubicle or partition it off. Your firm's guests and clients will appreciate the comfortable surroundings In fact, they'll be flush with comfort and just maybe they'll stay long enough to sign that deal!

So fix the leaky faucet, change the drab appearance and fix the broken partitions. If your business is state of the art, state of the art includes the restroom. You may even find better morale and greater profits!

It's the restroom, stupid!

Replay Your Whole Day For Me, Dear!

I love it when my wife gets home from work. She comes in, kicks off her shoes, gets a glass of wine and proceeds to replay her whole day for me. You know, who did what, a useless meeting, a useless person, how boring and unsophisticated engineers can be, this happened, that happened, lunch with so and so, someone got promoted, her boss called in from vacation, the project is over budget, blah, blah, blah. It's great; I love listening to the stories and hearing her version of everything. Then, after forty-five minutes or an hour, she says to me, "How was your day, dear?" "Oh fine," I reply. "What did you do today?" she inquires. "Oh, nothing. The usual," I say. "Ok, well I'm going to change now and I've got to call my sister," she explains. And she's off. Perfect timing; now I get to watch *Jeopardy* and make another vodka tonic. Who says married people never talk?

I love it when she replays her whole day for me!

SOME WHO ARE NOT PAID WHAT THEY ARE WORTH OUGHT TO BE GLAD!

Somebody who worked in a big corporation or government agency must have said this! I don't know who. But were they ever right! Think about this statement. How many people in your office deserve their paycheck? Do you earn every dollar of your paycheck? Did you put in a full eight hours today? Are you worth it? With the exception of very few professions, I think the answer for all of the rest of us is "no." Probably the only people that deserve what they make are trauma room doctors, nurses, paramedics, firemen and public school teachers. The rest of us are making salaries based on perceived value.

That's the key for all of us: "perceived value." No one really knows how to assess value because it is perceived. By you, by me, by our respective professions, by competition, by supply and demand, by geography and by whatever type of business entities are able to offer us employment. So market forces create certain salary ranges for similar positions and endeavors. This is all basic economics and value theory, right? Or, as the business gurus of the nineties like to say, your salary is a "value proposition."

B.S.

Stop perceiving.

Five Potatoes

If you were paid what you are worth you would be making at best minimum wage. Admit it, you don't do shit. You are useless. You come into work. You go to some meetings. You offer lame opinions, because it's all that's expected. Supposedly you manage some people, but they hate you. Yet everyday you say you don't make enough to do this job. Your efforts are not directly responsible for any company profits. Someone with less education and less time on the job could do it better. You've demonstrated no interest in furthering the mission of the company or in improving yourself or others around you. You offer no intellectual thinking to move things forward more efficiently. Your buzzwords are, "That's the way we've always done it." Your idea of analysis is, "That's the way they told me I had to do it." Your idea of following up is to provide no response at all. Your work product is paper that is out of date information the moment it comes off the printer. You take pride in moving paper off your desk. You take no interest in studying the competition. Someone else will do that and write a report. You've been around a while so you have no one to impress. Your very existence is an obstacle to a better work environment, a better product and more productivity. The business is so large that it can afford you and it can keep you there indefinitely. A lump of coal in your chair could do a better job.

You live on in your mysterious work existence. You survive every week. Your paycheck is never late. Your pay increases come once a year. Your benefits accrue. You grovel to the ever-changing cast of executives. You use every ounce of vacation and sick leave. You think others don't earn their pay. You perceive that they perceive that you are not expendable or replaceable. Your value proposition is that you are you and that's enough.

Be glad you are not paid what you're worth! You'd be paying the company!

Daddy, Where Do Interior Decorators Come From?

"Daddy, where do interior decorators come from?" "I don't know, dear. Go ask your mother—she used to be a legal secretary!"

Work Should Be Like School!

If school is supposed to be preparation for life, why do we get a three-month summer vacation, two weeks at Christmas and a week at Easter plus Spring Break? We don't get any of these things when we get a job! Christmas Day! Whoop di do! Thanksgiving Day! Yee ha! Fourth of July! Yeah, great! Where's the three months off in the summer? What about Spring Break? Work should be like school. That's what I was prepared for! What about you? No wonder everybody is messed up! The formulative years of our lives are spent on a certain set of givens. We are programmed from preschool to expect that it's over in nine months and you move on to something else after a three-month sabbatical. The past is mostly forgotten and we change and grow with new challenges, new clothes and new friends. We have no money but we have two weeks to shop for Christmas! I was really happy with that model. Why does it change when you get a job?

If you had a rough year at school with a psycho teacher or if you got picked on or beaten up all that will change during the summer. It doesn't happen that way at work. If you get a shithead boss you have to quit or request a transfer or plant cocaine in his desk. Or you're stuck for ten or fifteen years. No wonder there is so much depression and pain in our society!

The finest prep schools and the lousiest public schools in the country don't go to school between Christmas and New Year's! Why should we go to work then? Why should we work in those hot July and August summer days, when we could lifeguard at the pool?

There is some moron politician out there right now thinking, "Ah, ha. I'll improve our schools by . . . making schools like work!"

Don't even think about it, peanut-head!

You moron!

You probably had to go to summer school all your life!

Oh yeah! Well my dad can kick your dad's butt! I'll bet you ten million dollars!

Pizza face!

Your sister is ugly and fat!

Oh yeah! Well, at least she doesn't look like a troll like your mother!

FIVE POTATO: GUESTS

Making Faces

At parties or dinners why is it that women have a propensity for making faces while in the presence of others? This dramatic form of expression is based on something they see or something they hear. You can't understand why they just can't wait until you're back in the car on the way home or even wait until the next day. But no, they have to let you know their feelings right then. They think that you are the only one who can see their expression, when in reality, half the people in the room can see it. She doesn't notice that they notice, but it embarrasses the hell out of you. If she sees something disagreeable to her at someone else's home she just has to make sure you see it too by wildly contorting her face in your direction or just thrusting her elbow into your ribs. If someone says something that she finds deplorable or politically incorrect she cannot hold still but must roll her eyes dramatically or puff up with indignation. And everyone notices. Then no one can relax. The whole evening is uncomfortable and what are you going to do about it? Nothing! Because if you dare call her to the side or mention her behavior on the way home, she will deny it, then defend it. "I did no such thing! Well, their house was a mess and they ought to know it!" she protests. But it doesn't matter, because it's your fault!

Yep, it's your fault! Hell, you didn't know that Harry liked to leave his shoes by the front door or that his wife is a racist. But it's still your fault. This verbal barrage comes at you like a swarm of bees. When she finally shuts up, you sigh, realizing there will be no speaking tomorrow. And then, after a pause you shake your head ever so slightly and roll your eyes just enough to make it look like you're looking in the rearview mirror. But it's too late! Your extreme subtlety has been captured!

"Don't you make faces at me!" she screams!

Stop! Don't Tell Me Anything About our Guests!

When my son was two and a half, we went jogging. I jogged slowly and let my son run beside me. When we ended up going a mile and a half, I was amazed that the little fellow ran along without stopping or complaining. He had a big smile on his face the whole time. The point is that he didn't know he couldn't run a mile and a half, so he did!

If we don't know something, we're less prejudiced. Individual prejudice seems to work in the reverse of what we've been taught. The more we know about a person the more likely we are to judge that person before we even meet them. Once we meet them we start looking for the traits in that person everyone has already told us about. Sadly, that means we don't get to evaluate people on our own. The deck is already stacked. It's been my experience that men and women are equally guilty of the desire to talk about others as a way of informing. Sadly, it's usually negative information. It's as if we feel the need to warn our friends of the evil that lies ahead.

The more we know the less ignorant we are. Maybe that's true in world history or geometry theorems, but when it comes to people the less we know the better the opportunity for positive association.

Here's an example. A guy introduces his wife as his "fourth wife." If he had just said, "Let me introduce my wife," think of the difference in your thought process.

Ironically, if you don't talk about someone it's often because that individual is non-existent to you or inconsequential to you. That person isn't in a position to help you or hurt you, so what is there to talk about? I never talk about my neighbor because I hardly ever see him and I don't know anything about him. I have nothing to go on to decide if he is an ax murderer or a saint. Then the question becomes, "Do I want to know this person so I can be judgmental about him?" Probably not! And you know you will be judgmental. No matter what the guy says you'll be thinking to yourself, "What an idiot," or, "What an ego," or, "Who cares about his stupid cat." Admit it. You will do that. Knowing too much about someone you don't associate with just makes life more stressful, because you will spend time thinking about it, rationalizing it, and forming unfair opinions.

So I suppose we could just stop communicating altogether and watch as the world grows silent. But that's a little unrealistic. Let's not do that. Try an experiment. Next time you and your spouse/girlfriend/boyfriend go out with others, if one of you doesn't know someone in the other party, don't provide any advance information on that person. Then afterward ask your spouse/boyfriend/girlfriend to provide you with observations about the person they didn't know. Then compare. Maybe your observations will be the same, but maybe you might be surprised. You might just uncover your own prejudice and learn something about yourself. That's why you should bother.

And that is why no one is perfect and no one is above being talked about. Now go jog a mile and a half and clear your mind!

THANK MY WIFE!
SHE CALLED THE CATERER!

Men have a unique way of thanking their wives for things. Let me give you an example. In the beginning of the movie *Pretty Woman*, Jason Alexander is throwing a party at his Beverly Hills home. A guest at the party comes up to him to thank him for a great party. He responds, "Thank my wife! She called the caterer!"

In the movie, Jason Alexander plays a real prick of a lawyer. Of course, the line about thanking his wife was accurate but would have crushed his wife if she had heard it. It doesn't matter if all she really did was pick up the phone and call the caterer. It's her house! It's her party! It's her chance to show off her home and her jewelry and her good taste! It doesn't matter if she didn't even lift the receiver to call the caterer. Maybe a servant handed her the phone. Or better yet, an assistant called the caterer. It doesn't matter. It's her party and if she hears you say, "Thank my wife! She called the caterer!" she will cry if she wants to! And you, my friend, are toast!

Sadly, most idiot men think that by saying such a patronizing thing they are actually complimenting their wife. But what's really happening here is that the man's wealth and desire to impress his friends and simultaneously be funny is all about his ego. It's his house, his cars, his tennis court and his swimming pool. By the end of the evening the frou-frou food will be gone. The jewelry will be put away and the house put back to normal operating status. But his Harley and Lotus will still be all his and he gets to look forward to the "thank you" calls and copious complimentary notes that will be flowing in. On the golf course that weekend his buddies will be kidding him about his "niece" at the party.

So, if you don't have a Harley and a Lotus and you don't play golf and can't afford a tennis court or a pool or even a caterer, it's ok. Just invite everyone over for burgers on the grill. Buy the ground meat on the way home from work. Grill the burgers yourself. Show your friends the ball you caught at the baseball game. Then show them the antique desk your wife bought earlier in the week. Put on your favorite CDs. Make some margaritas. Have a good time and a lot of laughs. Then clean up the plastic plates and tell all your guests that your wife did all the work and you don't know how you would survive without her. When the guests are gone tell her how great the dip was that she made from scratch and how much everyone liked it. Act like you don't believe it when she says she bought it at the grocery store.

No, no, don't misunderstand, you guys. These words and actions toward her still aren't going to get you any sex that night. Why? Because you are too full of burgers and margaritas—even if she were to suggest it, you're too fat to move! But that's not the point. The point is that you have been sincere. You have communicated to your wife on many levels. She knows it. And when your friends call to say what a great time they had at your party, you can say, "Thank my wife! She calls *me* the caterer!"

"Thank You For Doing This—Ellen"

In the movie *Dave,* Kevin Kline plays a fictional U.S. President who must encourage his wife and First Lady, Sigourney Weaver, to participate in certain public events even though she despises him. In one scene he has to practice the words, "Thank you for doing this—Ellen." Afterwards when she refuses to do any more appearances and he realizes that she hates him, he says sheepishly to his advisors, "She hates me." They respond loudly in unison, "Yes!"

So next time you have to convince your spouse or significant other that she needs to do something you want her to do, and she doesn't want to do it, practice saying, "Thank you for doing this—." Try to sound sincere and grateful. You might get by. But most likely, if you have to practice, you have a major marital problem that all your friends already know about!

Have it Your Way!

Long, long, long ago in this galaxy, on this planet, in this hemisphere, in this country there were some unwritten rules about being the host and the guest for lunch or dinner at someone's home.

The host invited the guest. The host selected something to serve. The guests ate it. If you were the host and you were serving chicken, rice and broccoli, followed by apple pie, then that is what everyone was served. If you were the guest, then you ate it. If you were the guest and you didn't like what was served, you took a few bites and messed up the plate and said, "Gee, this is great. Thank you. Oh no, I couldn't eat another bite. It was so filling!"

Life was good.

Today, in this galaxy, on this planet, in this hemisphere, in this country there are some new rules about being the host or the guest for lunch or dinner at someone's home.

The "inviter" must now ask the "invitee" what food items and brand products they will consume. This must be asked a week or two before the event in order for the "inviter" to purchase everything and prepare the meal. The "invitee" must be sure and remember everything so as not to embarrass the "inviter."

This process is particularly stressful when people don't know each other well.

Inviter: "Hello, Jennifer. This is Meg Snosrean. We haven't met yet, but your husband Walter works with my husband Ted."

Invitee: "Oh yes, Meg. How are you?"

Inviter: "Wonderful, thank you. I'm calling because Ted and I thought it would be fun to have you two over for dinner on Saturday the 26th."

Invitee: "Why, that would be very nice. I'm sure we have that evening free, but I'll double-check when Walter gets home. It sounds lovely."

Inviter: "Wonderful! Shall we say 7:00 pm?"

Invitee: "That will be perfect."

Inviter: "Now I was wondering if I could ask you a few questions."

Invitee: "Sure, go right ahead."

Inviter: "Is either of you a vegetarian? Vegan? Fruitarian? Any diabetes? Heart disease? High blood pressure? Is either of you allergic to anything? Lactose intolerant? Are you a Muslim, Hindu, Jew, Catholic, Agnostic, Atheist? Do you have any ethnic or cultural preferences? Is either of you an alcoholic? Is either of you on the Atkins diet? The Scarsdale diet? The South Beach diet? Dr. Phil's diet? Oprah's diet? Weight Watchers diet? Jenny Craig diet? Lindora diet? Salt-free diet? Do you prefer bottled carbonated water? Bottled flat water?

Tap water? Ice? No Ice? Flavored water? Evian? Perrier? Arrow? During cocktail hour which brands of vodka, bourbon, gin, Scotch, etc. do you prefer? Are shellfish a problem? Do you prefer white bread, wheat bread, sourdough, pumpernickel, other? Oh and coffee, decaf or regular and particular brand or flavor? Cappuccino? Espresso? Port, Brandy, Cognac? Any particular brands? Five potatoes or just four?

"Ok thanks, I think I've got everything."

"Well Jennifer, I'm looking forward to meeting you and Walter. We'll have everything just the way you like it. When you are our guests, you can have it your way!"

"Oh yes, you can tell us if you're suffering from depression when you get here."

"See you on the 26th! Bye, bye."

My Wife Likes To Give Me The Finger!

My wife and I have had trouble over the years leaving parties and dinners and stuff like that. You know how all couples develop a signal to let the other one know it's time to go. We've tried everything: the pat on the back, the wink, the foot under the table, and nothing ever works right. These gestures might be too subtle or simply forgotten about during the evening. We never seem to be able to coordinate and pull off a timely, polite, joint departure with our little signals.

Last month we had to go to a housewarming party in West Hollywood. Beforehand, we had to come up with a gesture that we could use to announce silently to each other the intention to depart the party. So after trying a couple of ideas we landed on one we thought would be foolproof.

If one of us felt it was time to go, that person was to scratch their eye with their middle finger in a slightly exaggerated manner so the other would be sure to see it! This seemed like a great idea. It would be obvious to the other person but the guests would just think one of us was rubbing an eye.

It was a nice party. One of those standup affairs with frou-frou food and all you can drink. There were a lot of interesting people there. I enjoyed talking to many of them.

About two hours into the party, my wife walks up to me while I'm talking with another couple. Within a minute or two she puts her middle finger in her eye and rubs it. I just go right on talking. About a minute later she does it again. I don't notice. The guy I'm talking to asks her if she's got something in her eye. I still don't get it. Then the host starts introducing everyone at the party. That takes forty-five minutes. The host plays piano for another half-hour. When that's over, people begin to leave. But I start talking to someone else I've yet to meet.

A little while later I go up to my wife and put my middle finger into my eye and rub it.

To my surprise, she just gives me the finger!

Uh, I guess it's time to go!

Five Potatoes

You've invited friends over for dinner. Maybe they are colleagues from the office or just acquaintances. But they are "your" colleagues and "your" acquaintances. They're always "yours" even if your wife has known them for years. You want to impress them and offer them a fine meal. You have every yuppie cooking utensil on the planet and you have a pleasant home environment. All you need is food. You want to spare no expense. Ah, but your wife does! Remember, they are "your" friends. So suddenly the budget becomes an issue. This shopping trip she volunteers for because she knows you'll go wild and she has to control the money. Since they are "your" friends, "We don't need to spend a lot of money!" So much for filet mignon—bring on the chicken! But then, in an effort to save pennies, she buys only four potatoes! Hey, there are only four people at dinner, so four potatoes! Why does it never occur to the spousal unit that someone might want another potato, that the dog might eat one, that you might drop one on the floor? But hey, we saved twenty-five cents! Of course, heaven forbid you should suggest that she might have purchased five potatoes, because you know who has to get in the car, go back to the store and buy some more. You, buddy! Yes, you! Not to mention that this little trip will cause you to miss the fourth quarter! "Oh, by the way, dear, while you're at the store would you get some of that good dog food? The dogs really don't like that cheap stuff you bought last time!"

Your colleagues know you live in a nice neighborhood, drive nice cars and vacation in Maui, but once again you look like a cheap bastard inviting "your" friends over for a fabulous meal of chicken and four potatoes.

SIX POTATO: TRAVEL

Paris On $10,000 A Day!

My wife and I were thinking about taking all our money and moving into the Paris Ritz! Yes, we would take every last dime. Sell the investments, cash in the 401(k)s, the IRAs, the savings, sell the cars, the house, sell whatever else was of value and give the rest away. Then we would live in the Paris Ritz until all the money is gone! We would dine at the finest Parisian restaurants. Take all the time we wanted in the museums. We would picnic in the countryside and take in the opera. We'd have a chauffeur take us everywhere, enjoy the finest spa treatments, read Hemingway in the Luxembourg Gardens, brush up on Gertrude Stein and write in our journals.

Given the cost of a croissant in Paris, the money wouldn't last all that long.

I don't know what we would do when the money ran out. We could just kill ourselves! But, I was thinking maybe on the day we leave the Ritz, we would walk over to the Left Bank and sit at the café of Les Deux Magots and start writing a book called *Paris On $10,000 A Day!* For $10,000 a day, we'll always have Paris!

Ah, Paris! Le bon vivant!

"Ever Ride The Waves In Oklahoma?"
A Tribute To *Route 66*

Why is it with all the reruns available on cable television the programmers never put on the classic television show of the early sixties *Route 66*? For those of you who remember and those who don't, *Route 66* had the coolest theme music ever written by Nelson Riddle. Its story lines took the viewer from Boston to California. Two cool guys in a Corvette explored America, finding adventure, romance, good times, bad times, moral dilemmas and laughs.

At the time it was mature stuff. It was what many of us wanted to do the moment we had a car and a little freedom. At nine years old, I certainly pictured myself driving across America with my best friend one day. Honestly, I could never figure out how the two guys got the money for the car and the money to live, but it was the idea of traveling dusty roads and encountering all kinds of people and situations along the way that made it so intriguing. And they always just sort of rode off in the end, like Corvette-riding cowboys on to the next adventure. *Route 66* was a road map across America and it was damn educational.

Much of the time it was about risk-taking. It captured the imagination with surfers shooting the pier, risking certain death for excitement and then asking why; dirt farmers seeking water

Five Potatoes

from parched land to survive on their farm and ultimately giving up; kids vandalizing a monument to fallen men of the Revolution and learning a tough lesson. All this while the two guys in their Corvette became engaged and disengaged with the characters they met along the way and then moved on to next week's show to find new adventure.

Why would you drive across the country? Why would you take on others' problems? What is out there to conquer? Is it about ego, courage, challenge, or is it about justification or something you can tell your kids? "I did that once!" You can take pride in recounting the story. Why did you step off the precipice? Take me back to *Route 66*.

Next time you are confronted with a risk and you can't decide whether to take that risk, think of the surfer shooting the pier on a California beach; very dangerous stuff. Why? Why would someone take that risk? Then ask yourself, "Ever ride the waves in Oklahoma?" That was the title of the episode. I often find myself asking that question when adventure confronts my life.

I can hear the theme music in my head. I can picture the drives across the country. Take me back, cable programmers! And take me to Oklahoma. I want to make sure there are no waves there!

Strap Me In! Take Me To 35,000 Feet!

Do you want to have profound thoughts? Do you want to articulate your vision? Do you want to seek philosophic truth? Do you want to imagine yourself as President of the United States giving the State of the Union address, or Joe Montana driving for the winning touchdown in the Super Bowl, or Lance Armstrong climbing the Alp d'Huez? Do you want to write a speech that rivals Churchill? Do you want to plan your future? Do you want to relive a great moment in your life? Do you want to tell your boss what you really think of him? Do you need to make a decision on a tough business issue or family problem?

Ok then, bucko! Get on a big plane. It has to be a 747, 767 or 777. Make sure it's at least a cross-country flight. It has to last a minimum of five hours. Buy a first-class seat or upgrade if you can so you don't have to spend the money for first class. Make sure you have a pad of paper and a pen handy. Get your seat belt fastened and make sure you get a drink before takeoff, maybe two. Then as the plane reaches altitude and the cabin service begins, keep drinking. Two or three or four more should do the job.

Hey, you don't have to fly the plane! You don't have to get up. You have people bringing you drinks and by 35,000 feet you're well into trying to hold one up eyebrow at a time. The guy next to you is deep into the *Wall Street Journal*. So who cares? Who cares about anything that has been or will be? No one can reach

Five Potatoes

you and you're not going to call anyone on that expensive air phone. At this moment you're in a silver cloud, literally and figuratively. Safe in your inebriated state and locked in your seat your mind takes flight!

"I am Spartacus!" you think to yourself. Your philosophical thoughts make those of Alfred North Whitehead seem sophomoric! You are a genius! If only I was a political pundit, I'd give the press some answers! Suddenly, answers to questions about your life that you could never answer pop into your head. You find yourself arguing both sides of a political issue with ease! You can actually articulate the other side! Your lips are actually moving a little bit. You are damned good-looking and full of courage and confidence! You tell the flight attendant that if she will bring you vodka, you'll marry her! This doesn't even embarrass you!

How many countless times have you done this and not written down what you were thinking? But now you've remembered! Your pad and your pen are right there! You begin writing a bit slowly at first. Soon you are turning the pages of the pad! The guy next to you looks over but you know your writing is too messy for him to read so you keep going. The people you hold dear come to mind. You try and envision each one of them, one at time, at some age other than what they are now. This makes you sadly acknowledge the relentless passage of time, but this feeling is assuaged by consciously accepting the wisdom you have gained. Your thoughts are sometimes joyful and sometimes sad. The muscles in your face move your lips into a kind of smile that no one can see, but you can feel it from the inside. Ah, tender moments from decades past make your body warm and your mind fulfilled. Then you think of the things you'd like to do with the rest of your life.

Altruistically, your first thoughts are of your wife. What can I do to make her happy? How can I be better for her?

I've got it! I'll buy her diamonds and take her to Maui!! Excellent! I'm a genius! And that was really easy! It doesn't take a Thomas Paine to figure that out!

Now that you've got a plan, there are still two hours left to sober up, get over the headache, get some aspirin, bother the flight attendant for lots of water and go to the lavatory at least four times.

Strapped in at 35,000 feet is great!!!

The International Superstud
Or
I Should Have Been A Polyglot!

American men are such dorks! When traveling in foreign countries, we just can't pull off the James Bond thing. We can't blend in. We look bad in our American clothes and we can only speak three or four words of a couple of languages. We seldom have enough money to stay in the cool places and we certainly aren't driving around at light speed on the latest European motorcycle. Face it. We are pretty much ugly American tourists!

Come on. Admit it. You really don't speak Spanish or French or Italian even if you have been to those places five or six times nor do you really remember anything from four years of it in high school. Japanese or Chinese? No way, kemosabe! All my Japanese came from watching *Shogun*. Frankly, it's just plain embarrassing. Everyone should have to spend at least one year of high school in another country and become reasonably fluent in something other than English.

If only I had stuck with my French. I actually liked French in high school. Now I can only remember a few words and phrases. These might as well be forgotten too, because a few words ain't gonna cut it in France.

So, there I am in Paris trying to blend in. I'm with three beautiful women on the way to dinner. It's one of those splendid late-summer evenings in Paris. Ah, the city of romance, sophistication, fashion, wine, intellectuals. It just doesn't get any better than this! My high school French had not gotten me any disapproving looks on this trip to Paris. I thought I was handling things quite nicely.

I'm driving. Yes, I'm driving through Paris. No big deal, but I had to make it seem like I knew where I was going. I found that this is done successfully by just driving as fast as possible and following everybody else. I had become darn good at it, if I do say so myself.

The ladies are looking good in their recently-purchased French fashions. Indeed, I wasn't so bad in my $900 Italian suit. The concierge had made reservations at a particularly upscale, famous Parisian restaurant. It was halfway across the city from our hotel. (It was somewhere off the Place de la Bastille on a side street.) I got us there, flying through traffic, and found a parking spot, but none of us were exactly sure where the restaurant was located. We just sort of knew the general vicinity. So since we found a parking space on the crowded streets of Paris, we figured we would just walk about and no doubt spot the restaurant. After circling the area on foot it was apparent that we could not find the restaurant and we were going to have to ask for help. Damn.

Anyway, I'm about to ask one of the gendarmes for help when three attractive French women walk up and stand next to us while we're about to cross the street. Here it is! This is my chance to be James Bond. I am an international superstud! I am! I am! I can and will, in a debonair manner, ask the three attractive French women right in front of the three attractive American women if they know where the restaurant is located. This would demonstrate that I had taken control, knew a little French and was clearly a continental man. An international superstud! A

Five Potatoes

successful man! An educated man! A man of means and sophistication!

So I move forward to get the attention of one of the French women and as my eyes meet hers in an expectant way, my mouth opens and—I can't think of one word! Just air comes out of my mouth. I can't think at all in English, much less in French. My eyes start to get wider. My diaphragm is paralyzed. I can't think of anything. Not oui, not yes, not excusez-moi, not hi, not bon soir, not où est la bibliothèque? Nothing! Seconds feel like hours! The three French women all start to look at me curiously as if to say, "Is something wrong, sir?" Then my three attractive friends start to notice my discomfort. Now all six women are staring at me. I just don't know what happened. I am a mute idiot in an Italian suit! What a dork! The self-pride, male ego, the testosterone and the chivalry of the situation go right down the sewers of Paris! Damn that Jean Valjean! Merde, merde, merde!

Within a few more eternal seconds one of my female guests approaches, flashing me a pained frown, and asks the three French women where the restaurant is in plain English.

Well, I guess I'm not a James Bond international superstud nor am I a polyglot. Quelle bummer!

That's Bond . . . **Jimmie Bond!**

Club Dead

There are so many wonderful places in this world that we won't reach while we're alive. I think the best way to overcome this is to go to the places you always wanted to go during your life—just do it when you're dead.

I call it "Club Dead."

It's kind of like timesharing. Your ash urn is brought to, say, St. Tropez and placed on a towel on the beach for a week. Or it's put on a sailing yacht just off Barbados. Or you can purchase multiple destinations. If the estate can't afford much maybe your urn spends some time in the park overlooking the playground near your house.

Whatever your situation, give yourself something nice. You've "urned it."

If you and your spouse die together, Club Dead has no problem arranging separate destinations! Finally, a vacation without her!

Call us now and we'll add a free weekend for your urn in Orlando!

Mental Morons Moving On Planes! Or Plane Stupid!

Now that air travel has become what bus travel used to be, we have to have some rules! Here is what I recommend.

1. Anyone wearing a tank top on a plane (females included) should be shown the door. This is absolutely intolerable and unacceptable. It amazes me that people will wear a tank top on a hot summer day on a packed airplane. Yeah, I just love sitting next to sweaty pigs in tank tops and having armpit perspiration drip on me while the pig puts his or her bag in the overhead! Yeah! I just love turning to glance out the window and instead of seeing the clouds I find the tattoo-covered wart on your shoulder staring back at me!

2. All plane seats should be locked in the up position on flights of three hours or less. On longer flights people will be allowed to recline their seat if and only if they ask politely for permission from the person seated directly behind them and then raise their hand every time they start reclining the seat. I've had my knees crushed, my book pressed into my face and my drink go everywhere all because some schmuck wasn't polite enough to turn around and tell me that the seat was coming back. Look,

people, it's hard enough traveling on these cattle cars without making it worse for everyone around you.

3. Hello! Does everyone get it now? There is only one aisle on most planes! When the attendants are pushing the cart trying to serve drinks and snacks no one can pass them! By now just about everyone has been on a plane. Everyone should have figured this out! But no! People get up to go to the lavatory and stand behind the cart for an eternity. I think they try and make the attendants feel guilty for being there with constant body movements and eye movements like somehow there will soon be a passing lane installed! There is no way your toilet needs are more important than the vodka tonic I'm waiting for! Sit down! Shut up! You know there are about ten minutes after the seat belt sign goes off and before the attendants begin the beverage service. So get up then and get it the hell over with whether you have to go or not!

4. No one should be allowed to take their shoes and socks off while using the lavatory! I see people in their bare feet using the disgusting lavatories and on top of that taking their barefoot 3-year-old in there with them! Gross! Stop it! I bet you wouldn't do that at a stadium restroom! What makes you think a lav on a plane is any cleaner? What? You think because there is a carpet down the aisle of the plane all the germs, urine, snot and feces will be wiped off your feet on the way back to your seat? The lav on a plane is just a porta-potty in the sky. It's a flying outhouse! Would you go into a porta-potty in your bare feet?

5. If you are sitting near the front and there is no overhead space left and you have to put your stowaway bag way back toward the rear of the plane, then just sit there until everyone is off the plane before you knock everyone down trying to get to the back after the plane lands! Your baggage won't be

at the turntable yet anyway. So just sit there and wait! It's your fault for not leaving the lounge soon enough to get on the plane at the proper time. So accept it and give everybody else a break!

6. If you are fortunate enough to be seated on the aisle, then do the noble thing and tell the two people on the inside that you would be happy to get up anytime so they can get out! This takes the edge off. The two people on the inside are nervous the whole time because they might have to make you get up. And, of course, they think you will be pissed at them and they really don't need the hassle. So trust me, be a good neighbor: make the announcement when everyone gets seated before the plane takes off! This will lighten everyone up. They will probably be so relaxed that they will order multiple alcoholic beverages and you might actually get involved in some decent conversations! Who knows! You might get to interact with the human species while on this bus in the sky!

7. After watching the person next to you read the in-flight gift catalogue for the fourth time, offer them your magazine or newspaper. Is that going to kill you?

8. Don't bring stinky food on the plane! Ok, ok, so you can bring stuff from the airport onto the plane. Now that the airlines are cutting back on food service that's fine. But, good grief, don't bring some stinky sandwich and pickles on the plane. We hate you! It stinks all the way until we're at cruising altitude! And don't ask me to hold your greasy, smelly sandwich while you put your seatbelt on!

9. Don't argue with the attendants. If there are no more blankets then there are no more blankets! These people have a tough enough job as it is! And since I'm sitting next to you I would kind of like it if the attendant felt comfortable coming back

to our row so I can order my vodka tonic and forget about your mean spirit. Next time wear long pants!

10. Work cannot be done in coach class! I know you want to impress your boss and get a head start on those spreadsheets you promised. But they will just have to wait until you're off the plane. Pulling out your laptop and your three-inch-thick manual and your 50 pages of loose notes and your multiple highlighter pens just doesn't work. Bring a paperback, a magazine or watch the movie. Pull out your laptop when you're back at home in bed with your wife. See how much she likes it! Actually, if you're that type of person, she probably likes it!

If any of the indiscretions mentioned above occur, then the airline may deduct 25,000 miles from your frequent flyer account! That will add to the bottom line and help save our airlines! Maybe a little civility will return and society will advance just a tiny, tiny bit way up there in the friendly skies!

God, I wonder what bus travel must be like these days! I'll leave the driving to them! Yeech!

Prada, Prada, Prada

My wife is flying to Hong Kong next week. She and her friend are going shopping there.

"What's the matter?" I ask her. "Did the local mall run out of stuff? Is Rodeo Drive closed for repairs? Did Barney's go out of business?"

"No, no, no," she responds. "In Hong Kong you can get Prada stuff really cheap! Most of them are knock-offs, but who cares—they're really good! You can't tell the difference. My friend knows this back street in Kowloon where she can get anything we want. They say if you can spot the difference from the real Prada they'll take it back and fix it by the next day! It's going to be great! I was thinking about getting a few suits made while I'm there just for fun! I've got all the latest fashion magazines and I've been cutting out pictures. I hope they can make what I want. If not, I'll just go for Prada purses, belts and shoes. We've got upgrades to business class and we've got a suite at the Shangri-La. Did you know that there is a great shopping mall right under the hotel? Oh yeah, and we're going to go to one of those formal Chinese dinners with 12 courses. I have to practice with my chopsticks! Just think. I'll be able to pick up a few Christmas gifts for everybody and get that out of the way. We're going to have tea at the Peninsula. How much money should I take? Oh, never mind, even the vendors probably take Visa or American Express. Can you drop me off at the airport? Do you have that little head pillow thing you wear on long flights? Can I have a couple of your sleeping pills? I'd better call my sister and ask her what she wants me to get her. I think Prada purses for all the women in the family would be a great Christmas idea. I want to be sure and go to one of those little Chinese quasi-antique stores and get a neat little jewelry box. Did you know there are more Rolls Royce automobiles per square mile in Hong Kong than in any other city on Earth? I hope we have time to go over to Macau or if not at least get over to the Stanley Market and buy some cheap souvenirs. That's where the really bad Prada knock-offs are. But I'm really excited about the Prada stuff. I hope it's not too humid. It usually is horrible weather there. Should I take an umbrella? Well, no, I guess the hotel will have them. My friend said not to take open-toed shoes since it's so dirty in the streets over there. So I guess I won't take my Prada shoes. That's ok. Then customs won't question anything. Of course, I can't take any of my Prada purses for the same reason. But I just have to have something nice to wear out in the evening. Well, I'll have to go through my entire closet. What do you think about a hat? No, I guess not. Can you get the big suitcase out of the attic for me? What are you going to do while I'm gone, dear? Oh, you can watch football. That will be more fun without me anyway! You know there is some of that leftover chicken from last week in the refrigerator. Do you think you could get that railing on the back deck painted while I'm gone? It looks terrible. Oh, I almost forgot. The dog really needs to go to the vet and have that hot spot checked out. It looks like it may get infected. I wonder if they have little Prada dog collars. Wouldn't that be cute? Don't forget to put out the trash on Thursday night and the pool man comes on Friday. Have you seen my passport? If my family calls, you can reach me at the Shangri-La. Oh, wouldn't it be great to get a spa treatment there? I bet the Chinese are masters of great massages. If anyone calls from work, tell them I'm out of the country and take a message. But don't tell them where I am because I want them to think it's work, not some 9,000 mile Prada shopping spree. Oh, would you deposit this for me at the bank and try not to screw up the laundry like you usually do. And water the plants. They look terrible! If you get any e-mails from my sister or nieces changing their minds about which Prada purse they want, fax them to me at the hotel. I'm not taking my laptop. Those things are way too much trouble at the airport. Ok dear, is there anything else you need while I'm gone? No, ok. Well, are you going to miss me?" she asks.

"Well of course, dear, it just won't be the same without you, Prada, Prada, Prada!"

Survival

When I was very little my father would take the family camping near Big Sur on the California coast. I got lost in the woods one time. They sent a search team looking for me. I was only four but it must have been a traumatic experience because I haven't been camping since.

Yep, I'm not a camper. I don't own a single piece of camping equipment. I'm not a survivalist of any degree. In fact, if I was given a knife and a match and then dropped off in the wilderness and told I had to survive for three days and three nights, I'd be dead in twenty-four hours!

I'm a hotel guy. If wherever I'm going doesn't have a hotel with mints on the pillow, a mini bar, 24-hour room service, cable TV, and a blow dryer in the bathroom, forget it! I'm just not going!

You probably think I'm a wimp. Yeah, well, just try to survive in a luxury hotel when the mint for the pillow doesn't show up, all the vodka has been stolen from the minibar, room service doesn't pick up the phone, the cable company is on strike and you drop the blow dryer into a sink full of water while it's turned on! I'd like to see the Navy Seals, Army Rangers, and Delta Force guys survive that! Those wimps! Knife and a match . . . oh please, you guys! Get a room!

A Room With A View

When I travel and stay in reasonably nice hotels, particularly resort hotels, I want a room with a view. Yes, I know that a premium is placed on hotel rooms with the best views, but so what? Do you want to spend your vacation looking at the ventilation system on the kitchen roof? Even on a business trip, I want a room with a view. Maybe I'll only spend two minutes looking out the window, but I can't settle for looking at a brick wall fifteen feet away! If my company won't pay for a premium room then I'll pay for it just for the experience.

There is romance in a view. There is freedom in a view. People are more creative when they can see something out the window! Maybe you can't think outside the box, but at least you can see outside the box! If you are a leader of an organization you need to have vision! Get some vision with a view!

Imagine taking your family from the mainland to Hawaii for vacation. You check into your hotel rooms and find out you are looking at a banana plant next to the loading dock! No doubt some of your friends had this happen and shrugged it off as if to say, "Oh yeah, but we were hardly in the room. Besides, it was twenty bucks less a night." So you flew 3,000-5,000 miles and paid $7,000 for the airfare, hotel, rental car, food, gifts, snorkel rentals and tickets to the Polynesian Cultural Center, but you couldn't spend another $120. So you were in Hawaii for a week looking at the loading dock! Great!

Next time, pay the money, and get the view! Be a visionary!

Hotel Rooms You Should Know!

Room 731, Ritz Carlton, Boston
Room 4618, The Four Seasons, Chicago
Room 2350, The Broadmoor, Colorado Springs
Room 443, Grove Park Inn, Asheville
Room 71712, Hay-Adams Hotel, Washington, D.C.
Room 3902, The Pierre, New York
Room 1603, St. Regis, New York
The Valley View Estate House, The Greenbrier, White Sulfur Springs
Room 9919, The Ritz, San Francisco
The Honeymoon Suite, Grand Hotel, Point Clear
Room 420, Marriott Hotel, Annapolis
Room 148, Hotel Bel-Air, Los Angeles
The Sunroom Suite, The Awahnee, Yosemite
Room 1618, The Windsor Court Hotel, New Orleans
Room 123, The Hermosa Inn, Scottsdale
The Penthouse, The Delano, Miami
Room 3115, The Marriott, Maui
Room 601, Hotel Balzac, Paris
Room 209, Best Western, Fort Stockton, Texas
Room 710, Four Seasons, Philadelphia
Room 208, The Columns, New Orleans
Room 751, The Ritz, Paris
Room 303, Harvard Faculty Club, Cambridge
Room 7, Grand Wailea, Maui

Coming soon, more hotel rooms you should know. Solicitations welcome!

OH SHENANDOAH!

I like hotels! I like big ones, small ones, exclusive ones, expensive ones, and occasionally a clean cheap one. I like resort hotels and downtown hotels. I like historic hotels and contemporary ones. I like wild ones and conservative ones! I just like hotels. They make me feel good. They make me feel special. I like the sense that I am passing through like an extra in a movie. I like the pleasure of fine service and hospitality.

Of course, finding a moment of pleasure and hospitality in life has little to do with hotels or exclusivity or resorts or mahogany versus Formica. Sometimes, like a typical guy, I have to be reminded of this. I remind myself by thinking about a childhood experience. I think of special moments in my life that reek of warmth and fuzziness and family and I think of one weekend in the Shenandoah Valley of Virginia. I can see it.

I wanted to visit the famous caverns of the Shenandoah Valley. My parents planned a trip over a weekend. We drove from Washington D.C. out through Harpers Ferry, West Virginia then across the Shenandoah River and into Virginia.

It was so beautiful. There was gentleness to the roads and even the highway. It was as if the other cars were in slow motion. The evening mist hung over the mountains and stretched out onto the trees in the valleys. This was the kind of place that made me want to get out of the car and go lay on the grass and watch the night cover the view like a blanket slowly pulled over your head.

We stopped at some anonymous one-story motel with a built-in restaurant. I'm sure it's long since been torn down. I don't remember the name or whether it was associated with any of the chain motels of the era. But it was uniquely sited on a hill overlooking the Shenandoah Valley. There were little terraces off each room. They were perfect for sitting quietly and talking with my parents. We talked about things. They liked to have a cocktail or two before going to dinner. I played catch with myself on the sloping hill of freshly cut grass beyond the balcony. The grass seemed to go for acres and acres. The only lights were from the restaurant and a few very distant farmhouses. The mountain forest was behind the motel and made for a nice contrast to the open space and view in front. The motel served as not much more than shelter between the two.

There might have been other people staying there, but I didn't see anyone. Yet it was not creepy or scary. It was mesmerizing. It was tranquil. Time had stopped just for us. We had no other place to get to. No one would be calling. The old manual TV didn't get anything but fuzz in the mountains so there was no point watching it. It was just a time to sit on the terrace and watch over the countryside and listen to the quiet.

My mind can clearly see my father. I can see and hear my mother. No one else knew where we were. There were no problems to resolve. There were no family issues. The world situation was not a concern. Money was not a topic. There was no place we had to be. It was the absence of all these things both profound and mundane that was the source of the pleasure. The hospitality was created not by service or accoutrements but by the very fact that the motel existed in that particular setting at that particular time.

Oh little motel in the Shenandoah! You have given me that memory and it has been a lasting one. It has been a faithful memory and a warm, sympathetic one. Maybe you are the reason I like hotels.

SEVEN POTATO: THE CAR

Temperature Control

Why is it that when you were dating, the girl always sat in the passenger seat and never complained about the temperature in the car? Despite being very polite and always asking if she was too hot or too cold, she told you she was very comfortable. In fact, it seemed like your temperature comfort zones were exactly the same. What a perfect match!

Ah, but then, after a while or after marriage, whichever comes first, suddenly your temperature comfort zones are exactly opposite and you are the one who must adjust (of course your zone has never changed). "Are you hot, dear? Why is your window down? I'm freezing! Put that window up!" she exclaims. "Are you cold or something? Feel my nose! It's numb! Turn off the heat; I'm dying in here!" she shouts. "Don't control my window! I'll put it up or down when I'm ready! I hate that when you put my window down!"

It's then that you realize that you will never be able to maintain your comfort or hers and you are going to suffer a verbal attack every time you leave the driveway, so you start thinking ahead. You have to take off your jacket or sweater before getting in the car. You have to pretend you don't notice that one of the rear windows is down about an inch, letting in some fresh air so you can breathe. But, don't worry—before you can get out of the driveway she's spotted that window! "Put that back window up, I'm freezing!" she exclaims. You roll up your sleeves.

At stop lights you put your window down and quickly stick your head out to get a breath of fresh air, and just before she shouts, "Put your window up!" you have hit the up button and she can't quite get the words out in time. Whew, what a relief! You can make it to the next stop light before succumbing to heat exhaustion!

But most importantly, even though you are the driver ninety percent of the time, she somehow has become the captain of the temperature controls. Guys, don't even consider reaching for the AC button or the fan switch. It belongs to her! Your comfort as the driver of the vehicle is no longer her concern. And yet she wonders why the back of your shirt is soaking wet!

All that's left to you is the ten percent of the time that she drives and you're in the passenger seat. At last, you get the controls!

Wrong, bucko!

"Dear, we don't need any air conditioning—it's a beautiful day. And besides, I'm driving. I'm the one that should be physically comfortable. It's a safety issue!" You give a sigh that you hope she won't hear and you roll your eyes as you turn your head to the right and stare out the window, wondering if you could have stayed home.

Road Trip!

Have you driven across America lately?
Hello, Fort Stockton, Texas!
Hey, Grand Junction, Colorado.
What's happening, Elmira, New York?
Yo, Baker City, Idaho.
Ciao, Eureka, California.
Nice to see you, Bay City, Michigan.
Hey y'all, Boone, North Carolina.
Lovely day, Fair Hope, Alabama.

If you haven't driven across, around or through America lately, I highly recommend it. Instead of going to Florida for a week or two, take a drive. See some stuff. Stop at the Snake Farm. See Rock City. Walk through the Alamo. Follow the Little Big Horn. Check out Madison's birthplace.

Visit West Point. Drive around the Rose Bowl. Go to a ballgame in another city, like in Pittsburgh's new stadium. Actually pay the money and spend some time looking at the Impressionist work at the Chicago Art Institute. Buy a book on the Impressionists to bring home. Go up in the Space Needle. Stop at the outlet mall. Play putt-putt and drive go-carts at some cheap roadside amusement park! Check out a National Park. Visit Antietam and stand in the bloody lane or walk across the Burnside Bridge. Feel the presence of those gone before. Take the ghost tour in Charleston. Rent a carriage in Central Park. See a play at a small town theater.

Take your kids. And spend the time talking about stuff. If one of them doesn't want to go, leave him/her at home. The other kids will get attention and love the trip so much that everyone will want to go next time. If they want to put on their MP3 players and their headphones tell them to go ahead. The only requirement is to look out the window.

Why will they love it? Because you are really not going anywhere. Maybe there's vague plan; something like driving to Chicago using different routes there and back. See what you find. If the kids see a water park on the way, stop. If you don't get to Chicago it doesn't matter. Maybe you go out of your way to see Mount Rushmore instead. Don't make any hotel reservations. Just stay along the way in safe, clean places.

Who am I to give you vacation advice?

Nobody!

I have no credentials in this area. I don't write travel books. I've never been in an RV.

But every time I pull out my photo albums of our road trips, I just can't believe we did all that and saw all that and had a hell of a good time!

And don't forget—take a camera!

I know about photo albums!

She Can't See Beyond The Hood Of Her Car! Or, I Was Right In Front Of Her But She Still Couldn't See Me!

This is not what you think. I don't have a problem with women drivers. They're fine. This is really about vision. I wish I had counted over the years how many times I've crossed paths with my wife or other female friends on the road. It's been hundreds. I see them and I wave. I honk the horn. I try to get their attention. I could be walking the dog and see her at the stoplight. I step to the side of the road and I wave. It could be a friendly wave or a wild wave, but whatever the type of wave it is very visible. If I'm at a stoplight in my car and see her coming the other way, I wave out the window and honk the horn. But nothing! No response. She just stares out the front window as she drives by. There is no recognition. No return wave.

What is she thinking? How can she drive a car? Hey, it's not much to honk and wave. Why can't they see beyond the hood of their cars? Is this some childhood thing that involves Easy-Bake Ovens instead of Hot Wheels? There seems to be no recognition of the automobile in the female mind. Cars all look alike to women so they can't pick out yours. Actually, it seems they don't even look at other cars while driving or at stoplights. Yet women get lower insurance rates than men! How do they have so few accidents? Clearly, they are aware of nothing around them. Could it be they are thinking deep thoughts as if in a trance? Maybe so; after all, they are away from you! I guess that gives them time to think of things you didn't do for them today!

THE SHAGUAR

The Jaguar is the sexiest car on the road! The rest look like jellybeans! One must make it a priority in life to own a Jaguar. Any one will do, from the 50's models to about the 1996 models. Buy a used one! But why, you ask? What about Ferrari? What about Porsche? What about Mercedes?

You guys don't get it. It's not about speed or handling, workmanship, technology or engineering. Those cars are all better than Jaguars. It's about being called a Jaguar! A car that's named after a sleek, fast, sexy animal, not a dead white guy! BMW? What is that? Sounds like a laxative! Mercedes? They all look alike and everyone has one (unless you live in the Midwest). It's about imagery. It's about looking good! It's about SEX! You morons! Jaguars look different, particularly the older ones. Jaguars don't have the most gadgets. They don't go as fast as Porsches. They don't have German engineering. At one time they even had the worst reputation for falling apart of probably any car in history. But, you see, it doesn't matter if a rubber band makes it go. You look good in it! She looks good in it! And you don't look like everybody else on the road in their jellybean cars!

Austin Powers, International Man of Mystery, knows this! And he gets all the groovy chicks in his Shaguar! "Shaguar baby! Yeah!"

If She Loves You For Your Car, You Probably Don't Want To Marry Her!

Over time my friends have owned almost every kind of car. Several have had Ferraris. Another had a Jag convertible. Several have owned Porsches. There were lots of Mercedes and BMWs. A couple had Corvettes, Mustangs and Firebirds. My roommate even had a '72 Nova! Years ago there were Triumphs and MGs and a couple of jalopies. I even had a Cadillac with fins that my uncle gave to me. It was so cool at the time.

Guys love cars. Even lots of gay guys love cars. One of my gay friends had a classic BMW Tii. He loved that car. He drove it every day and managed to keep it in perfect condition.

Some women like cars. Some women recognize the joy that fine automobiles bring to men's lives. Some women are even like men when it comes to cars! If you can find a woman who gets it, you should learn more about her.

But here's the catch. You'll be able to tell right away if she really knows anything about cars. Usually she's just impressed with your car because she thinks she'll look good in it and if she's not looking good for you, who is she looking good for? But how do you tell if she's just using you for your car or if she really knows some stuff?

Here's how.

Next time you're out driving with her keep an eye out for old Triumphs and MGs. When you are far enough away that she can't read the name on the car, ask her what kind of car that cute little sports car is. If she can't tell the difference between a Triumph and an MG—forget her!

If she owns a Triumph or an MG—marry her!

Footnote: Ladies, feeling lousy about driving around in that old Honda while watching guys go by in Porsches? Don't! Just remember the old joke: What's the difference between a porcupine and a Porsche?

A Porsche has the pricks on the inside!

LIKE A ROCK!

I can't stand commercials that repeat themselves for fifteen or twenty years. I have to hit the mute button when they come on. Chevy trucks are the best example. That stupid theme song, *Like a Rock,* has been playing as the background for what seems like an eternity. I doubt Bob Seger had Chevy trucks in mind when he wrote it. So I guess he sold himself out to some moron executive at the ad agency for GM. Who wants a truck that's like a rock? Static, motionless, hard, inert, immobile and heavy is what I think of when I think of a rock! Let's not forget crushable!

Imagine how non-English speaking people must react to this when they're trying to learn English. They must scratch their heads and think we are all idiots. I doubt they'll be willing to buy a Chevy truck! Who would buy one? Chevy trucks should be boycotted until they change the theme song of the ads. Maybe they could change the song to *Truckin'* or *American Pie,* you know, "*got a pink carnation and a pickup truck.*" Obviously, General Motors isn't selling many trucks anyway because they don't seem to have the advertising budget to change the theme song! Like a rock! Not me! I want a truck that's like a truck! If I want a pet rock then it's ok for my pet rock to be "like a rock."

Actually a boycott is a pretty good idea. Let's boycott products if the majority doesn't like the ads or if they play too long!

"As General Motors goes, so goes the economy." Remember that line?

Yeah, GM—we're sinking like a rock! So get rid of that ad!

How about this: "Chevy Trucks: Like Ford Trucks! Like Dodge Trucks!"

Passenger Seat Driving!

I drive too fast! I don't pay enough attention! I like to look at stuff when I'm driving. I get lost in thought. I talk to myself. I get distracted by my cell phone and the radio. I look at attractive women on the sidewalk or in the car next to me. Sometimes my foot slips off the gas pedal. Sometimes I put my seatbelt on with both hands while the car is moving.

My wife sits in the passenger seat and blasts me for all the horrible things listed above. "Watch out! Stop! Where is you head today? Why can't you just wait until we're stopped to put your on your seat belt? What are you looking at? The road is straight ahead!"

I can't do anything right when she's in the passenger seat. She makes me nervous. When I'm alone I never have any problems. I've never had an accident. She's had three! Nah, nah, nah, nah, nah!

Well, I take that back, I was backing out of the driveway in the Jaguar when I hit the Porsche! Damn, that set me back about two grand! Man, how often in life do you get to say that? "I crashed my Jaguar into my Porsche and did $2,000 damage! In my own driveway!"

But guess who was in the passenger seat?

I never say anything to her when she's driving. Hmmm, maybe that's why she's had three accidents!

CRUISING THE GAP

A friend of mine told me about cruising the gap. Cruising the gap is a lifestyle or philosophy of living that is analogous to groupings of cars on a big Interstate highway.

Have you ever noticed how herds of cars somehow get grouped together and then split, forming a gap between the herds that leaves about a quarter-mile or half-mile of empty highway? My friend suggests getting caught alone in the gap is like being alone on the road more taken. Alone in the gap, there is personal freedom. He can speed up or he can slow down. He can change lanes. He can relax. He can look at the scenery. He can be alone with his thoughts. He is isolated from the group mentality. His actions are not dependant on the actions of others, nor do they affect the actions of others. He rides apart from the crowd. The cars in the herd are affected by the movements of the members of the herd. They are controlled by the actions of others. They are the mainstream.

Most importantly, he wants to be in the gap. He finds ways to position himself to be there. There is no choice of roads diverging in a yellow wood. He's already on the road more traveled, so he might as well go down it in a dash of individuality.

Somehow, over time, the gap closes, the herd size changes. Freedom is overtaken and the search for the next gap begins.

Williston Lamar

All things must pass on the road more traveled on which most of us find ourselves. At least, when possible, we should cruise the gap. And that can make all the difference.

OIL AND WOMEN DON'T MIX!

Oil changes for the family automobile do not exist in the mind of women. Women believe that gasoline alone runs the internal combustion engine. No other fluids are required. It's just a fact. Certainly this fact is somehow physiologically tied to lubrication!

Self-service

Just as a crude survey, ask yourself how many times you've pulled into a gas station with your wife in the car with you. Ok, then ask yourself how many times she has gotten out of the car, used her credit card and put in the gas while you got to sit there and listen to the news? I bet the answer is never! If it's not, you were driving the car with a broken leg and she felt bad for you.

Women can do this little chore; they just won't do it when you're in the car, and they won't volunteer. Yet if you weren't around they would pull up, hop out and fill it up!

Lou Holtz, the great football coach, tells a funny story about a place kicker who just couldn't seem to make any field goals during practice. So Coach Holtz walks up to him and asks, "What's the problem?" The young man responds, "Coach, I can't make 'em when you're watching me!" Coach Holtz says, "Well, son, I plan to be at the game on Saturday!"

So next time you pull up to a gas pump and your wife just sits there, just sit there yourself. Don't make a move to open the door. When she says, "What are you doing?" then you say, "I'm waiting for you to fill up the car. I plan on driving it this week!" So maybe she just couldn't fill up the tank because she thought you would be watching!

White Asphalt

I don't understand. Then again, I don't understand most things. Why are our road surfaces black? Why are tires black? Why does oil turn black? Why aren't all streets and all tires white? Everything would be so much cooler in the summer. Instead of whitewall tires, there should be blackwall tires. Instead of blacktop there would be whitetop. Have you ever stood in a Wal-Mart parking lot in Phoenix in the summertime? No wonder global warming is getting worse! You might as well stand in an oven! We could reverse this environmental nightmare if everything paved was changed to white paving. Most pool decks at hotels use some type of topping to keep them cool so your bare feet don't burn. So why can't we do that with roads and parking lots?

I know, I know! If it could have been done in white it probably would have been done by now. Not to mention the cost; it's obviously cheaper to create black asphalt and black tires than white versions. But why? Am I that crazy? Come on—this is a good idea. The automobile industry could use a different look. It can't be that expensive to take the black out of petroleum-based products and vulcanized rubber. Oh sure, it would take a long time. We would still have people running over white Interstate highways with black tires and we'd still have white tires getting black by running over black highways. It would probably take two or three generations. But think of the WPA and all those projects; they put people back to work and they helped build some of the most functional and monumental construction projects the U.S. has ever seen! Besides, it's really getting hot out there. We could do test roads and test tires in Iraq while we rebuild the place. It's really hot over there! We don't need any more power failures and strange, harsh weather conditions. I say we go with white asphalt! After all, who would have thought five years ago that the best rapper would be white and the best golfer would be black? See, it can work!

Anyway, I took my ideas to several major associations: the National Asphalt Paving Association, the Association of Asphalt Paving Technologists, the Asphalt Paving Alliance, the Tire Industry Association, and so on. I even went to Mike down at Western Tire Supply in Burbank.

Basically the responses were all the same. They first thought I needed a rubber room, then they thought they would tar and feather me, and in the end, wishing only to avoid any bad publicity for their industry, they just said, "Get your white asphalt out of here!

Geez, I was just trying to think outside of the black box!

Driving Mr. Lamar!

My mother will be ninety this year. She was smart enough to stop driving. I'll be fifty this year. I want to stop driving too! I want a chauffer, even if it's my wife!

You know men tend to be the driver all the time. Short trips, long trips, it doesn't seem to matter. The father, the husband, the boyfriend always seems to be the driver. I think this is one that the feminist movement overlooked. Women should demand to do the driving. Besides, they're always telling us how to drive. "Look out! Didn't you see that car? Slow down! Pay attention! Do you want me to drive?" My answer is, "Yes, you can drive!"

I've been assuming the driving responsibility ever since I could drive. Now, as more of the highways of life have passed under me, I finally figured out how much better it is to be a passenger and let "the wife" drive the car!

Every time we took a weekend trip or a long vacation I did all the driving. Driving is more stressful and energy-consuming than I ever realized. The physiological process of driving into fatigue is a slow and unnoticeable one. I could never understand why my wife was so relaxed after a weekend trip or why she had so much energy to unpack and put things away.

Then one time we were leaving Las Vegas and driving to LA. As the valet pulled the car up under the porte-cochere this sense of inner peace came over me. I said to my wife, "Honey, I'm a little tired—would you drive for a while?" Shocked by my lack of male assertiveness, she responded, "Well, ok, I guess."

It was great! I was so relaxed; I could look at the desert scenery and read the billboards. I could lean back and close my eyes. I could fool with the radio buttons. I wasn't tense. It was like a ground-level plane flight. Strapped in at one foot off the ground! Hell, I might even order a cocktail! I'm not driving! This is great! Hey, look at the mirage over there! Check out this Porsche coming by us! Hey, any Twinkies back here?

My wife is stressed. She says her back hurts. She calls other drivers names. She gets terribly upset when we're stopped for a half-hour for an overturned truck. She wants to know if I've had the oil changed lately. Funny, she hasn't mentioned oil in ten years of marriage. I didn't know she realized that cars need oil changes. Oil and women don't mix.

Meanwhile, I enjoy waving to little kids in cars next to us. I get to hear the news and sports, cycle around twice on the all-news station. I study the road atlas and find places I've never heard of. My shoes come off. I scratch my toes and loosen my belt. When we get home I'm ready to barbeque, walk the dogs and clean the garage. Life is good! I'm never driving again!

"Mr. Lamar will not be driving today. Oh honey, one more time around the park, please!"

"Look out! Didn't you see that car? Slow down! Pay attention! Do you want me to drive?"

WHILE MY OLD CAR GENTLY WEEPS

Did you ever have a car that someone gave you? Maybe they sold it to you for a pittance. Or maybe they just said something like, "I always wanted you to have this car." Whatever the case, you needed a car at the time and it sure felt good to get one so easily. And maybe, just maybe, it was an interesting car. Perhaps it was an old Cadillac, or your brother-in-law's three-times-used Pontiac convertible. Or maybe the death of an aunt or uncle left the family wondering what to do with the old Comet Uncle Gifford had driven for twelve years. And you were the one saying, "I'll take it. I need a car for school."

The day you take possession there is already an ancestry combined with ownership. The car was someone else's, but you know who had it and that makes you feel better than if it was off a used car lot. You feel good! The car is yours. There are visions of shining it up, getting that fender repainted and replacing the radio with something way more sophisticated so you can play your favorite stuff all the time as loud as you want. Hmm, maybe even get some new, wider tires.

Then the minor annoyances start. A week later the battery is dead. After that the carburetor starts sticking and won't let enough air in to allow the car to start. The knob comes off the light switch and you can't find it in the dark. Then you step on it and crush it. While attempting to change the oil you misunderstand the calibration on the dipstick and overfill the oil. The next thing you know, you're driving down the highway putting out a blue smoke trail that gives cause for everyone driving by to scream environmental epitaphs in four-letter words.

All this passes. It's your car. It gives you freedom. One of the windows stops working and the brake lights no longer work. It takes an entire weekend to buy the right bulbs and install them yourself. Then, on the way home from downtown after a night out, the car runs out of gas. Fortunately, the flares your mother gave you as a gift when you got the car are still in the trunk, although slightly damp from the leak in the dry-rotted trunk insulation.

Friends get rides in your car. The dog rides in your car. Several different girlfriends ride in your car. You pick up your dad from work in your car. You pack the car up for school. You receive many parking tickets and only two or three speeding tickets over several years. The transmission goes. But, having only enough money saved for a few days of cheap meals, you beg the "Dad" for the money for repairs. You know every engine noise and what it means. You know what to do when the horn gets stuck. You know exactly which speaker wire comes loose and which tire usually needs air. This is your property. This is your car. This car is part of who you are. Your friends recognize you by the car.

You have carried everything you own in the car. You carried plants for your first apartment and wood from the lumberyard that had to stick out the window. Your roommate borrowed it countless times for beer runs. There must be the hardened remains of a couple dozen french fries under the seats and at least $1.67 in change in the ashtray.

There was the night you slept in the car when you locked yourself out. And the time you hid the car around the corner so her parents

Five Potatoes

wouldn't know you were at her place. There was the time you tried to stop but you hit and killed a bird and felt so bad about it you still think of it. And remember exactly where it happened.

Then thoughts of restoration seep into your mind. "Well, maybe someday this old car will be worth something," you say to yourself. You're thinking about new paint and some upholstery work. Maybe you could even get the bumpers re-chromed. You're thinking this car would be really cool. You fantasize about new carpet and a new windshield without a jagged crack in it. Ah yes, you should steam clean the engine and maybe put some chrome parts in there just for effect. How proud your uncle would be if you could fix it up.

One afternoon, you find yourself in a part of town you rarely travel. It's kind of auto repair row. There are transmission shops and muffler shops and auto body repair guys and just about every auto specialty you can imagine. So, driving by, you pick out a friendly-looking shop with good graphics that advertise car restoration and auto body and paint. On a whim you pull in. In these kinds of places you always have to seek someone out. The guy is usually in the back or in the supply room or under a car. You look at some of the cars randomly aligned in the shop. All are in various stages of repair or disrepair; it's hard to tell. But one thing is for sure. There is no one working on any of them. Some filthy old boom box on a workbench is tuned to a Spanish station. Finally, after you trip over a muffler pipe and make a racket some guy looks out of the storage room. He sees you and yells out, "Just a minute, bud." Finally he comes out, wiping his hands on a rag that's covered in black stains. "Good afternoon," you say cheerfully. "Do you all do restoration work?" You put in the "you all" to make yourself sound like one of them. The guy responds, "Yeah, we can paint your car, what do ya got?" Now you're thinking this is a huge mistake. Why didn't you pick another shop? You point in the direction of your beloved car.

"This your car, here?" the guy asks. "Yeah, it needs a complete paint job. Some upholstery work and a new windshield, probably some work on the window mechanisms too," you mumble. He's not impressed with your car. Obviously, he's seen hundreds in the same shape. He doesn't walk around it or even look closely at it. "Yeah," he says. "If you want to spend the money, we can do this. You're lookin' at about $3,200 for paint, another $400 to $500 for carpet and about the same for the seat repairs. Re-chroming those bumpers is about $200 each not including labor to get 'em off. And the windshield; I'll have to check my price book, but that's about $200. So you're talking 5 grand and maybe more."

Trying not to look shocked, you say, "Wow, that's quite a bit. I had no idea it would take that much." "Yeah," the guy says. "If you want it restored good, that's about the damage." "Well, let me think about it. About how long would it take?" you ask humbly. "Oh, depends on when you get it in here, but you're lookin' at three to four weeks," he responds, turning to go back in the shop. "Ok, I'll look at my finances and let you know. Thanks," you say, knowing the whole thing is out of the question.

Driving home, you feel that warm and comfortable feeling of knowing that at least your old car is running and the heater still works. And surely, Uncle Gifford, God rest his soul, knows that you tried to keep it in good shape and you tried to invest in making it like new. The thing is you just don't have $5,000. And even if you did you have to admit that the car will never be classic. It wasn't even that nice a car when it was new. It's just yours. It's your vehicle of freedom.

Months go by. The raise you expected comes through. Driving home one night you see the lights of the new car dealership and dream of one day buying a new car.

A week later the old car won't start for the hundredth time. But the hassle and burden is too much this time. The responsibilities of life can't wait for the repair of the infirmed vehicle. You try and calculate the value of trading it in and monthly burden of a new car. Another week goes by. It looks like the front end needs alignment. The front tires are wearing severely on the inside edge.

That's it. Life must go on. Maybe the local high school can use the car for their tech class. Maybe you can just take it down to the Goodwill lot. It will never pass inspection without a couple hundred dollars of work. But it still runs fine, you say to yourself. Nevertheless, the time has come.

The salesman at the new car dealer gives you a couple hundred bucks for the car in a moment of pity. Your new car is being prepped for you to drive off the lot. The papers are signed. The deposit is made. Cleaning out the old car you find a Valentine's card wedged in the trunk from several years ago. Glancing at the card you place it back in the trunk as if the valentine was meant for the car, your true love. In the glove box is the St. Christopher medal your mother gave you for safe travels when you drove off to college. This you keep and realize that it will go in the glove box of the new car. The old french fries stay under the seat.

One last look, and a rush of memories come forth. The college sticker is still on the back window. Running your hand down the fender and across the steering wheel you say a quiet "thank you" and turn to leave.

After the salesman shows you all the gadgets on the new car, it's time to drive away. The new car smell overwhelms your senses and blocks out any sadness over the old car. But there it is. Making the turn onto the main street, there it sits waiting to be taken away.

One last glance before paying attention to the road ahead; I turn and drive on, while my old car gently weeps.

MORE . . . SPUDS

DIE LAUGHING

Have you ever run across people that you realize instantly are the type of people that really don't like anyone? They have a mean look. They breathe out the air of superiority and aloofness. There is sternness in their face that is frozen even in lighthearted situations. Whenever I encounter a person like this I get away as soon as possible. But also, I stop and think. How does that person communicate decently with all the people that one encounters in life?

Obviously, they must have had some problems in childhood and/or been really hurt in some way that over time builds up a defense shield so strong that nothing and no one will ever break through.

I have a couple of neighbors like that. Two different neighbors have this problem and they don't seem to know it. I'm not even sure where on the street they live. Just somewhere down the street.

One of them tears off down the street in her car. I wave every time, but get no response. Her eyes stare harshly, straight out the windshield. She drives so fast that she's going to run over her own child someday. Frankly, I don't know how she ever conceived a child! She gets up to about thirty-five miles an hour in a hundred feet and then slams on the brakes at the stop sign which has been there for forty years. With a look of distaste at another driver who has the right of way she tears off down the street to whatever world-saving thing she must be doing today. Her look at all times of the day is one of, "I'm pissed and I want the whole world to know it. Don't even think about talking to me! Obviously, whatever I'm doing is far more important than anything you could want to stop and talk about! I don't have to say hello, because I'm superior to you. I interact with no one—no exceptions; and obviously my life is more important than yours!" If this woman were to meet Mother Teresa, she would probably shake hands as a tiny gesture of courtesy, but then walk away thinking to herself, "Obviously you can't help me because I'm not starving like the ignorant, meaningless rabble you work with." And I wonder: how does she do it? How does she maintain that distance, the aloofness, how can she be like that every single time I see her? She has a job. She must interact with someone, sometime. She has to put gas in her car. She has to buy groceries. She must interact with a few other human beings! Do you know someone like this?

Then there's the other person that lives down the street. She's a walker. That is, she walks the neighborhood in a high-speed walk with a pissed-off look so she won't have to stop and talk to anyone. She doesn't have a dog to walk so she can just keep moving at a constant rate. Obviously, she read somewhere that walking is good for your health. But, this person is so angry at the world she's never going to be healthy anyway. She never smiles and it's not like all this exercise is going to make her a babe. She really does look like the Wicked Witch of the West without the bike. She's dog ugly! She's not going to have anyone find her attractive. Her youth is gone. It's over. Why do you want to try and be healthy and live longer if you hate life anyway? Why doesn't she just sit in a dark room in her house and wait to die? Get it over with!

Thank God I like everybody! I might die young. I might die old. I might die of cancer or heart disease, but I'm going out laughing with the mailman and the dry cleaner and the auto shop guy and my tax guy and my stock broker and my dogs and my family and my friends and the airline counter lady and the waiter and my college buddies and my colleagues and the random taxi driver and the person in the toll booth and the obnoxious timeshare salesman and the cleaning woman and the receptionist and the plumber and my dentist and the nurses trying to resuscitate me. I'm even going to clown around with Saint Peter! Because he'll be the last person I need to communicate with and the last person to make a decision about my future so I will need to summon up all of my communication skills and good manners!

Besides, if I end up in hell, I'll need to have a few laughs first. I'm sure to cross paths with my neighbors who did not die laughing!

I like everybody!

All Dressed Up! As Nuns!

My mother loves nun movies. She watches them over and over. She watches everything from *The Bells of St. Mary's* to *Sister Act II* and *Heaven Knows, Mr. Allison*. She loves them all. Of course, back in 1918, she did get shipped off from her tiny hometown to a Catholic school in Baltimore when she was only five. That could have something to do with it! Now that she's too old to drive herself to mass, I think she watches them even more because they are much more spiritual than watching Reverend Relevant on Sunday morning TV. Also, I think there is a kind of esprit de corps among nuns that relates to women who didn't grow up during Title Nine. I don't know anything about this, but clearly, it's a good thing.

Now like I said, I don't know very much about these things, but I have been witness to one of the funniest nun stunts ever. It happened in Rome.

While I was a student in Rome, my female classmates were harassed endlessly by Italian men. Italian men are particularly notorious for harassing females, verbally and physically, particularly non-Italian females. Their harassment escalates beyond anything we see here in the U.S. Don't get me wrong, I'm not singling out Italian men. All men are scumbags. But Italians are particularly good examples and they live in a predominantly Catholic country. So anyway, these two girls from our class had had enough from the Italian men. So they bought some material, made some patterns and sewed up their own habits and garb.

Five Potatoes

They pulled their hair back and tucked it in. They bought some long Rosaries at the flea market and got all dressed up every day and went about Rome as nuns!

We would follow them just to see what happened. They certainly never got a second look from the Italian men. They never got pinched or patted on the butt. No problems!

Here's the good part. Their boyfriends would show up. They would find the most public place and then grab the fake nuns and kiss them passionately, bend them over backwards in Fred Astaire-like forms and squeeze their asses. The girls would put up no resistance and seem to enjoy it and then squeeze the guy in various places and kiss him back all over the neck and face. Then they would just stop and calmly walk away in different directions! God, it was funny! I wish they had video cameras back then. I think one older Italian gentleman had a heart attack watching this and a woman in a café passed out! But, believe me, those girls never got hassled! I only wish they had mooned the crowd as they walked off!

I've never heard of anyone getting arrested for impersonating a nun. But there is definitely a movie in this story. My mother would love it!! Very spiritual! Well, uh, probably not!

I Wonder What The Poor People Are Doing Today?

I don't know how this little colloquialism got started, but I don't get it. Who cares what the poor people are doing? You know whatever they're doing, it's bound to be depressing.

I want to know what the rich people are doing today. I fact, I want to know what they are doing right at this moment.

Ask yourself, what is Julia Roberts doing right this second? What is George Bush doing this hour? What is Robin Williams doing? How about Bill Gates? Is he sitting on the can right now? Is Jennifer Aniston picking her nose?

I wonder if the poor people sit around asking each other what Oprah is doing while they pitifully suffer. Well, I guess we can read about what the rich are doing in the gossip magazines. Maybe we really do need a source of information on what the poor people are doing.

If I were in the tabloid business, I'd start a new tabloid. "Enquiring minds want to know, what are the poor people doing?" I'd call it the *Welfare Enquirer*.

Think of the headlines. "Glue on the back of food stamps causes cancer." "Mother gives birth to alien child under bridge where she lives." "Shelter dog cares for shelter cats." "Six hundred pound

Five Potatoes

man called 'cannibal' of homeless shelters." "Man robs convenience store, takes Twinkies not cash." "Doctor transplants redneck's brain into pig—no discernable difference in pig behavior." "Study shows West Virginia residents all have the same DNA."

A more worthy journal might be like the Poor Picayune from the south or the Poor Post from the north. These scribes might feature some articles like: "Friends have crayfish boil, dance to Cajun music, get drunk and want to do it again next week!" "Man spends life savings to buy fishing pole, wins $1 million in bass championship." "Unemployed Boston woman bakes cookies to feed homeless kids." "Car wash supports local athlete's trip to state finals."

If you are asking your friends what the poor people are doing today, just read the *Welfare Enquirer.* Or maybe, if you are asking your friends what the poor people are doing and getting some answers, you might even recognize yourself!

"When Are They Going To Play Baseball?"

If you don't live in New York, it's always good to check out a Broadway play while you are visiting the city. When my kids were quite young, I took them to see *Damn Yankees*. I believe it was at the Marriott Theatre at the time. I believe Bebe Neuwirth was the lead as Lola. It was a very good production.

We had the cheap seats near the back. It was very exciting for the kids. They love plays and all three had participated in a lot of small school productions. To encourage them to go we told them that this was a musical about baseball and that it would be fun and lively!

We got there on time and took our seats. The kids were excited and sitting on the edge of their seats. Actually, I'm not sure whether they were sitting on the edge of their seats because they were excited or because they were too short to see over everyone in front of us. Regardless, they were excited. The play begins.

It takes a while to get the story going. Joe Boyd, the frustrated Senators fan; his wife, the frustrated wife of a fan; the deal with the Devil and the addition of the "escape" clause all leading to the sad rendition of *Goodbye Old Girl*.

About this time my youngest, who's only six at the time, gets bored and puts his head in his hands and starts swinging his legs

Five Potatoes

that don't reach the floor. He manages to kick the back of the seat of the nice old lady in front of him several times without even realizing it. She responds with a few half turns of her head to let us know she has noticed the kicking. I begin to wonder if this was a good idea. Are the kids going to fade and lose interest? So far my two older kids are still into it.

Then with no warning, the six-year-old stands up and shouts out, "When are they going to play baseball?" Horrified, I grab him and sit him down and put my index finger to my lips and give him a close up view of the negative look on my face. I don't think the stage heard him, but certainly the immediate twenty rows in front of us heard it loud and clear. I look up to see if anyone is coming to kick us out. But fortunately all I see is a few faces in front of us turning around and a few quiet shhhs. The guy behind me thought it was funny and let out a little laugh.

My little one turns to me and in a whisper says. "Well, you said it was about a baseball game. So, when are they going to play baseball?" I told him to be patient a little longer. He was fine after that. And as I reflected on it afterwards walking back to our hotel, it occurred to me that he had been to a couple of real professional baseball games where he was allowed to yell and cheer and give gaff to the batter and the pitcher and boo the umpire. Why was this any different? Here we were in New York City and it was, after all, the Damn Yankees! That's my boy! You tell 'em!

I Can't Remember The Brilliant Thought I Had Two Seconds Ago!

Boy, getting old sucks! I can't remember things I thought about two seconds ago, but I can tell you the score of Super Bowl III! I can't remember who called the house this morning but I can remember February 5th, 1972! You know, there are all these theories on short-term and long-term memory, but nobody thinks that's going to happen to them. Why? Because they don't remember it's supposed to happen to them! So it goes unnoticed.

A couple of years ago I was in Charleston, South Carolina. On the way there I was telling my kids about Rainbow Row. Rainbow Row is a beautiful stretch of row houses in historic Charleston painted very elegantly in soft rainbow colors. Together they form a kind of elegant, classic Southern façade. We had been in Charleston a day or two when we ran across Rainbow Row. The kids said, "Hey Dad, there's Rainbow Row." I said, "What's that? I never heard of it!" My kids went wild! "Dad, you've been telling us about it for a week!" they responded emphatically. "No I haven't! I don't even know what Rainbow Row is! What are you talking about? I don't see any rainbow!" "Dad, have you lost it?" my oldest says to me. "I swear, I don't remember. What are you talking about?" I'm incredulous. Then my wife chips in with,

Five Potatoes

"Dear, have you been drinking? You couldn't stop talking about this on the way down here!"

That was the beginning. It was December 1999. The beginning of the end of my short—and long-term memory! That was the beginning of my realization that my memory was not distorted, prejudiced or exaggerated, but I was actually blanking out. Part of it I blamed on thinking about too many things at once; therefore, some stuff got lost in the mess. Then I thought it might be a sign of early Alzheimer's. I was wondering if I was eating the right things. Well, I knew that couldn't be right because I've never eaten the right things. So if this was going to happen because of poor brain nutrition, it should have happened a long time ago. Maybe it's the NutraSweet in Diet Coke and Diet Dr. Pepper. Maybe I just need a long rest. Just maybe my little brain had absorbed just about everything it could. But I really was worried.

I couldn't help but wonder what things I had blanked out on like that at work or at home. I was trying to think of all my recent phone calls and messages. How many meetings had I just blanked out on? Was I supposed to have done things I didn't do?

That was four years ago. I think about my memory cells every day. I've forgotten a lot of stuff since then. But I did go to conscientious list-making. I write down everything I need to do, should do, want to do. I write down phone calls I should make. I have lists of things to do a mile long. Sometimes I wake up and can't remember what season it is and sometimes when writing a check I have to think about the year. I definitely can't remember the date. I do remember that I have a couple of lists ongoing. So I try to remember where I put them.

Well, there's lots of stuff published on memory loss these days. Sadly, no one has the magic potion. In the meantime, I just hope

223

I don't forget my pants one day. I've already forgotten to pull up the old zipper a bunch of times.

I guess I can understand the aging process. But, I really get scared about instant forgetfulness. That's when I'm driving along and I think of something. It's usually something I want to remember or write down. The thought could be anything, but the overlay track on my brain says to the original track, "This would be a good thing to remember." I pull the car up to a stop sign and watch a lady and her dog cross the street. And then it's gone. I can't remember the thought I just had two seconds ago. I mentally beat myself up. But I can't even remember the gist of the subject. After a couple of hundred feet, I pull the car to the side of the road. I put the car in park and rub my eyes. I close my eyes and try to think of what happened before I pulled up to the stop sign. Where have I just been? Did I stop at the stoplight a mile back? What was I doing out on this errand? What was that important or interesting thought?

I hope my kids will benefit from medical research and not go through what I am experiencing.

I received a postcard from my oldest the other day. It was a pretty picture of Rainbow Row in Charleston, South Carolina. "Dear Dad," it said. "We were here, where were you?"

How nice of them to remember!

Don't Cry For Me Bethesda

With regards to Andrew Lloyd Weber and Tim Rice
Sung to the tune of *Don't Cry For Me Argentina*

I can't be calm
I think you're lame
Though I tell you, I think it is real
That I'm ready to move
Because there is no fun
You've changed so much
All I can see is a bank I once knew
The town by restaurants defined
And crowded beltway around you
I had to move on this way
I had to change
Could have stayed all my life in my car looking out of the mirror
Out of the humid air
So they chose layoff
And I found I had to start anew
Things impressed me as I recall
I really expected them to
Don't cry for me Bethesda
The truth is I really left you
All through my wild plays
My poor judgment
You were so white bread
Now you're so P.C.

Williston Lamar

And as for crawl and as for sprawl
You've given in to them
Though it seems to others it's just urban planning
Creating confusion
And adding to pollution
You and I can see
The demographics are right in line
Still I just love your green trees
Don't cry for me Bethesda
Don't cry for me Bethesda
The truth is I really left you
All through my wild plays
My poor judgment
You were so white bread
Now you're so P.C.
Have you heard too much?
I've gone away, now listening is over for you
But all you have to do is follow me and move away
You know it's true

Coming soon! DON'T CRY FOR ME PASADENA

Late-night Radio

Troubled? Can't sleep? Depressed? A lot on your mind? Worried? Anxiety-prone? Overwhelmed? Tired? Regrets?

Happy? Engaged? At peace? Doing well? Full of good humor? Good relationships? Job ok? Everything going great?

Somewhere in between?

Your state of mind doesn't matter. Darkness is all around. The curtains are drawn. All is calm. White noise pervades the air. It's 2:00 a.m. You have no responsibility to anyone or anything at this hour. You breathe. It's warm in your bed.

Turn on your transistor radio! Listen to a late-night station! No, I'm not talking about political talk shows. I'm talking about replays of radio shows from long ago or current broadcasts about aliens, time travel, ghosts and the paranormal.

The stories take you away. The guests are interesting. In your dark room your eyes are the cameras registering the vision your imagination has created. The stories unfold while you witness them in your mind.

You don't have to believe. You just have to listen. Even for just a few minutes. Until you fall asleep again. You see, these sounds take you away. They give you another life. Even if it's just for a minute, they remind you that it's not all about you.

When you wake up tomorrow nothing will be different. The facts of your life will still be the facts of your life. All of the unsolvable problems of your existence will awaken with you.

But you will realize when the sun comes up that you are still alive and there is still time to live and maybe even time to resolve some things, and that the grain of sand that you are in this universe is just that. So maybe you'll be better today.

All this because of late-night radio!

SHE LOVES THE DOGS MORE THAN ME!

My wife and I rescued two old dogs. They are sweet, gentle, old golden retrievers. After a few days with us, both of them ended up in the bedroom every night. We bought them special sleeping cushions and even put out an extra bowl of water in the bedroom. That was ok for a while. But, of course, after a few days on their beds they wanted to be in our bed. It was cute the first time. Sort of funny the next night, but after three or four times I had to leave. Thank goodness we have other bedrooms to go to. While in bed one of my dogs starts licking my foot, coating it with warm dog saliva. This makes me a little nervous. Then the other one gets in between us and looks at us as if to say, "Well, is this all that happens up here?" My wife hugs and kisses both dogs. Then she talks baby talk to them, massages their necks, and then kisses them some more.

When she is away on a trip her first words to me over the phone are, "How are the dogs? Did you feed them yet? Did you check their ears and brush them? Don't forget their allergy pills! Put the phone up to their ears so I can talk to them." So, while holding up the dog's long, floppy ear, I place the phone up next to the dog's head. She speaks to the dog for at least a minute. Then she asks me, "Well, did he have any reaction?" So although the dog had no reaction I don't want her to think the dog is sick, so I say, "Oh yes dear, he wagged his tail and moved his head all around and his eyes got big." Then we go through the same process with the other dog with the same result. "Your dogs love you, dear," I tell her.

When she gets home the dogs run to greet her, She drops her purse, gets on her knees and hugs and kisses them. She scratches their tummies and asks them if they were good dogs today. She asks the dogs in baby talk if "Dad" has fed them yet and if "Dad" has taken them for a walk. She waits on her knees pointing to her cheek awaiting the affectionate dog kiss from both dogs.

Then she asks me if I paid the mortgage.

Alas, I'm just the two-legged, saliva-covered husband.

"The Last Time I Saw Him, He Was Having A Good Time!" (Al Ward)

Alan Ward left this world last Saturday. He chose to leave it. He was a complicated man. Sincere, yet softly amusing; talented, yet unfocused; friendly and calm despite a troubled soul. He had already died twice as a result of wounds received in the jungles of Vietnam, yet was miraculously brought back from the brink each time. These experiences gave him a kind of presence and charisma as if he had already done everything there was to do in and out of this world. He was a bit of a scoundrel and a con man, but always for fun and only for small profit. He never took from anyone he knew. We attended college together. He was like an older brother or young uncle; more experienced in everything and wise beyond his years. Peaceful in his pursuit of happiness, he liked everyone. Everyone liked him. Though he was a student like the rest of us, his six or seven additional years of life made his demeanor appear to be that of a pipe-smoking college professor with no particular political agenda. He was like a teacher. His stories of war always stirred our imaginations and scared us a little. He never raised his voice in anger. He was generous beyond his means and was continually in search of genuine friendship. He was on permanent disability from the Army, but I never heard him place any blame for his physical ailments or his lost youth.

Distracted and frustrated, I think he just wanted to continue down the road sooner rather than later. I don't know of his rationale, of course, but I can hear him saying, "OK, old buddy. We better get going before they drop a frag on us!"

He was one of those guys you tell your kids about. Despite his dalliances with alcohol, drugs and sex he was not running from anything; he was just experiencing things with no particular zeal or addiction but in a rather thoughtful way. All these experiences just added to his list of things to keep us, his little brothers, in awe of his every word. He had a traditional response when asked where someone was. He would say, "I don't know, but the last time I saw him he was having a good time!"

He once told me he wanted to have three wives at once. That way he could do drugs with one, drink with the other and have sex with the third. Each one would be very talented in her category. This theory may seem offensive at first but he didn't mean it in its literal sense. At least he pretended not to. He meant that he enjoyed many things and how life would be perfect if he could find the female version of himself. After college I lost touch with Alan Ward or "Wardoid" as we use to call him. Twenty-seven years later, it's too late to talk to him again to ask him questions about his experiences. But I have a pretty good idea that through his action last Saturday, he's telling us about his new experience in ways we will just have to ponder silently and wonder if keeping in touch would have changed the outcome.

This last time I saw him, twenty-seven years ago at our graduation, he was having a good time.

The Other Side Of The Aqueduct

There's a beautiful place on the Wellesley College golf course. It's an aqueduct. It is a very large structure, Romanesque in design with ornate iron railings. A large berm curves its way along the wooded edge of the campus golf course, rising in height as it gets close to the aqueduct. Walking on top of the berm toward the aqueduct is like a train coming around a long, slow curve toward a tunnel. You know it's coming but you sort of don't want to get there.

I haven't been there in years. Last time I tried to walk down that path I found out you can't park your car and they won't let you on the golf course so it's virtually inaccessible. I don't know what the big deal is. It was just such a pleasant place to walk on a summer evening.

The really intriguing part of walking up there along the berm and then standing on the aqueduct was that no one went to the far side of the aqueduct. It seemed that the path just ended where the structure ended; sort of like a tunnel with a wall at the end. There didn't seem to be anyplace to go. The aqueduct served as a place to stand and look at the Wellesley bell tower over the green, green golf course and occasionally served as a launching pad for throwing little pebbles to the still pond water some sixty-odd feet beneath. Standing on the aqueduct on a late-summer evening was like being within a classic landscape painting by Washington

Allston or Ashur Durand. For me, it was literally like being a brush stroke on the canvas. I loved standing there, hands on the rail, lost in all the brush strokes of the superbly-contrived composition of architectural grace and benign nature.

I never ventured to the other side of the aqueduct. It always looked a little scary and dark and pathless. Even if I go back someday and stand on the aqueduct, I'll just look over to the other side. I don't want to go to the other side of the aqueduct. It's selfish, I guess, but I just don't want to be out of the painting.

EIGHT POTATO: THE FAMILY

I Want To Go Home!
Or
There's No Place Like Home!

We grow up, go off to school, begin building a career and in the process we meet someone. Then, through our influence or theirs we move away from home. Sometimes finding a job or just doing what we want to do or going to a place we think is nice is the rationale. We even move away just to be cool. Yes, just to be cool. We move to places like San Francisco, Boston, New York, and London that seem hip.

My observation is that while men and women move away from their roots with equal zest, it's the women that lose it every six months. It begins with, "I miss my family!" That comment leads to, "They're all at the town festival this weekend." Which in turn leads to, "I want to go home!" And of course, this becomes the mantra for the next two weeks.

As the days go by the endless rationalizations for a trip to her family home become dinner conversation. "Oh, did I tell you I checked into cheap fares?" she gushes. "No, but please tell me about them," I reply. "We can go for a week for only $X and if we use frequent-flier miles we could save half of that! Or, if we stopped in Denver we could save $100! Of course the tricky part will be getting time off." She says this with great anticipation. "Can you get the time?" she inquires. Of course, your first thought is that you'd rather sleep with your boss, who you hate, than spend six days with her family! "Can't she just get over it?" you think to yourself. "She's all grown up now. It's ok to stay away from home for a long time! Besides, we live in San Francisco, probably the coolest, most beautiful city on Earth. If they really loved you they would find a way to get here."

Then you offer up the ultimate sacrifice. "Why not have your family come here?" you ask sheepishly. "They've only been here once and they seemed to have a good time, as I recall." "No," she says. "No, Mom's on too many medications and Dad doesn't like to fly and my sister and her husband don't want to miss the end of the soccer season with their kids. We need to go there." Oh God, I've lost this old argument. So I try a new one. "Hey, let's go, but let's stay in the local hotel down the road. I need more points with that hotel chain. Think about it. There will be room service, mini-bars, and a workout room. We can actually have sex! What a concept!" She was actually thinking about it until I said, "What a concept," as if I was somehow declaring that we hadn't had sex in a while and it was all her fault. After a moment of silence she says, "No, my parents would be insulted. They would think we didn't like them or my mom's lasagna. Dad wants to watch some games with you and Mom wants to go shopping and my sister is going to want to us to come over and see her new interior decorating scheme. I want to go home!"

Epilogue:

You end up having a much better time than she does. You watch football with Grandpa and some cousin. You can't remember the cousin's name, but he's really good at making margaritas. You eat, you drink and you do as you're told. You go where you're told with childlike obedience.

Your spouse shops with her mom and shares family gossip, family feuds and minor family disgraces. Her brother doesn't like her politics and tells her so. Her dearest, best friend tells her she has gained weight; and finally, no one can agree on where to go out to dinner so they all argue about it for an hour and then complain because your other sister got her way with the chain restaurant choice and the service sucks. Of course, her nephew shows up with his slut girlfriend. Both them are dressed like they just came off Melrose. At least they're interesting. The others are obsessed with telling the same stories over and over again. This time it's the wedding story about the gay photographer who hit on the bride's father. Nothing new here! Except there are more insults about why we don't move back to be closer to the family. We're the only ones who left this marginal existence and so we have to be berated about it for days.

Then it happens. She says it, not you. "Let's move the plane reservations up and leave a day early. I don't care if I have to pay a $100 fine for changing the tickets. I can't stand it here. Thank God we don't live back here! I want to go home!"

THINGS MY FATHER LOVED, LIKED, DISLIKED AND HATED: MAYBE YOURS DID TOO!

- He loved "rathskeller"-type places.
- He loved afternoon naps on Saturday or Sunday.
- He loved azaleas.
- He loved birds and bird watching.
- He loved Bob Hope.
- He loved *Bonanza*—particularly Hoss and Pa.
- He loved boxwood, peonies and dogwoods.
- He loved Chinese food—lo mein and chow mein.
- He loved cocktail hour.
- He loved cold, frozen beer mugs—with beer on a hot afternoon or evening.
- He loved collegiate Gothic architecture.
- He loved crab cakes.
- He loved diner-type restaurants.
- He loved games that ended in a tie.
- He loved golf—he liked Gary Player and Gene Littler.
- He loved *Hawaii Five—O*.
- He loved hemlock hedges and English boxwood.
- He loved his 1920's wooden shaft golf clubs.
- He loved *Ironside*.
- He loved Johnny Unitas and Y.A. Title.
- He loved Lancer's Rose Wine.
- He loved *Lawrence Welk*.

Five Potatoes

- He loved little children who were too young to understand anything yet.
- He loved Louis Armstrong.
- He loved *M.A.S.H.*
- He loved *Magnum P.I.*
- He loved old houses.
- He loved Polynesian restaurants—Trader Vic's, etc.
- He loved poor, honest, good, hard-working, genuine people.
- He loved Roger Staubach and Drew Pearson.
- He loved Ronald Reagan.
- He loved San Francisco.
- He loved *Sonny and Cher*.
- He loved sport coats and interesting ties.
- He loved Strauss waltzes.
- He loved the American Indians.
- He loved the Dallas Cowboys cheerleaders.
- He loved the evening and when it was dark he loved to name the stars.
- He loved the French, the Italians, the Chinese and the Swedes.
- He loved *The Golden Girls*.
- He loved the Hawaiians and anything to do with the Polynesian culture.
- He loved *The Mary Tyler Moore Show*.
- He loved the place he grew up.
- He loved *The Smothers Brothers Show*.
- He loved the song *When You Wish Upon A Star*.
- He loved the stock market.
- He loved the tropics.
- He loved *The Wizard of Oz*.
- He loved to go to the annual boat show at the D.C. Armory.
- He loved to leave football games and church early.
- He loved to play 9 holes of golf in the evening.
- He loved to read *Barron's* every Sunday.
- He loved to watch big, long freight trains.
- He loved to whistle to the birds and try and get them to eat raisins on the railing.

- He liked and always wanted a 30- to 36-foot cabin cruiser.
- He liked Arnold Palmer and Jack Nicklaus.
- He liked big trees and dogwoods when they bloomed.
- He liked Bing Crosby—but he liked Bob Hope more.
- He liked black leather dress shoes—even for yard work.
- He liked boxer shorts.
- He liked cars with stick shifts and a hand brake.
- He liked Cesar Romero and Ricardo Montalban.
- He liked chestnuts.
- He liked Churchill and Roosevelt.
- He liked Elizabeth Taylor.
- He liked everything to do with Egypt and the pyramids.
- He liked Fords.
- He liked Georgian-style architecture.
- He liked girls with beautiful curls.
- He liked his old friends from long ago.
- He liked holly trees with lots of red berries.
- He liked hot dogs on the grill and barbequed chicken.
- He liked Hugh Hefner.
- He liked Ike.
- He liked Jack Parr.
- He liked Liberace.
- He liked Lobster Newberg.
- He liked most of his clients.
- He liked the movie *Love Story*.
- He liked Nat King Cole.
- He liked Paul Harvey—particularly his Christmas Eve sketch.
- He liked Pebble Beach.
- He liked people to display emotion and sympathy when it was genuine.
- He liked people with personality.
- He liked Peter, Paul and Mary.
- He liked Pierre Salinger.
- He liked Richard Nixon and John Kennedy for serving in the Navy.
- He liked slot machines.

Five Potatoes

- He liked squirrel, rabbit and quail hunting.
- He liked Sunday afternoon car rides to look at houses or property for sale.
- He liked the annual trek to the in-laws to pick up big boxes of Christmas gifts.
- He liked the Cub Scouts and the Boy Scouts and gave them money.
- He liked the guy at the service station who used to put new tires on the car.
- He liked the Osmonds but preferred Sonny and Cher.
- He liked the song *Tie Me Kangaroo Down, Sport* by Rolf Harris.
- He liked *The Flintstones*.
- He liked the underdog in sporting events.
- He liked the woods.
- He liked the Ziegfeld Follies.
- He liked to buy "socks for Mom"(stockings) for Mother's Day and Easter.
- He liked to buy drinks for the ladies of the family.
- He liked to carve the turkey at Thanksgiving and Christmas.
- He liked to cut down his own Christmas tree.
- He liked cedar trees more than pine trees.
- He liked to drink bourbon with his brother.
- He liked to drink gin.
- He liked to drive the kids over the fords in the creek.
- He liked to eat grilled hot dogs in bed while he watched football games.
- He liked to eat out—anywhere; he loved cafeteria-type places with lots of choices.
- He liked to fish.
- He liked to leave church at communion and read the paper in the car.
- He liked to listen to the all-news station on the radio.
- He liked to look at the lawn and shrubs when he came home from work.
- He liked to plant his garden.

- He liked to play golf on late summer evenings.
- He liked to put his socks and shoes on before his pants.
- He liked to say "bullshit" whenever he was talking to his brother.
- He liked to see antique cars go by.
- He liked to take flowers over to his parents' gravesite.
- He liked to take the most scenic way home from work.
- He liked to talk to door-to-door salesmen.
- He liked to trap raccoons and possums and then let them go.
- He liked to trim the hemlocks.
- He liked to visit colleges and universities.
- He liked to watch animal/wildlife shows like *Marlin Perkins' Wild Kingdom*.
- He liked to wear his bathrobe with holes in the elbows.
- He liked Walter Cronkite.
- He disliked Chevys.
- He disliked *60 Minutes* being called a "news magazine"—it was a TV show!
- He disliked *All in the Family*.
- He disliked women with men's names like "Billie."
- He disliked Elvis.
- He disliked Frank Sinatra.
- He disliked his brother.
- He disliked Jimmy Carter.
- He disliked modern art unless his kids were the artists.
- He disliked police.
- He disliked squirrels who ate the bird food.
- He disliked talking about the war.
- He disliked the Beatles.
- He disliked *The Godfather*.
- He disliked the Pope and thought the church was behind the times.
- He disliked the Roosevelt Bridge across the Potomac—not enough stone.
- He disliked watching baseball on TV.
- He disliked women who smoked or who were taller than him.

Five Potatoes

- He hated cold air blowing on his neck from the rear window of the car.
- He hated dogs peeing in his yard or garden.
- He hated highway design.
- He hated midnight mass because he wanted to go to bed.
- He hated modern architecture—glass boxes.
- He hated motorcycles.
- He hated *Rowan & Martin's Laugh-In*.
- He hated sauerkraut.
- He hated the 10 foot basket in basketball
- He hated to pick up the phone on weekends.
- He hated to touch things in public restrooms.
- He hated to see people cry.

Condescending Celebrities!

My son is a drug addict. He's been arrested multiple times. He's currently in rehab. My daughter is twenty-six. She doesn't work or do much of anything. She dropped out of high school and ran off with a folk singer. But she's back now living at home. After her DUI she's only been stopped once for speeding. She has gotten help for her anorexia. My wife is obsessed with plastic surgery and she is a functional alcoholic. She's my third wife. She doesn't work or volunteer, but gives my money to the Cancer Society. The other two wives took the money. I report to a therapist after a bout with kleptomania. My therapist discovered I suffer from a severe persecution complex stemming from guilt over my childhood behavior. My lawyer is handling my tax evasion case. I haven't spoken to my sister in years. I'm being sued for leaving the scene of an accident. The tabloids say I'm having an affair with a married woman half my age. I'm suing. My agent isn't tough enough to get me what I deserve. I had to fly commercial to Cannes. My father is in a home in Kansas. I hope they are taking good care of him. I haven't seen the place, but for what it costs it better be nice.

So have dinner every night with your kids! Because I'm a big network star and I know what's good for you!

I'm Able To Sit Up And Take Liquid Nourishment!

Back then, there was Uncle Gifford. The black sheep of the family. The character. The crude, rude one. He was gruff. He was fat. He resembled Fred Flintstone. He was loud and obnoxious. He didn't get married until he was fifty-five. He had no children; although my sisters and I were his only nieces and nephew he never gave us a gift or a Christmas present. We were scared to death of him. He'd slap us on the back and say to my sisters, "Got a boyfriend yet? Don't forget you can love a rich one the same as you can love a poor one!"

We never knew if he was drunk or not. He loved bourbon, even on Sunday morning. On the few occasions a year that my father would make us visit him, he would give all of us bourbon on the rocks whether we wanted it or not. And age didn't matter. When I was ten I got bourbon on the rocks. "Here, kid," he would say. "This won't kill you!" Twenty-five years later he was still handing me bourbon on the rocks. My mother couldn't stand to be in his presence, but when he came over she would hand him bourbon.

Gifford was the youngest child of three. His older sister used to tell us that when her mother was in labor with Gifford, she struggled so hard to deliver him that she nearly died. My aunt swore that this was a precursor to how difficult he would be in later life. He was difficult. He was selfish. He was lazy.

Gifford was a surveyor by trade. But really, he was a hired gun for a survey company to get projects finished or difficult projects fixed. I think he had this role because everyone was scared of him. He seemed to work when he wanted to and do nothing when he wanted. He had no schedule.

Uncle Gifford's life was about as self-centered and miserly as it gets. He saved his money. He never traveled anywhere. He never spent any time with his nieces and nephew. He lived off his parents for many years, but no one would confront him about it. He was constantly playing the stock market and looking at real estate. I think he may have bought and sold some land from time to time.

One time he stopped by our house on a Sunday afternoon. My father noticed the rear fender of his car was crushed like a tin can. My father asked what happened. Gifford responded in his gruff voice, "Drunk as a skunk last night, I backed into a fire hydrant!" Gifford thought it was funny as hell. My father and I just sort of looked at each other.

One of Uncle Gifford's favorite things to do in life was to watch the Miami Dolphins play football. He used to say, "Boy, you watch that Bob Griese now. That Bob Griese, he's a winner, boy!" One of his other favorite things to do was to call my father and talk about the stock market. It was the only time I ever heard my father use four-letter words. The two of them communicated with very few words other than "horseshit" and "bullshit." I guess it was their way of being brothers. My mother would just roll her eyes.

What Uncle Gifford lacked in terms of manners and class he made up for by being a character. His colleagues at the surveying company used to call him "Old Giff." And Old Giff he was. He was a character who lacked character.

For the last twenty years of his life he moved into a small historic house in West Virginia. He stopped working completely and

Five Potatoes

never came to see us anymore. We would visit him maybe two or three times a year. He bought a huge Cadillac and mostly sat around reading stock reports, watching the Miami Dolphins and drinking bourbon. He would sit on his front porch and watch people go by. He got to know a few locals and as long as he could be the center of attention and play "the character" he enjoyed life.

One of the last times I saw Old Giff he was sitting on the front porch when I arrived. I shouted to him as I walked up, "How are you, Uncle Gifford?" Without getting up from his chair, he responded, "I'm able to sit up and take liquid nourishment! Bourbon, that is!" I thought that was just about the funniest thing I ever heard him say. I guess that saying is sort of a colloquialism. I'm sure it wasn't original, but I had never heard it and I thought it was a great statement on many levels; a sort of quadruple entendre. It's like you're ninety-five years old when you're not. It's like you're in a nursing home when you're not. It's like you can't eat solid food when you can. With all those potential maladies you can drink bourbon, when you can't! One can even adjust the ending to suit your personal tastes: vodka, scotch, brandy or whatever. I remembered that moment with Old Giff and I started using the phrase myself. I thought it was a very funny, albeit a unique way of describing one's well being and it's a whole lot more original than saying, "I'm fine." The only thing is that every time I've ever used that phrase, no one ever laughs. I don't get it. It's a very funny expression!

Old Giff has been gone twenty years now. Maybe it's a genetic thing, but I think the older we get the more we adapt to and appreciate our family history.

I'm going to keep using that phrase in response to the question, "How are you?" until someone finally laughs when I say it. Until then, I'm able to sit up and take liquid nourishment!

You're Not Going To Wear That, Are You?

Double standards are just part of life. We kind of have to live with them most times. Like when guys have bad clothes days. Women just jump all over us. "You're not going to wear that, are you?" As if all her friends might see you and think she's with a dork. "Here you go. Try this and this," she says. You have to change. There is no choice. You will look like she wants you to look. Sadly, this doesn't work when the proverbial shoe is on the other foot.

You know there are certain outfits of hers that are just unbearable for you to see her in. There's the one that makes her look like Annie Oakley and the one that makes her look flat and don't forget the shoes that make her look like she's an Army Ranger. Then there are the jeans that are either too loose or too tight (ass is important, you know), and the winter jacket that makes her look like a troll. Oh, did I mention the gold shoes that look like slippers from a nursing home? Your brain says to ask her, "You're not going to wear that, are you?" But you can't. Asking is the kiss of death. So you just think it. After a pregnant pause, she asks you, "How's this look?" Now, you have to say something. "Fine," you say as you raise your eyebrows. "Fine," she retorts. "What's wrong with it?" "Nothing," you respond sheepishly. "You look great. Let's go." "No, no. If you don't like it, what else can I wear?" she demands. "I don't know, but we're late." "Oh God, get me out of this one!" I'm thinking. "I don't know, but how

Five Potatoes

about the black outfit?" I offer. I can only imagine that she has a couple dozen black outfits. One of them has to look better than the ridiculous stuff she's got on! Soon she's found something. But changing means everything. She has to change the shoes, the jewelry, her hair, her make-up, even her underwear. You know you can't say another word since you are responsible for both of you being late. So what else are you to do but wait and wait and wait and wait? Sounds a lot like the trail of refugees going from Casablanca to Lisbon!

Time passes. Your daughter grows up. She's sixteen. I don't know what evil lurks in the hearts of the boys she's going out with (actually I do know), but I know I'm going to take out my revenge on my daughter for the years her mother spent torturing me. "Hey, young lady! You're not going to wear that, are you?"

WORLDS COLLIDE!

The most insightful episode ever of *Seinfeld* was not "The Soup Nazi" or "Master of Your Domain" or even the final episode. The greatest episode ever (in my opinion) was "Worlds Collide." Watch it! You'll see!

I find myself becoming a different person in each piece of my life. Maybe you do too. I'm a different person at work than I am at home. I'm a different person with my relatives than I am with my friends. I'm a different person in public places than I am in private. I'm a different person in big meetings than I am in small meetings. Maybe "different" is not the right term. Really, it's kind of a multiple-personality thing. I have good moments and bad in all these circumstances, but it's particularly interesting to me when worlds collide. My wife is many different people in many different situations as well. Only no matter how long we're married, there are occasionally collisions of my wife's world and my world, where one of us is embarrassed by a "different person" we hadn't seen before.

Sometimes there are good moments that seem to extend and compliment the person you think you know so well, but sometimes there are awkward awakenings! Sometimes there are things you don't want your wife to know and vice versa. But they have a way of coming to the surface when worlds collide. Usually, it's when you show up unexpectedly at her workplace, or she at yours. Or it might include one of you walking into a conversation with a family member that's obviously not meant for your inclusion. The situation really doesn't matter. When worlds collide more planes of the dodecahedron of your personality and hers become visible to each other no matter how long you've been together. It makes a person anxious and a little lonely. You're the last person they want to see, but hopefully, to quote Sheriff Matt Dillon, you're still the first person they call.

Sometimes we experience one of those awkward awakenings and start to get a little edgy about it! We wait until we're alone and then start piling on the questions. Who was that guy? You never said you liked *CSI* before! How come when they're here you laugh at that movie, when you won't watch it with me? You won't get in the hot tub at a hotel but it's ok here at the Snosreans's!

Anyway, you get the idea. It happens to all of us. But I have the solution to worlds colliding and it works.

Just shut up! Say nothing! Do nothing! Physically ignore it, but mentally record it! Then the next time you are embarrassed when worlds collide, and she confronts you, have three examples ready to relay right back to her! Sit back and watch as worlds avoid!

Mom

Everything Freud, Jung, Maslow, Pavlov, Harlow and Piaget and their buddies said about a man's relationship to his mother is true! Think about it!

To My Daughter: No Boys Until You're 45! To My Mother: No Boys Until You're 85!

"Dad, this is Paul," my 16-year-old daughter says. "His parents own an island in the Bahamas!" . . . "Holy shit, honey! Want to get married this summer?" I say. "Just kidding, dear! Sorry, no boys until you're 45!"

"Mom, have you met that nice old widower down the street? He's really good-looking for his age! I think he's lonely! He talked my ear off," I confide to my mother. "Why don't you introduce yourself? Maybe you can go to lunch together. Oh, I forgot, no boys until you're 85! What's that? Oh, you're 89! So you've been running around for four years now! Oh! Well stop it! No boys until you're 95!"

Mom, when I was 16 why didn't you tell me, "No girls until you're 45?"

Swan Lake

My sister has a small pond in her front yard. She really wanted to get a pair of live swans to swim around and sit on the property and look good. She harassed her husband endlessly with a kind of obsessive-compulsive behavior that makes everyone around her nervous. Anyway, she eventually found a place to purchase the swans. She bought them and some special food that they're supposed to eat. The swans settled in comfortably in the front yard pond.

My sister's neighbors have a pond also. It's slightly larger than my sister's pond. One day when my sister came home from shopping she couldn't find the swans. After looking everywhere in her yard she eventually went over to the neighbors' property, where she found the two swans gracefully floating. With much encouragement she tried to lure them back home, but with no success. This infuriated my sister. She took it personally. She went home and brought back their special food and tried to bribe them to come back but they just wouldn't move.

The neighbors began to get frustrated as well. A swan can really make large excretions and with more frequency then a large dog!

So my sister gets this brilliant idea. If dogs can have electronic dog collars and electronic fences that keep them on the property, why can't swans have them too?

Five Potatoes

She calls the local sales rep for electronic dog collars and asks if they can be used on waterfowl like swans. I would have loved to see the expression on the sales rep's face when this was asked. After considerable discussion and some remarkable coercing by my sister the rep agreed to come have a look. My sister insisted that it would be a marketing coup for the dog fence company. She would also grant permission to use photos of the swans with the dog collars for the company's marketing material.

Eventually the beautiful, sleek, long, white necks of the swans were fitted with electronic dog collars. The guy from the dog fence company came out and installed the wire for the fence and helped my sister attach the collars. My sister didn't understand why they couldn't make them in white to match the swans! But anyway, this seemed to work for a while.

Alas, the joy of watching the grace, nobility and elegance of the swans was a feast of splendid repose. Knowing they would stay put was less romantic but still comforting.

Eventually, my sister noticed that the swans were wandering farther and farther from the pond. They seemed to be going beyond the carefully concealed wire fence. It was soon determined that the little battery boxes on their collars were allowing water from the pond to penetrate to the battery and thereby rendering the whole system useless. My sister thought that some kind of caulking or sealant might do the trick, but caught up in the more mundane matters of day-to-day living she never got around to fixing the problem. Nevertheless, the swans never left the property. There must have been a kind of human-to-fowl mental connection that helped the swans understand their place. Perhaps the whole scheme was simply a birdbrained idea, but the swans were in a good environment, well-fed and secure. Selfishly for us, the birdbrained humans, the visual pleasure was intoxicating.

The swans lived on in my sister's pond. Their earlier transgressions were forgiven and Tchaikovsky can make claim to another Swan Lake.

Epilogue: The female swan attacked a stationary lawn tool, cut herself, contracted an infection and died. The male, in his loneliness, wandered far away. The family searched for days. He was found in a much larger pond, frozen to death from the cold winter. Thus even the life of swans imitates art. Siegfried and Odette win again at goodness, beauty and love.

What!

"What!" she screams over the phone to her sister. I hear this all the way from the garage. So my ears perk up a little and I keep listening to the phone call, all the time thinking something is drastically wrong back at my wife's family home. Two minutes later she screams, "What!" Now you know something bizarre has happened. She hasn't said much on her end of the conversation. I'm thinking that soon there will be tears and the suggestion of a trip back home. Maybe someone had a heart attack! Then it happens again. "What!" she exclaims. So, I go into the house and watch her pace around the floor with the phone. Eventually, I make eye contact. After a few hand and eye gestures I convey that I now have a need to know if something is wrong. She waves me away as if she can't deal with me and the phone conversation right now. It's too serious a situation. I'll have to wait until she's off the phone.

Trying to brace for the worst and all the travel arrangements that need to be made, I wait patiently for the end of the call. She walks in calmly and doesn't say anything. After ten seconds I can't stand it anymore and so I jump in with, "What's wrong? Is something wrong? You sounded really distressed on the phone." "Oh yes! Can you believe it?" she pronounces. "Saks wouldn't let my sister return her Prada shoes without the receipt. She went to the manager and he apparently doesn't believe that the customer is always right and then she had a parking ticket on her car when she came out of the store!"

All I can say is, "What!"

NINE POTATO: KIDS

God And Man, Cognac And Cigarettes

Spirituality often takes place in God's cathedral, not in man's architecture to God. A couple of years ago I was driving across country with my sixteen-year-old son. On the way we stayed at the Broadmoor Resort in Colorado Springs. After dinner one night we went and sat on the benches just outside the lounge. It was dark and quite stormy out. The only illumination was from the lightning strikes on the mountains. The waitress came and asked if we wanted anything. I said, "Two cognacs and a pack of Marlboro Lights, please." She looked at my son and me kind of quizzically. She knew he was a long way from twenty-one, but she saw the seriousness in my face and heard the thunderclaps from the distance over the mountains and rushed off, back to the bar. Then my son looked at me kind of quizzically and said, "Dad? Cigarettes?" "Yeah," I said. Now I don't smoke and never really have, but this was just the night to sit quietly and have some cognac and smoke a cigarette or two or three with my son. It was my way to be the dad and his moment to be a man with his dad.

To look at the eastern edge of the Rockies at night is to look at all the obstacles a man can cross. The lightning was silhouetting the top of the mountains in a constant bombardment of strobe-like intensity. Rain was falling heavily, but we were sitting just under a small, green awning that provided barely enough cover so that only the occasional stray drop made it to where our feet rested. We were alone on the terrace.

The cognac made the feeling warm and the cigarettes were like silent peace pipes where there was already peace, but the spirit of God's power was plainly visible in the night sky. Those few moments were informally ceremonial. The passing storm was a kind of soft changing of the guard. Few words were spoken. No impossible questions were asked. No expectations were set. There were no wishes made; no promises, either.

I'll remember that night always. We were together, God and man, cognac and cigarettes.

My daughter will be sixteen this year.

Popsicle Sticks

Parents! Are you tired of buying expensive computer games? Are you sick of *The Simpsons*? I bet you don't want to shell out over a hundred dollars for a ball game, right?

So try Popsicle sticks!

Buy some Popsicles at the grocery store. You and the kids can enjoy eating them on a hot day. Save the sticks. Ask each child to write their name on their stick or make up a name, you know, something like "Old Silver" or "Benji." Write these names in permanent marker on both sides. Then go get the garden hose, place it in the gutter and turn it on. Then have Popsicle stick races down the gutter. Talk about cheap! Nothing to make! Nothing to spend money on! Talk about low tech! Talk about fun! Excitement! Competition! Immediate gratification! The family and their friends can play this for hours. First Popsicle stick to the sewer grate wins the race!

Martha Stewart, eat your heart out!

Sunday Syndrome

September 1963, a Sunday afternoon, fifth grade; homework due on Monday: English, math and social studies; it's quiet. That day was the beginning of a lifetime of Sunday Syndrome.

Tonight is Sunday night. It's September. My young son is going to high school tomorrow. He seems calm enough. He seems to be happy. Deep down I know he is like me. He's squirming a little bit inside. He doesn't want the day to end and night to fall. He's paralyzed into inaction. He's procrastinating about getting his books together and his room organized for tomorrow. There are so many other things he'd rather do. If only the Earth would stop turning.

Maybe my son is thinking, "What will happen tomorrow? Did I buy a nerdy notebook? Will someone make fun of it? What about my locker? What if I can't get to class on time? They will all see me coming in late and I'll be singled out. What if that algebra teacher is as mean as they say and calls on me on the first day? What about study hall? There won't be a teacher there and I might look the wrong way at some cool kid and get razzed."

I'm thinking, "What will happen at work tomorrow? Did I remember what I'm responsible for tomorrow? Will I have all the answers for the status meeting? Did I forget the most important thing? If I read this material, will I be informed? What about the scheduling? What about the budget? Can I get an answer to a question before 8 a.m. so I can provide the response in the meeting at 8:30? What should I say in the presentation? What are the key points I want to focus on? What will the results be? Will I be accused of not doing my job just because I didn't do enough on the weekend?"

Sunday afternoon is so quiet. There are so few cars on the road. Even a sunny Sunday afternoon seems dull like a gray day, full of dread. So much work to do. So much preparation is necessary. But Sunday is the day of rest, of freedom. It should be fun, not pensive. It's not fun. It's eerily quiet. All Sundays are eerily quiet. But I know I have to look at the work I brought home on Friday. I have to find the will to start. But I don't want to start. I'd rather clean up the den. I have some family things to attend to. If I can't do them on Sunday when can I get to them? Next weekend? What about those bills that need to be paid this week? It's all too much. As I find more distractions, I worry more and the Sunday Syndrome becomes deeper. The Syndrome wrestles with my mind and my body with agonizing slowness. Every sound seems muffled. Yet I can hear the constant hum of the refrigerator. The afternoon progresses and the time to do a good job on my appointed tasks has grown shorter. I procrastinate. I just don't want to have to think too much and the work will make me think. I want to rest. I don't want to look at the huge stack of paper. I want Monday to be a holiday. Then I realize that there is not enough time. Then I begin to think of creative ways to abbreviate the work ahead.

I encourage my son to get started with his schoolwork. He shrugs. I feel the same.

Fear consumes the afternoon. Fear that I will fail. Fear that my son has the same fear. Fear places a barrier in the path of preparation. Fear that nothing I can do at this point will be enough preparation. Why didn't I try and get some of this done on Saturday? I think of things that will consume the time I should be using to prepare for Monday and I want to do all these things before starting my work. The car needs gas for the week. I didn't read the editorials in the Sunday paper. I need to do some laundry for the week. How can all of this fit in this day?

I'm not organized. Maybe if I just start to collect things and straighten things up I'll find that I don't have as much to do as I thought. Evening is coming. Soon I'll have to have dinner. After dinner it will be dark. Maybe I'll call a friend who will distract me and lighten my spirits. Maybe they haven't done anything either. But what if they did all the work? I can't bear knowing that someone else has it all done. That will scare me.

I think of the people I know who never acquired Sunday Syndrome. Who seem happy-go-lucky on the weekends. They're never worried about Monday. They never seem to bring work home and they never seem unprepared on Monday. I wonder if there is a specialist who can tell me how I can be like that. Has the shrink community dealt with Sunday Syndrome? I don't know. It's too late for me after 42 years, but maybe someone can save my son from this plague.

I think about crawling into the corner in the fetal position. I feel like I need a drink. But I know the moment my lips touch the alcohol the day is really over and absolutely nothing will be done this Sunday evening. I can't let that happen. My son actually volunteers to do the dishes. He's rebelling against doing his homework. He definitely has the Syndrome.

We're on the East Coast. Night has covered the scenery. I flip the channels on the television. There is a game on from the West Coast. It's bright and sunny still on the West Coast. I think, if only I were on the West Coast there would be three more hours to use and I could get everything done. On the television there is a preview of *60 Minutes*. It looks really interesting. Ten till seven. I can gather up my work and sit in front of the TV and wait for *60 Minutes*. But if I watch it, then it will be 8 p.m. I will be getting tired by nine. I have to get sleep because it will be hard to get up tomorrow. That will only leave an hour this evening to get everything done. The work really requires a whole day. Sunday, Sunday. Slow-motion. Tired. Worried. Fearful. Sunday Syndrome.

It's one minute to seven; papers in my lap. My son's schoolbooks open. Two seconds of silence from the television. It's 7 p.m.

There it is! That damn *60 Minutes* stop watch!

Tick, tick, tick, ... tick, tick, tick . . . . Sunday Syndrome.

Son Of A . . . Golfer!

Golf has to be the single most difficult sport on Earth. It is also the most embarrassing. Do you think public speaking is tough? Try standing on the first tee with a couple of foursomes backed up and every one of them watching you tee off. You slice one into the woods and they roll their eyes at their partners and whisper, "Can you believe we got behind this guy?"

Frankly, I don't understand how so many people learned to play golf so well. It takes years to gain any consistency and you must be either a driving range owner (à la Kevin Costner in *Tin Cup*) or retired or a doctor to have the time to play five or six times a week. The rest of us poor slobs who only get six or seven opportunities a year will never play worth a damn.

I've hit about a million ground burners, half a million slices and hooks, a quarter million direct in-the-lake shots and countless other poor shots. Hell, I've even ten putted! Let's see Tiger do that! My handicap should be about one million! About half of all those embarrassing moments were in front of strangers. Occasionally, a moment comes along that makes up for at least ten of those humiliating ones. Recently, my fifteen-year-old son gave me that pleasure.

Picture this: seventh hole, par 5, championship Robert Trent Jones course. My son and I are playing just for fun by ourselves. We are taking our time, enjoying the day. We are having a great father and son bonding experience. Only a few people are on the course.

Five Potatoes

I'm thinking that this is why golf was invented. After slicing my last drives (one hit a house, one hit the top of a palm tree and birds flew out, the last one bounced off a retaining wall and went into a lake) I decide to just drive the cart and watch my fifteen-year-old son smack 'em down the fairway.

So, of course, since only one of us is playing, we move along quite quickly. Then we catch up to a foursome on this long par five. They are hitting their approach shots to the green. I want to sit in the cart, talk to my son and have a beer while the foursome ahead of us finishes up. From several hundred yards away they look like the typical country club scratch or nearly scratch golfers. They are no doubt old buddies that move around 18 holes without ever taking a mulligan. Regrettably, they see the two of us sitting in the cart at the tee box and start waving for us to play through. I hate that; I want them to just keep playing. I'm happy to wait. Maybe, if we wait, I might even feel like playing again. Why can't they just keep going? But no! They keep waving and waving us on.

So my son hits a decent but short tee shot. I drive him to his ball. The foursome has now reached the green and continues to wave us on. My son hits his second shot, which stops just short of a big lake in front of the green. The foursome is just standing around on the edge of the green, talking, laughing, and schmoozing. I can just tell they are arrogant, country club, prick, white guys. I wish each of them would just pick up their balls (all four of them) and play on. But no! Now that they have waved us on, they must watch us. Since I'm just driving the cart, I tell my son, "Let's just skip the rest of the hole and drive by these guys and give them the old 'thank you' wave." I'm nervous for my son. I'm worried he'll drop one in the water or miss the green completely and four putt and die of embarrassment. Then these guys will be wondering why they let us play through. And my son will be discouraged about the game of golf and give it up. I guess this is how fathers unintentionally suggest the wrong thing and provide their kids with a bad example.

My son says, "Dad, I can do this." He was more than right. With all five of us watching, he pops one up over the lake and plops it down four feet from the pin. Calmly he walks up to the green and says hello and thanks the foursome for letting him play through. He walks up to his ball, looks at the putt for about two seconds and with complete cool, drops the putt for a birdie.

Small moment in life? Hell yes, it was a very small moment! Of the six of us that saw it, I will be the only one who remembers it.

If I never hit a golf ball again, it will be ok. That moment was this middle-aged man's small triumph, a father's pride. That moment made up for countless embarrassing shots I had made over the years. And I wasn't even playing!

My son had the confidence. He made the effort. He delivered! Yet it was my victory. That was my trophy moment. My son had released me, at least temporarily, from the demons that haunt the game of golf. Of course, I won't ever win the Masters or even the club championship. I'll never even beat my friends. But on this occasion, my son won this small moment for me!

I haven't had an opportunity to play golf since.

Would I Like Her?
A Story Of Father And Son

There's nothing as overrated as your last relationship and as underrated as a cold martini! But when you can share these things with your father, that's really cool! Remember that classic scene in the movie *You've Got Mail*? Tom Hanks has left his relationship and his father, Dabney Coleman, has left his marriage realizing that his wife dumped him for the nanny (a great concept all by itself)! They meet up on his father's yacht. As Tom makes the martinis they confide their stories of relationships gone wrong and, eventually, the real manly men come out. After Tom describes his ex-significant other and her personality traits, Dabney asks Tom, "Would I like her?" What a great line! Anything will do! Your throwaways! Just bring me a woman! Being alone on a yacht with only a martini is just too much to bear! But those martinis get you through. Could there be any conversation more revealing between a father and a son? Those Nora Ephron romantic comedies are great! All guys should watch them even if they think they're chick flicks. Trust me, listen to the dialogue, and it will help you with all your female relationships. Hell, they may even help your relationships with other men!

It's too bad we guys only talk to our fathers when our relationships with women are failing. Think what it would be like if you had a great relationship with a woman. Lots of love and sex and you were really happy. So you tell your dad how great it is over a martini. And he says, "Would I like her?" Whoa!

Sittin' In The Ritz!

So my daughter and I enter the cocktail lounge of the Ritz in Boston. The evening is one of those very cold, crisp December nights. Holiday decorations glisten all over the hotel as shoppers, guests and business people fill the lobby and the lounge completely. Every seat is taken with Bostonians in their long, elegant camel hair coats and cashmere wraps sittin' in the Ritz. The cordovan mahogany woodwork, plush suede-covered chairs and dark carpet provide the background to the mesmerizing tapestry of sparkling jewelry, crystal-like glasses housing shimmering ice cubes, clear flowing vodka and golden hues of Scotch.

The view out the large picture window to the sidewalk is like a scene from a Christmas movie with holiday shoppers rushing by carrying their purchases, no doubt bought on Newbury Street. Taxis drop off and pick up guests. The snow-covered Public Garden across Arlington Street is dark, yet streams of people continue to rush in and out.

Inside the place is alive. It feels good. The tumbling of ice, the martini shaker, glasses toasting and soft piano renditions of holiday favorites forces the normally quiet conversations to a higher pitch. People are happy and laughing. You can see it in their eyes and hear it in the cacophony of sound. If you dropped dead right here with all the people sittin' at the Ritz, it would be a good place to die.

Five Potatoes

There was one seat left in the entire lounge and it was at the bar. I help my daughter into the high bar seat. Standing behind her I got the attention of the bartender and ordered the usual Grey Goose on the rocks with a twist for me and ice water with lemon for my daughter. She's just seventeen, sittin' in the Ritz.

Stockings, high heels, perfume, jewelry; she's all grown up now. I need to take some deep breaths and take in this moment. I finish my drink and look around the room and whisper in my daughter's ear that she looks very nice and notify her that I need to find the men's room. Leaving her sittin' at the Ritz, I go off in search of the men's room.

Returning to the lounge, I stand in the entry and survey the scene in Cary Grant style. It makes me wish I could reach into my breast pocket, pull out a sterling silver cigarette case and catch the eye of Ingrid Bergman across the room. Alas, sans cigarette case, I glance across the room scanning the people sittin' in the Ritz and catch a glimpse of my daughter . . . talking with some guy! She has her back to me, but he is facing me. Jesus! He's older than me! My daughter is laughing and carrying on with this man. "Ok, ok," I'm thinking, as every conceivable thought rolls through my mind like a bowling ball. "Be cool."

I approach slowly from behind her while taking a close look at this guy. He is hitting on my daughter! As I move toward her, the chemical balance in my brain shifts instantly from skeptical thoughts to amusing ones. This is good! Maybe I should keep walking and see what happens. There are still no other chairs at the bar. After surveying the room one more time, I walk up behind my daughter, placing my hand on her shoulder and say, "Come on honey, our table is ready," hoping that this phrase will keep this guy guessing about our relationship. But then, in a moment of pure innocence my daughter says loudly, "Oh, hi Daddy, this is Bob Martin." Did she have to say "Daddy"? My cover is blown. I just wanted to be the cool older guy with the beautiful brunette, thirty years younger. "Damn!"

We say good evening and happy holidays to Bob. I help my daughter with her coat and we head arm in arm for the dining room. As we step up the few steps leading out of the lounge, I just can't help myself. When we reach the top step, I just have to turn quickly and see if anyone is watching us. There they all are, sittin' at the Ritz. No one is even looking in our direction! It's ok. It gives me more time to look back. Tugging on my daughter's arm, I turn her around so we can both look back into the lounge. I whisper that she should remember this moment. The feeling of it will never be captured in a painting or a photograph. Now it's time to go to dinner and talk about where she would like to go to college. But first, I tell her how very proud I am of her.

Before turning to go, I reach in my breast pocket for my imaginary sterling silver cigarette case, and look at all the merry people sittin' in the Ritz.

This Is Your Day!

Every couple of months when my kids were little, each child got their own special day. When that day arrived I spent the entire day doing whatever that child wanted to do. It was exclusive; just Dad and my son, or Dad and my daughter. The other two kids had to stay with their mom or grandmother. It was usually a Saturday or a Sunday but not always. We would get going fairly early and they would get to have breakfast out wherever they wanted. After breakfast, we would get back in the car and I would say, "You can do whatever you want. This is your day!"

Sometimes it meant going to the zoo or a movie. Other times it was a long bike ride and a picnic. One time we went hiking and played in a creek and got all wet. Another time we went to the "airplane" museum. I think one of the best times ever was a train ride from Washington D.C. to Harpers Ferry, West Virginia and back. That was great. My youngest son, no matter how old he got, always said the same thing on his special day. "I want to go to Grandma's house!" He loved being at Grandma's house. Her house was his security blanket. But that was ok because it was his day!

Somehow the words "this is your day" stuck with my kids. They're mostly grown and I don't see them as often so it's hard to have a whole day with just one of them. Besides, they have other things to do now and lots of friends and activities. Hanging with Dad isn't so cool anymore.

Now when they're home from college, usually on some holiday or spring break, I am off as well. We'll all drag ourselves out of bed and straggle into the kitchen. The smell of coffee, bacon and eggs permeates the kitchen and den. For college kids it must seem like every day is a day off. For me it's mostly a chance to worry about the things I didn't get done at the office. But at least I know that for a few days I'm with the kids and I don't have to be anywhere.

As we sit eating, talking and flipping channels on TV, I ask them what they would like to do today. My oldest son looks at me quizzically and proclaims, "Dad, we can do whatever you want. This is your day!"

I smile, quietly honored, and say, "Thanks."

Hey Mom, I've Got A Bone In My Ice Cream!

So I'm seven years old. I got the ice cream out of the freezer and dug out three or four huge scoops. I took the bowl of ice cream down to the basement to watch TV and enjoy this masterpiece of a dessert

After a scoop or two I took a bite and lo and behold I bit down on something like a small steak bone. Hard as a rock. You know the feeling when you encounter something so diametrically opposed to the sensation you are expecting.

I bit down again. Again my jaw could not close as my teeth hit this incredibly hard object.

"It has to be a bone," I thought. "How could a bone get into the ice cream mix at the ice cream factory?" I pulled this big chuck of ice cream out of my mouth along with whatever was in it. Not wanting to look at it, I yelled upstairs, "Hey Mom, I've got a bone in my ice cream!"

She yelled down the stairs for me to come up. I brought the whole bowl along with what I had extracted from my mouth. Patiently she took the bowl and the remains and dissected them.

"What do you know!" she exclaimed. "You really did have bone in your ice cream! You've lost another tooth!"

I thought it was funny. She did too. But when I told my friends of this little tale they thought I was so stupid. They made fun of me for years whenever stupid stories of childhood came up. "You bonehead!" they'd say. I never should have told them. It was between me, Mom and the tooth fairy.

Of course, in the forty-four years since then, I've never again purchased that brand of ice cream! Maybe Ben and Jerry should concoct "Bone Crunch": I might try that!

Midday In The Sculpture Garden Of Good Kids And Evil Humor
Or
Learning From Art

When my kids were little I would take them to the Capital Mall in Washington, D.C. Occasionally, we would ride the merry-go-round or go to the Air and Space Museum. Sometimes we would play tag on the Mall. Often we would end the day in the sunken sculpture garden of the Hirshhorn Art Museum.

Like most kids they never ran out of energy, but I did. The sculpture garden was my rest period. I would sit on a bench and make up a game for them. I asked the kids to follow the path, turning left, turning right, turning left again. I picked out a particular sculpture for them to get to by following these directions. They had to read the title of the sculpture and the artist and return to me by a different route and they had to stay off the grass.

From my vantage point on the bench I would try and pick something that looked interesting. On the count of three they would race to the sculpture. Of course the two little ones couldn't read so the oldest would tell me the title and the artist. Then I would pick another sculpture and give directions and off they would go. They would run so fast and laugh all the way to the sculpture and back again. The little one mostly ignored the rules and ran across the grass laughing so hard he would fall down. The security guard didn't seem to mind. The kids were usually the only ones there and they were a joyful kinetic force in the static green garden punctuated by blackened bronze shapes.

After a while they would settle down. At such tender ages I was surprised to see the concentration in their eyes as they sat with me looking at the random placement of the massive, heavy bronze monoliths. We started giving our own names to the various pieces. It was really fun. It was sort of like "Name That Tune" for sculpture. I would come up with a title and then they would have to do the same. So we had titles like "Headless, Armless Man Runs Four Minute Mile" and "Fat Woman with Tiny Head" and "Man from Stony River." My daughter came up with some good titles like, "My Teacher" and "Black Pig Sunbathing."

I don't know if Henry Moore and Alexander Calder would be offended by my kids' giving their masterpieces new titles, but surely at some point they had to come up with a title themselves. I wonder if their kids gave them some ideas. Given the amorphous, amoeba-like mass of most of them it's not surprising that my youngest used the same title for all of them: "Poopy." No offense, guys, but you've got to admit some of your bronze blobs do appear to be super-sized dog defecations!

One assumes these artists actually wanted the public to look at their works. Well we did, and midday in the sculpture garden with good kids analyzing their masterpieces certainly was a creative and artistic experience; the kind I think the artists would have appreciated.

The kids are grown now and I can't help but think that joyous memories of the sculpture garden helped guide them to the things they do now—the oldest, architecture; the middle, children's theatre and music; and well . . . the youngest . . . golf. After all, it was the youngest that always broke the rules and ran across the grass!

TEN POTATO: JUST FOR GUYS

Kilts

What were we thinking? Men in pants! How did this evolve? Did anyone look between our legs? Pants make no sense on men! We should wear kilts or skirts or dresses. Women should wear pants. Look at their anatomy! Whose idea was this? The Romans had it right. Togas! Ok, somebody 'fess up! It had to be someone or some empire after the Romans but before the Dark Ages that made pants the attire for men! Talk about a cultural fight for freedom! Let freedom hang, not ring! Cross-dressers have figured this out! Why can't everyone else? Let's face it: the whole zipper thing is insane and deadly! So, my fellow men, let's all do a paradigm shift and get rid of our pants and start wearing skirts!

I can't wait to go shopping for shoes!

One Berating Is Not Enough! Hurt Me! Hurt Me! Beat Me! Beat Me!

A friend of mine is constantly worried about stuff his wife remembers but he doesn't. In fact, he doesn't remember anything his wife ever says or tells him to do. No big deal here. So what guy remembers anything his wife jabbers on about? The thing that really upsets him is when he gets nailed for forgetting something she told him to do and then before she's finished berating him she happens to remember another thing he forgot that she had told him to do!

That really hurts!

Tribute To *Top Gun*

I love the movie *Top Gun*. I have never met a guy who didn't like the movie and I've never met a woman who at the very least didn't get hot over the volleyball scene! The writers of *Top Gun*, Jim Cash and Jack Epps Jr., should have received awards and praise from men and women alike. They captured so much of what it is to be a real guy's guy. In fact, they pretty much captured in brief sentences and phrases the life of a man. There are guys I know who live their whole life using *Top Gun* as a guide. True!

For instance, did you ever notice how as a man gets older, after sex he needs to discuss it? The answer is right there in *Top Gun*. Viper (Tom Skerritt) to Maverick (Tom Cruise): "A good pilot is compelled to always evaluate what's happened so he can apply what he's learned."

In *Top Gun*, Carol (Meg Ryan) explains the image of the perfect husband when she describes Goose (Anthony Edwards) to Maverick: "My little angel, Goose, always goes home and goes to church!"

Career decisions are an important part of a man's life. Goose to Maverick: "Holy shit! Maybe I could learn how to be a truck driver! Mav, do you have the number of that truck driving school we saw on TV? Truck Master, I think it is. I might need that!"

Guy talk is a big part of every man's life. This is manifest in one of the most classic guy scenes in *Top Gun*. Maverick to Goose: "This is what I call a target-rich environment!" Goose to Maverick: "You live your life between your legs, Mav!" Maverick to Goose: "Goose, even you could get laid in a place like this!" Goose to Maverick: "I'd be happy to get a girl to talk dirty to me!" Later on, Goose to Maverick. "Ok, twenty bucks. You have to have carnal knowledge, of a lady this time!" . . . Maverick to Goose: "She's lost that loving feeling!"

Then there is every all-American male's dream wife, Carol, saying what every man wants to hear-—a lot. Carol to Goose: "Goose, you big stud! Take me to bed or lose me forever!" Goose to Carol: "Show me the way home!"

In every guy's life he learns that he has to be brought down a notch or two. Usually, it's your father, your coach, a boss, a teacher, an opposing athlete or most often your wife. In *Top Gun*, Maverick gets his. "Your ego is writing checks your body can't cash! You screw up just one time you'll be flying a cargo plane full of rubber dog shit out of Hong Kong!" My dad used to tell me I'd be digging ditches! This line from *Top Gun* is much more potent and funny! I really thought I might be digging ditches. Flying rubber dog shit out of Hong Kong can't be all that bad!

Then there are the lines that have no doubt been made part of your life by your best friend or your fiancée. "You've violated a major rule of engagement!" and "You have a confidence problem!"

Top Gun is literature and film for the ages. It's lyrical poetry with sounds of fighter jets, explosions, bars, volleyball, rock music and dialogue like, "Goose, you're such a dickhead!"

The movie is an incredible story of camaraderie and esprit de corps among men. Viper: "You're the best of the best! We're going to make you better! This school is about combat. There are no points for second best. Just remember: when it's all over out there, we're all on the same team!" God, it just doesn't get any more guy-like than this!

As you know, when the movie concludes, Maverick has his confidence back and his girl and all is well in true Hollywood fashion.

So what are the most important lessons a guy can learn from watching *Top Gun* a couple of hundred times? There are two very important things!

1. "There are two O's in Goose!"
2. "Never, never leave your wing man!"

SUNKEN GRAY HULLS OF STEEL

Standing on the shores of the Hawaiian Islands, a melancholy feeling comes over me. In contrast to the amazing combination of air, water, green foliage and volcanic rock that composes the islands, I can't help but be mesmerized by the knowledge that hidden from the powerful blue-green hues of the great Pacific Ocean are hundreds of barnacle-covered, rusted, sunken gray hulls of steel throughout the entire ocean. All of them are quietly resting in peace, undisturbed on the ocean floor. All of them were once alive with the voices of men and the grinding of machinery. Now one can only imagine the dark caverns, silent hulls and lightless openings that must lead to a kind of twilight zone.

Who were those men? What were their last thoughts? Are their souls captured in the wreckage? Do their voices continue down there? Are the Sullivan brothers together? How long will generations of men and machines sail off toward their demise on an ocean the name of which means "end of conflict"? Would some of them have been my friends or even relatives if they had not been committed to the deep?

I ponder what it would be like to magically drain the Pacific Ocean and walk among the vessels lodged in the silt. I think what it would be like to stand upon the bridge, look out across the foredeck and to go below and inspect the living quarters of those lost. Among the remains, I might find a personal item that could be returned to a grandson or granddaughter. I imagine the

Five Potatoes

soul of the ship, and the soul of the ship would want someone to do that before the waters return and the passage of time turns the sunken gray hulls into anonymous grains of sand. Personified as a form of honor and recognition, the gray hull would want to feel the sun dry off her decks and see the moon and the stars guide the way. Just once more, in tribute and in recognition of the innocent and needless sacrifice.

It is not to be. But I can think about it and hope that the souls in the sunken gray hulls of steel will know about it.

OF COURSE I WASN'T LISTENING!

I'm reading the paper, watching ESPN, scratching my crotch and paying the bills. Of course I wasn't listening to you! Could you whittle it down to just what I need to know in a life-or-death situation? Then, come over, sit on my lap, grab me by the chin, force me to look at you and tell me what the life and death situation is and how I'm to deal with it.

Then go away. Don't go away mad, just go away! But do come back later today and tell me again because I'm sure I will have forgotten whatever it was by then!

The Martians Are Coming!

There's a secret little game I play in my mind from time to time. It goes something like this. The Martians have just invaded. They plan to destroy everything on Earth. Just for the fun of it, I guess.

You are standing in line at the post office or in the grocery store. Maybe you are on an airplane or in an airport. You could be in line at the bank or in a seminar. Wherever you are, you need to be with between a dozen and a hundred people to play this game.

The Head Dictator of all the Martians has given the people of Earth a proposition that will save the Earth from destruction. However, you are the subject of the proposition. The Head Dictator Martian has picked you out of all the humans on Earth. He tells you that you can save the Earth from destruction if you will pick a woman in the room with you at that moment and marry her and then spend the rest of your life with her until you die! No divorces or the deal is off and the Earth will be destroyed.

Talk about the power of observation! Try this. It's fun! You never know with whom you'll have to spend the rest of your life.

Before you try it, realize that this works both ways. Your spouse might be playing this little mental game herself. The only difference is that the Venusians are coming!

THE MOST ROMANTIC SCENES IN THE MOVIES—MADE ESPECIALLY FOR YOU, DEAR!

Women want romance. Men want sex. Ok great, we figured all that out in the nineties. Blah, blah, blah. However, what no one has really offered up yet is how to get the men to be romantic and how to get the women to want more sex. Since I'm just your basic guy, I can't help on the women part of the equation, but I have an idea for the men to help them be more romantic.

If you are unable to be romantic or unable to think of anything romantically original, guys, try watching some of these scenes from the movies. You've probably seen them all before, but watch them in the context of just one romantic scene. You must play them over and over so they stick in your mind. Then videotape them all together and play it for her on Valentine's Day or her birthday or your anniversary. This is not the usual stuff the media shows us over and over again and labels romantic. You know, stuff like, "Frankly, Scarlett, I don't give a damn!" from *Gone with the Wind*. Or, "The problems of three little people don't amount to a hill of beans in this world," from *Casablanca*. Some of the movies are great and some aren't, so forget about the movie. This is about the romance of a particular scene. For those of you who are romantically challenged this is

Five Potatoes

"romance," not sex, and not toilet humor! Sorry, fans of *Austin Powers*!

So here it is. I humbly offer this list as a gift for men and women.

1. Paul Newman and Katherine Ross in the bicycle scene in *Butch Cassidy and the Sundance Kid*. Perfect music, perfect couple, great scenery and Katherine Ross flipping her robe over her legs. Paul Newman's blue eyes.

2. Julia Roberts and Hugh Grant in the press conference scene in *Notting Hill*. You can see the love in their eyes as they exchange questions and answers in the press conference at the Savoy Hotel in London.

3. Jimmy Stewart and Donna Reed in the telephone call scene in *It's a Wonderful Life*. Look closely at these two great actors. They are literally shaking with the excitement of realizing they are in love.

4. Humphrey Bogart and Ingrid Bergman driving down the Champs Elysées in *Casablanca*. Although this is just a studio shot, there is pure joy on their faces as they cruise in a convertible down the most famous street in the world with the Arc de Triomphe in the background. Both are genuine in their acting. They are smiling, in love and looking good in the most romantic city on Earth. Footnote: In my opinion, if you have never driven in a convertible with someone you love on a beautiful day—you better go buy a convertible.

5. Gregory Peck and Audrey Hepburn in the final scene of *Roman Holiday*, as the Princess (Audrey Hepburn) looks longingly at Joe Morgan, the reporter (Gregory Peck). They both know that the last twenty-four hours have changed their lives forever, but now they must walk away.

6. Rene Russo and Pierce Brosnan in *The Thomas Crown Affair*. The dance scene is followed by sex on the staircase. Romantic, passionate, artistic and hot!

7. Ingrid Bergman and Cary Grant in *Notorious*. Intensity, danger and romance all come together. In the last scene as Cary Grant reaches a desperately ill Ingrid Bergman, they look at each other with looks that define trust. He carries her right out the front door past the Nazis.

8. Harrison Ford, Greg Kinnear and Julia Ormond in *Sabrina*. Or Humphrey Bogart, William Holden and Audrey Hepburn in the original *Sabrina*. When Sabrina (Julia Ormond, Audrey Hepburn) returns from Paris she is all grown up. It's the North Shore of Long Island, a summer night, the orchestra playing *How Can I Remember, The Shadow Of Your Smile, When Joanna Loved Me, Moonlight*, etc. Men in white jackets, women in beautiful gowns, money, champagne. Sabrina is already in love with David. Now it is David's turn. He falls for Sabrina on sight! They dance.

9. Meg Ryan and Kevin Kline in *French Kiss*. When Kate (Meg Ryan) visits Luc's (Kevin Kline) boyhood home in Southern France, he takes her to his bedroom and shows her a school project he made about wine and explains to her how wine takes its taste from the earth and the air. Ok, ok, I know Kevin Kline should have washed his hair!

10. *Shakespeare in Love*. Gwyneth Paltrow and Joseph Fiennes in the bedroom scene and on the stage at the end of the movie are just fantastic!

11. Nicole Kidman and Ewan McGregor in *Moulin Rouge*. Every guy I know can't get into this film at first, but then after twenty minutes he's hooked. This is an outstanding romantic tragedy. Take a look at the last ten minutes and add it to the collection.

Here are some others you might consider:

12. *Bridget Jones's Diary*—The blue soup scene, funny and romantic.

13. *The Family Man*—The home movie birthday scene. Great stuff!

14. *City of Angels*—I don't know—anything with Meg Ryan.

15. *Kate and Leopold*—Dinner on the balcony.

16. *Pride and Prejudice* (the A&E version)—the ending, what else?

17. *My Best Friend's Wedding*—The phone call at the end from across the room.

Once you've completed the video, wrap it up and give it to her as a gift. Make sure you have a really good wine or champagne ready to go as you watch. Light some candles. Turn down the lights. Don't talk during the video, just cuddle with her and the champagne. As the video ends make sure you have the soundtrack from *French Kiss* or the soundtrack from *Sabrina* ready to continue the evening. Then tell her, "You complete me," (*Jerry Maguire*). Well, maybe not. That's getting really trite.

If you're still not there yet or it's not working, use the volleyball scene from *Top Gun*!

If all this fails to enhance your romantic capabilities, give it up, dude! Finish the champagne and put in *Animal House, The Jerk, Caddyshack* or *Porky's* and at least have a few laughs after she's gone upstairs to bed!

Don't Get Married 'Til You've Seen The Taj Mahal!

My dad told me not to get married until I saw the Taj Mahal. He actually took this advice and went there way back in the thirties! The rationale here is that the Taj Mahal is a bitch to get to, thus delaying any marriage opportunities and forcing you to be older and wiser. Just think. If it's tough to get there now, think how tough it must have been in the thirties!

Did I listen to my dad?

No!

What a dumb ass! Always listen to your dad on these things!

Pass this idea along to ten single friends and you'll be entered in the "Trip to the Taj Mahal" sweepstakes! Significant other not included!

Definition Of A Noun

A noun is a person, place, thing or idea. That's what my grammar school teacher taught me. You probably got the same definition. Remember, I'm talking about nouns, not nuns!

"What in hell is this about?" you're asking yourself. It's about evaluation of women! Come on, you buttheads! You know you do it! You have evaluated every date you've ever had—including many you didn't have but sounded good over a beer. You've even done post-date critiques! Don't lie, you savage male bastards! Ok, ok so you're never going to be the thoughtful, ever-smiling, gentlemanly Mr. Darcy in *Pride and Prejudice*, but who is?

When you evaluated a woman, what did you do? You check the boobs, the face, the ass, and the legs. Maybe if you are not a total male idiot you look at the eyes, the teeth, and her clothes and maybe even talk to her! Yeah, yeah, yeah, this form of evaluation is never going to change. This is the human male animal. But guys, if you want the right woman, take it a step further.

Try this. Evaluate a woman along the lines of the definition of a noun. Is she a people person? Is she a place person? Is she a thing person? Is she an idea person? Make a chart. On the left-hand side from bottom to top write 1 through 10. Across the bottom of the chart write the categories: person, place, thing and idea. Check out the highest category and the lowest. Take an average. Ask your friends if they agree with your rankings. Then rank yourself in the same categories. How do you compare to her? Similar? Opposites? Ask your friends.

Look, the divorce rate is 50% and it's financially and emotionally costly. So add this evaluation method to your selection process. It may not replace boobs, face, ass, and legs, but you'll know if she's going to like your friends, make love in the Paris Ritz, dig Porsches and let you be unemployed while she works! If she does these things she's a hell of a Compound Personal ProNOUN!

Keep Breathing!

Things so rarely turn out as we expect or want them to. Despite careful planning and attention to detail, despite discipline and energy, all too often whatever it is, is not what you thought it would be! So your life is in the toilet! So it's ninety-five percent your fault! So you were lazy! So Bart Simpson is your role model! So your wife is banging a used car salesman! So you're way overweight! So you lost the kids' college money in Vegas! So your dog bit the neighbor's dog and you have to pay the vet bill! So your credit cards have been cancelled! What are you going to do?

You're going to keep breathing! That's all! It's easy! You're going to go on and be better for having expanded the bandwidth of your life experience. Maybe you'll get it right on the next try or maybe you'll screw it up again and again. But you're going to keep breathing.

I Don't Know!

"*I don't know!*" I wonder how many times I say that a day. Some people find it difficult to say. *I don't know.* I find it remarkably easy to say, although occasionally frustrating. For example: if someone asks you, "How big is the universe?" it's pretty easy to say, *"I don't know!"* Yet people will go on and on about black holes and big bangs and Stephen Hawking and God. That's one kind of *"I don't know"* answer to a question.

Another kind of *"I don't know"* answer to a question is usually something basic, like your wife asking, "Honey, did the mail come?" It's 3:45 p.m. The mail almost always comes by 2:00 p.m. But I know that if I answer, "Yes dear, it's probably here," she'll go out to the mailbox and check and it won't be there and then I'll get blasted with, "I thought you said the mail was here! I went all the way out there and it's not here!" So, not wanting to risk that kind of repercussion, I answer very politely, *"I don't know."* That's when we men find out how useless we are and how we men pretty much don't know anything! At least *I don't know* anything.

She asks, "Did the package come from my mother?" It's hard to understand how to answer this question because I've just said *I don't know* if the mail came. So after a moment of thought I answer, *"I don't know."* Then she asks, "Where is the mailman today?" Once again, I respond, *"I don't know."* "Did the neighbors get their mail today?" she asks a few moments later. Once again, all I can say is, *"I don't know."* Continuing, she asks, "Is our

Five Potatoes

mailman on vacation?" Trying to be expressive this time, I answer, "Hmmm, *I don't know.*" That's followed by yet another question from my wife. "Do you think he's down the street talking to Mrs. Gibson again? You know their sons are both in the Army." Trying to change the tone just a little bit more I respond, "Uh, no, oh, *I don't know.*"

Then she gets pissed and impatient and goes to check on the mail, rolling her eyes as she leaves the room, and no doubt thinking, "You are a lazy schmuck," which is an overstatement in her opinion.

Later in the day, all is quiet. My wife is happy that the mail has come and the package from her mother is with all the bills. She's lost in thought.

Then I ask her, "Dear, how big do you think the universe is?"

She thinks for a moment and then responds, "Oh, well, let's take the age of the universe to be 10 billion years. In that time light travels 10 billion light years, and some people stop here. But the distance has grown since the light traveled. The average time when the light was traveling was 5 billion years ago. For the critical density case, the scale factor for the universe goes like the 2/3 power of the time since the Big Bang, so the universe has grown by a factor of $2^{2/3} = 1.59$ since the midpoint of the light's trip. But the size of the universe changes continuously, so we should divide the light's trip into short intervals. First take two intervals: 5 billion years at an average time 7.5 billion years after the Big Bang, which gives 5 billion light years that have grown by a factor of $1/(0.75)^{2/3} = 1.21$, plus another 5 billion light years at an average time 2.5 billion years after the Big Bang, which has grown by a factor of $4^{2/3} = 2.52$. Thus with 1 interval we got $1.59*10 = 15.9$ billion light years, while with two intervals we get $5*(1.21+2.52) = 18.7$ billion light years. With 8192 intervals we get 29.3 billion light years. In the limit of very many time intervals we get 30 billion light years.

"Another way of seeing this is to consider a photon and a galaxy 30 billion light years away from us now, 10 billion years after the Big Bang. The distance of this photon satisfies D = 3ct. If we wait for 0.1 billion years, the universe will grow by a factor of $(10.1/10)^{2/3}$ = 1.0066, so the galaxy will be 1.0066*30 = 30.2 billion light years away. But the light will have traveled 0.1 billion light years further than the galaxy *because it moves at the speed of light relative to the matter in its vicinity* and will thus be at D = 30.3 billion light years, so D = 3ct is still satisfied.

"If the universe does not have the critical density then the distance is different, and for the low densities that are more likely the distance to the most distant object we can see is bigger than 3 times the speed of light times the age of the universe."*

"Oh, God!" I say. *"I didn't know that!"*

*Quoted and paraphrased, probably poorly, from www.astro.ucla.edu/~wright/cosmology_faq.htm

ELEVEN:
JUST FOR WOMEN

THE FRECKLE PILL

Taking this pill may cause some side effects, including: headache, diarrhea, constipation, flu-like symptoms, high blood pressure, increased risk of heart disease, colon cancer, backache, hot flashes, heartburn, psoriasis, skin lesions, tooth decay, gingivitis, hair loss, impotency, yeast infections, temporary blindness, kidney stones, poor liver function, prostate cancer, bone degeneration, excessive perspiration, neuron depletion, and gas.

But your freckles will be gone. We guarantee it or your money back!

John Henry Newman— The Gentleman

Civilization would have moved forward so much faster if all men were forced to live up to the expectations set forth in John Henry Newman's classic 1854 essay *The Gentleman*. Find this essay and read it. I think by extrapolation you will find that had nations, led by men, followed its creed, there would have been no wars to end wars, no international terrorism and no religious zealotry. But, perhaps even better, there would be no offensive, argumentative, scream-fest, political, network, cable and radio talk shows! Bye, bye!

Another upside is that women would then have only courteous, chivalrous men to commandeer rather than falling for absolute bastards that ruin their lives! Allowing the good guys to finish first for a change and preventing the publication of a plethora of books on "good women and their bad choices!" What about good women and their good choices? Please, someone write a book on that!

How about you, Hillary?

Seventy-five Percent Of All Men Live Their Lives Between Their Legs!

THEORY NUMBER 37

Women, be warned! Seventy-five percent of all heterosexual men live their lives between their legs. The other twenty-five percent like good sex as much as the next guy; they're just distracted by a few other interests that occupy their time.

Be vigilant! Choose wisely!

I've had the opportunity to describe this theory to a number of educated, worldly women over the years. I usually bring it up after several drinks.

I thought the very suggestion of Theory Number 37 would stimulate hours of discussion and thought-provoking anecdotes. But the reverse is true. My theory is met with a moment of silence and disbelief.

"Oh! No!" they all say. "It's at least ninety-eight percent!"

End of conversation. "Waiter, check please!"

Williston Lamar

Dear Self,

    You're an idiot! You didn't have to make up some fancy theory. It was pretty much common sense, Sherlock! Do you think women don't figure this out in junior high? Way to go, stupidicus! They'll probably never have drinks with you again!

With regret,
Male

Sylvia Plath and The Silver Bullet Martini

I wish I had met Sylvia Plath. She ended her life when I was only ten. She had been a friend of my aunt's in the forties when she lived in Wellesley. She was probably the first real person I had ever heard of who had committed suicide. At that time I had no clue why someone would want to take their own life. Now, with half of the passages of my own life behind me, I'm beginning to understand more, but I'm still perplexed.

I can remember standing in the dining room of my aunt's house and hearing the news. I was shy and quiet so I didn't ask why. All I could think of was that it must have been something very complicated, some sort of deep emotional thing and that I should not ask any questions. Nevertheless, I have always kept her name in my mind.

I tried reading *The Bell Jar* in high school because my aunt gave it to me. But I wasn't ready. I didn't understand the intricacy and complexity of the writing. I didn't understand the talent. I didn't appreciate the degree of thought and emotional depth a writer could achieve, nor how that could be conveyed and understood by so many. I didn't want to open my eyes to the dark, disturbing view from the bell jar. It scared me. Life for me was football games and school and homework and playing in the creek. It was wiffle ball and bikes and weekend trips in the pursuit of happiness.

I was afraid if I read the book, I might not recover, like trying an addictive drug and never escaping its powerful hold.

I had read Salinger by high school, *The Catcher in the Rye*. It didn't bother me much. It did widen my perspective on failure and non-conformance. But it was just what everybody thought was cool to read, so ho hum. *The Bell Jar*, while sometimes thought to be the feminine version of a Salinger novel, is much more tragic and in my opinion considerably darker. Nevertheless, only now, at fifty, can I begin to understand the anxiety, the depression and the rationale behind the slide into insanity. How could she have known so much and conveyed it so well in just thirty-one short years? Through her prolific writing, Sylvia Plath helped me to begin to understand these things. I still can't read the whole book. Sometimes I just open it to a page and read that page and become unfocused. Sometimes I just look at her sketches in the book. There's one sketch that depicts a pub in London called The Anchor. In 1971, I went to a pub in London called The Anchor. I wonder if it was the same one in her sketch. I didn't make the connection then, but I wrote a short story in college that took place at The Anchor. It is still my favorite writing achievement.

My aunt died in 1971. She had been a widow for ten years. I can remember spending summer nights with her in Wellesley when she would say, "Let's go down to the Ritz on the Boston Common and have cocktails." Even though I was only in my middle teens I was always up for the excitement of going downtown and going to the Ritz. I wasn't of legal age, but it didn't matter to her. She would introduce me to the waiter as her young nephew and order two Silver Bullet martinis. I would just take a sip of one and give it back to her. Then as the alcohol dispersed into her body she would tell me of Sylvia Plath with a haunted look that revealed she understood these things. I couldn't understand, but at least I had the grace and presence to listen.

Five Potatoes

I think about my aunt often. Last night I made a Silver Bullet martini and took it to my study. I dimmed the lights and pulled out *The Bell Jar.* My dog curled up at my feet. After a few pages and another Silver Bullet my understanding was no better and my wisdom no greater but I know that at fifty, I've experienced the distortion of vision and the fear that comes with the thought of the descending bell jar.

BERMAN & BERMAN

For those of you who don't have cable, there is a great "just for women" show on one of the channels called *Berman & Berman*. The Berman sisters are brilliant women. They are sophisticated, educated, and great-looking. They talk expertly on every imaginable topic involving women. I find them informative and worldly and more than courteous to all the guests they invite to their show as well as to their audience members. I've told my male friends about the show. I tell them they could learn quite a bit about women, life, love, body parts, marriage and happiness if they tuned in.

Sadly, they all watch the show on my recommendation but can never remember what it was about because they are too busy thinking about which of the two sisters they would like to boink!

BABY, YOU CAN RIDE MY BIKE!

Ladies, are you lonely? Looking for Mr. Right? What's wrong with you? If you want to meet guys just go cycling. Go to a popular place for cycling like the Rose Bowl in Pasadena or Rock Creek Park in Washington D.C. or the Levee in New Orleans or Grant Park in Chicago or Boulder, Colorado or Bloomington, Indiana. Cycling is everywhere and everyone can ride a bike.

Think about it, ladies: tight asses, very muscular legs, flat stomachs, wide shoulders, big chests full of lung capacity, and these guys have road manners! Why aren't you out there?

I haven't even mentioned the sweat or the athleticism.

If women would pay attention to cyclists, at least the semi-serious ones, they would find some great guys. Just watch the Tour de France and learn about it. Read Lance Armstrong's book, *It's Not About the Bike*. All these guys speak three or four languages. They travel the world. Most are well-educated and do pretty darn well financially. This sport should attract a huge following, particularly among women. It's free for all spectators. The athletes are totally accessible. Most of them are stunned that you know who they are! But it's just about never on TV. That's because the really big races take place in Europe and because no one in the U.S. understands the sport.

Everyone in America thinks the first guy over the finish line is the winner. It's nothing like that. Bike racing has incredible strategy and positioning and endurance. There's climbing and sprinting and time trials and team time trials. It's amazing. I can't understand why ESPN doesn't cover it. Ok, so they would have to do a special show that teaches people about the sport, but so what? Everyone has ridden a bike at some point, so the market should be huge. Everyone knows how your legs ache when you try and go up a hill. How many of us have thrown a touchdown pass in the NFL? See what I mean?

Besides, the Tour de France (the greatest cycling race in the world) is 22 days long and is something the French organize and do very, very well. And after all, we can't have that these days! We need a Tour of America! But it has to start with the women. Don't worry about those tight outfits! Wear whatever you want! Get out there! Get out there on your old three-speed with fenders from junior high! Get some exercise! Meet some guys! I've even seen undeserving women snagging some real studs! Join a cycling club. Go to a race in your area. Write ESPN or the Outdoor Life Network and tell them you want to see more cycling coverage. Come on, don't go to bars or join a computer dating service. Please don't end up with a chainsaw murderer! Really, don't go that route. Take the high road!

Here, baby, you can ride my bike! But please wear a helmet!

No Man Is An Island

No man is an island! Men are atolls!

In Praise Of Glasses!

I love women that wear glasses. I say the hell with contacts or laser correction surgery. Glasses are cool! They look cool! Women look even smarter in glasses. There's that beautiful librarian fantasy thing going on. Glasses are like a window on the soul. They're sexy. But more importantly and more romantically, glasses are sensual; they're one last thing to take off!

And besides, you can actually see what's in the mirror across the bedroom!

WOMEN I'D LIKE TO HAVE COCKTAILS WITH!

Think about it! The Venusians invade and tell you that you can have cocktails with any woman—past or present—that you want. You get two weeks and one woman per evening. There's no sex, just cocktails and conversation. Who would you pick and why?

I thought about this for a long time!

It was hard! Er, I mean, difficult!

There are the classics like Cleopatra, Mary Magdalene, Joan of Arc, Mona Lisa, Mother Teresa, Catherine the Great, Katharine Hepburn, Natalie Wood, Marilyn Monroe, Eleanor Roosevelt, Amelia Earhart, Lady Di, Imelda Marcos, Shirley Chisholm, the Mata Hari, Queen Isabelle of Spain, Ingrid Bergman and on and on.

Then there are those that are still with us. Julia Roberts, Jennifer Aniston, Pamela Anderson (remember, it's just drinks), Hillary Clinton (remember it's just drinks), Halle Berry, Barbara Walters, the earthquake lady at Cal Tech, Martha Stewart, Oprah, the Dixie Chicks, Sally Field, Meryl Streep, and on and on.

It's impossible to choose!

Then, after weeks and months of thought, it came to me.

I'm sure it would be a great benefit to talk to some of the people above, but that's for someone else, maybe historians or pop-culture gurus.

So I've decided.

First, I'd like to order a couple of vodka martinis on the rocks with a twist. Actually, I'd like to be in a cocktail lounge at a Ritz Hotel. Any one will do, but San Francisco, Paris, Boston, or New York would be nice.

Then I want to spend the first evening with my grandmothers on both sides. Then I want to spend the second evening with their mothers and so on for fourteen evenings.
Wouldn't that be cool? It would be total of fourteen generations or up to about four hundred and twenty years of family history as told by mothers. That would take you back to 1584 or so. That would be good. Those are women I'd like to have cocktails with!

TWELVE POTATO: MONEY

THE LESS MONEY I HAVE, THE MORE CREATIVE I GET!

Money, power, sex! The big three! When you have a reasonable amount of money or income everything is easy. But let's face it, life with a reasonable amount of money is not very creative. Why? Because you can just go out and buy some dumb gift or repay a favor with a dinner out. You can purchase the jewelry that insures at least one sexual encounter, but has no meaning. You can pay for your children's education. You can get the flat screen TV. You can put gas in the car or buy a new car. You can vacation in nice places. You can save for retirement. I bet you can't name any of the gifts you got last Christmas or who gave them to you. Why? Because the gifts were just another ill-thought-through purchase. You bought them because it was easy to buy them and because you have the money to pay for them, at least eventually. What would you have done if you didn't have any money? What would you do if you had no job and no money? But hey, my gifts are creative as hell and they're from the heart, not the wallet! Money dulls the senses, stifles creativity and is generally way overrated.

Has Bill Gates done anything creative since he was a starving computer geek, busy pitching DOS and Windows? Why do you think poor, starving artists do their best work when they're poor, starving artists? They have nothing to lose! As soon as you get some money you spend 90% of your time trying not to lose it. And in the process of protecting it you lose all the time you might have spent doing something fun, creative or memorable. Living this way, one's literal wealth may find salvation but the figurative richness of life just evaporates!

Ever try and figure out how you're going to get your kids through college with no job? The pressure is on. Pressure produces fear and fear of failure is the greatest motivator. Fear enhances creativity! The very process of trying to solve this problem keeps you alive, stimulates your mind and takes you in new directions. That's what the richness of life is all about. It's the journey, stupid! Ok, so you've got the money. Then your efforts can be directed to other things. But whatever the challenge, try to be creative and pull the game out in the fourth quarter! It's much more exciting! No one remembers the games that end up 44 to 0!

Just try and figure out how you're going to retire and live decently if you have no income. That takes talent and guts.

This reminds me. Why is everyone in America obsessed with retirement? Is the journey over at age 60 or 65? You're probably going to die of heart disease or cancer before you get to use your retirement anyway. Then the kids just fight over it and lose all their creativity and the close-knit family you tried so hard to create. You say you need to work hard and build your retirement nest egg so you don't have any financial worries. So you'll be secure. No one is secure! Just ask the people at Enron! They are all greeters at Wal-Mart! Are you going to sit in a chair and watch *Seinfeld* reruns and think to yourself, "Hey, I'm financially secure and the other guy isn't?" What fun is that? Life might be a show about nothing, but it's your nothing!

Just because you're old and your mind and body are slowing down our society says we should have enough money to give up living, play cards with the blue hairs and sputter around the golf course!

How about this idea? At age sixty, if we haven't retired already, we must give up all our money. We get to keep the house we're in, the cars we're driving at the time, all personal mementos of our lives, but most importantly we stop doing whatever it was we were doing for a living. The money goes into a giant pool that pays our medical costs, prescription medications and any special care that might be required now or in the future. It also covers all reasonable lifestyle expenses. Then, there is true retirement. Only the creativity you've longed for all your working life is finally available. The protections and security you sought for so long are built in. You have aged and experienced life enough to become a non-starving artist! You're free to be creative! You can stop the rat race. You'll be daring, not protective. You'll take risks. You'll invent and create. You'll be free to take the time to appreciate the richness of life! You can become politically active. You can play more with the grandchildren.

I think this is called socialism!

Say, does anyone know of a job I can apply for? I need to get busy saving for retirement!

Maybe I could be a sociologist! Do they have a union with a 401(k) plan?

If You Dropped A Bowling Ball Into The Ocean, How Long Would It Take To Hit The Bottom?

This is a great question. Ask it sometime in front of a group of people. You will learn more about each individual in the group from their answers to this question than you could learn from spending a week camping with them. Some people will analyze the hell out of the question and end up asking more questions. Others will use formulas and weights and distance and gravity. Others will guess based on some broad estimates like how fast the Titanic went to the bottom. Some will simply throw out an answer or ask for more information because they don't care or don't want to waste time on such a ridiculous exercise. From these responses you will be able to tell an anal engineer from an artist. It's amazing!

However, if you ask your wife this question, I guarantee her response will be, "How much did the bowling ball cost?"

Ninety-five Cents Now Versus a Dollar Later

The world is full of rip-offs. They piss me off. For example, I can order the same thing at a drive-up restaurant three days in a row and pay three different prices! Another example is restocking charges, which are usually ten percent of the price of the item you're returning. Bull! The store should pay you to bring the item back plus your mileage and time! Then there is the real estate deposit that you can never get back in full or in a timely manner.

A friend of mine got into it with his wife over the return of the real estate deposit. They found a house they both liked and put down the required deposit. Apparently, there was a clause that said something about the deposit being non-refundable after the inspection was approved. My friend didn't like the inspection report so he asked for his deposit back. This sounded reasonable to me. But no! Five percent of the deposit would be forfeited. Basically, this five percent went to the owner. Why? I guess because his house sucked! I guess if your house sucks you get to keep some of someone else's money for your trouble.

My friend was not too concerned about a couple hundred bucks. But his wife sure was! What a battle! She wanted it all back and she wanted it now! It was all or nothing! "I'm not going to give them a dime of our money!" she protested. The couple spoke with their realtor. The realtor tried to help through the owner's realtor, but without success. Now she was really pissed and there was no sign of any of the original deposit money! The owner of the house in question wasn't budging and became defiant based on his perception of her attitude.

My buddy was losing sleep. He was becoming certain he would never see any of his money again. Finally, we had one of those heart attack lunches together. You know: cheeseburgers, fries, etc. Guys always seem to get things done over this type of lunch. Anyway, we decided his wife needed the old "ninety-five cents versus a dollar" lecture!

Basically, it goes like this. "Dear, let's take the ninety-five cents now and we'll fight for the other five cents later. By the time we get the five cents back we'll be able to get some interest on the ninety-five cents. It's better to get just about all of it than none of it. Ok?" What you are not saying is that it was all your money to begin with and you don't want to lose it all because of her bitchy, fighting, adversarial mood which could lose it all for you.

It's like sex. Take it whenever you can, even if it's less than perfect. Because if you don't, you're sure not to get anything! Give it your best shot! About ninety-five percent!

Exact Change Only!

What form of early childhood training is it that teaches women to drive us crazy with the exact change policy of buying things? We can be at the drive-up window with twenty cars behind us or in the grocery store line with eight people with filled carts behind us or in any crowded store, when the cashier says, "That will be fifty-two dollars and thirty-six cents." I start to hand the cashier three twenties when my wife jumps in and says, "No, wait, I have exact change!" Then she has to pull up her purse, search for the change purse within her purse, and then dig for the change. The line behind us starts to get impatient and then she drops the change. Eyes are rolling. Heavy sighs are coming from the rear of the line. I offer to help pick up the change to speed things up. This only causes more delay. The bag guy leaves that cashier station to go to another one. This exasperates the cashier since he will now have to pack the groceries for the remaining people in line. Your wife just giggles and says, "Oh, I have so much spare change and I need to get rid of all these pennies!" Finally, the moment arrives when it's all counted and you can be on your way. But, you can't say anything about it because you know she'll snap back, "Well, I've got to get rid of some of this change. What's the big deal? Oh, get over it!"

Since I don't have this little problem, I always pay with bills and keep the loose coins and fresh change in my pocket until I get home. Then I carefully divide the change into various denominations and place them in plastic cups in a drawer in the kitchen. The other day, I came home and tried to put some change away. I found that all of the change was missing. She had taken all the coins to the bank, cashed them in, and collected $383.42! My hard-earned coins! Gone! Cashed in! She gives all of her change to the clerks behind the counter, but I so carefully save mine! This seemed terribly unfair, like robbing my piggy bank! So, I confronted her: "Where's all my money?" "Oh!" she exclaims. "Look at this hot pair of Manolo Blahnik shoes I bought at Barney's with all that change I found in the drawer!"

DEEP THROAT

I've read all the Watergate books. Deep Throat is Fred Fielding! That's my final answer!

If I'm right, I want Woodward and Bernstein to give me a million dollars. I'm sure they've got it in a slush fund somewhere! If I'm wrong, I'll settle for the $32,000 and an autographed copy of *All The President's Men.*

I wonder if the Las Vegas bookmakers are calculating odds on the outcome of the Deep Throat mystery!

Here's a thought. You know there are "sports books" at the major Las Vegas casinos. They should have "court books." That way the public could gamble their hard-earned money on life or death, 15-20 with no parole, suspended sentence, juvenile detention, guilty-not guilty, or whatever! "Yeah, honey, sorry! Dropped a couple hundred today! Thought for sure O.J. was going to the chair!"

Better yet, a reality show along the lines of *Divorce Court* on amphetamines! Place your bet on joint custody, single custody, length of alimony, or bet on who is the "real innocent" one!

But one thing is for sure: if you bet on Deep Throat the odds are against you!

The $1 Purchase Value Reduction Theory Of Home Economics (PurVrt)

What if you reduced the cost everything you have at home by exactly one dollar every time you use it? If you turn on the dishwasher deduct one dollar from the cost of the dishwasher. If you wear your Calvin Klein underwear, black Polo shirt, your khaki golf shorts and leather belt plus a pair of topsiders, that's going to deduct five dollars from the combined cost of those items. It will cost you one dollar for each item. If you sit down on your leather couch, deduct a dollar from the cost of the couch. Check your e-mail on your home computer, another dollar. Every time you use an object for its intended purpose you have to deduct one dollar of its purchase price value. Each time you turn on the television it will cost you one dollar. Then figure out how many dollars it takes to live for one day, a month or a year.

The purpose here is for everything you own to cost one dollar every time you use it resulting in a zero sum over time.

Let's use the dishwasher example. Say your new dishwasher cost $329 including sales tax on sale at Best Buy. Add $50 for the price of installation. That's $379. Every time you use the dishwasher reduce the price by one dollar. When you've done the dishes 379 times the item has earned its price tag. After all, it's certainly worth one dollar to do the dishes!

If your TV cost five hundred dollars to purchase, will you turn it on five hundred times this year? Probably. If your new Armani suit cost twelve hundred dollars, will you wear it twelve hundred times before it's worn out or out of date? Probably not! Maybe you should consider a two hundred dollar suit. If your athletic shoes cost eighty-seven dollars, will you wear them eighty-seven times? Yeah, I guess so. Will you drive your new SUV forty-five thousand, three hundred and forty two times in the five years you told the dealer it would take you to pay for it? That would mean you would have to drive it 24.844 times a day for five years. Not including maintenance, gas and insurance. Hmmm. Maybe you should consider a scooter!

Ok, ok! Now think about this economic theory in terms of your wife. If she does the laundry, one dollar! Dishes, one dollar! If she makes the bed, one dollar! Escorts you to dinner, one dollar! Wears her "La Perla" underwear, one dollar!

Sex . . . priceless!

Suze Orman won't tell you this!

She might think this theory is debasing, misused or corrupt. It's really not too deviant; it's just PurVRT. You know someone out there must be working on the software! *PurVRT Money Manager!*

Less Is More, More Or Less!

Famous for his axiom, "Less is more," the architect Mies van der Rohe strove for structural integrity and material honesty in his buildings. From the Czech Republic to Chicago, his contributions to the aesthetic credos evolving from Prussian Classicism, Russian Constructivism and the philosophies of the Bauhaus are among the primary theoretical and literal design components of the 20th century.

If only there were dedicated thinkers and doers like Mies in the fields of money and power. Today, as throughout history, nothing has really evolved. It has always been that more is more. More money and more power lie at the root justification of everything. I suppose it's a leap to think that aesthetic theory can apply to financial, legal, political, social, cultural and economic functions. But then, form does follow function, so why not?

Just think if the words "integrity" and "honesty" played out on the global scene like a fashion trend. Imagine Wall Street, Hollywood, Washington, Beijing, Seoul, Baghdad, Rome, Tel Aviv, Jerusalem, Paris, Belfast, Bogotá, Manila, Bangkok, and Tokyo all following a global trend toward honesty and integrity. I guess that sounds too much like John Lennon. Maybe it's just that no one can define honesty and integrity anymore. Everything is so cluttered; we'll never know the truth about anything. The people that think they're telling the truth have even been misled. Even when we think we know the truth about a person or an event it's likely to be misinterpreted by the audience or spun to meet the audience's expectations.

I think it was John Rockefeller who was once interviewed by a reporter back when he was the wealthiest man in the world. The reporter asked how much money is enough money. Mr. Rockefeller responded, "Just a little bit more!"

It's always more is more. I'm sure if you asked any politician how much power is enough power, the answer would be the same as Rockefeller's. Even if you asked your next-door neighbor if he had enough money for retirement he'd say, "No, I need just a little bit more!" Certainly if you asked Tim the Tool Man Taylor, he'd say, "More power!"

So the next time you're driving by a significant building in your travels, look at it closely. Is less really more in the aesthetic, ethereal sense or not?

Mies is long dead and much of his work is surrounded by the clutter that is the built environment. But it would have been interesting if Mies had been a politician or a mogul. He may have still uttered the phrase and be remembered for it, but he probably would have added, "Read my lips, less is more, depending on what the definition of is, is. More or less!"

THIRTEEN POTATO: POLITICS

Middle-of-The-road Extremist Or Radical Fence-sitter: I'm Not Sure!

I'm trying so hard not to be a liberal; I'm trying so hard not to be a conservative. Every extreme point of view is so divisive. Everyone is so in your face, I don't know what's right anymore, and frankly, I haven't done the personal research or taken the time to attend lectures or write papers on any of the controversial topics that divide us. I don't know who's telling the truth. I don't know if the people speaking on the left or right know the truth, or if they have done their homework, or if they truly believe what they are saying but have been misled by someone else. Therefore, I don't feel qualified to have an opinion.

Like everyone else, I watch and listen to the news. I read the papers when I can and I read magazines. But honestly, even with this kind of input, I just don't know who is right. I don't know if anyone is right and I don't know if what I'm seeing, hearing and reading is accurate and factual, opinionated, marginalized, or even the whole story. I know I'm opinionated about my own work. I have to think that people who report and write the news or act as representatives of some agenda must be jaded in some way.

Why aren't things more clear? Why aren't there answers to some basic things that we worry about? Why can't society move ahead faster with answers instead of dueling groups that stiffen the resolve on both sides and slow us to a crawl?

I know politics is a tough game. I know economics is hard to comprehend. I know the environment is not fully understood by science. I know that society has diverse and selfish interests. I know that law wins over justice. I know that blood is thicker than water. I know we all need to soften our stance and think first.

But I just don't know the answers. Do you? Are you right about every belief you have? Were your parents right? Were your teachers right? Is your husband right? Did you believe them? Or were they just the home team that you rooted for? Can a social policy or an economic policy or a political choice be resolutely explained by a few magazine articles or interviews on the *Today Show* or talk radio? Can you intellectually separate yourself enough from your preconceived or long-held beliefs to actually listen long enough to the other side to be able to represent that side if you had to?

I try to ask myself these questions, but the same answer keeps coming back to me. And that is, "I don't know." Why, I ask, does everyone else seem to think they have the answers?

Therefore, when it comes to taking a position, I'm just not qualified. I am an interested person, but I just don't know who's right—I can't decide on my position. It's not that I don't have the courage of my convictions. It's just that someone else always seems to have a good point or counterpoint that I'm not prepared to answer with a better point. Sometimes, when I think I have an excellent counterpoint I worry that I will not be able to articulate it or that it will come back immediately at me with a slam that is unrecoverable or worse, uncomfortable. Therefore, I hesitate and let it go. That makes me a radical fence-sitter! It makes me a middle-of-the-road extremist!

Someone explain this to me, please. My ass is starting to hurt from sitting on the fence and when I move to the middle of the road I get run over.

Is anyone with me on the fence? Does anyone share my uncertainty? I'd like some company and some certainty that there are others with me. I hope of that I can be sure!

WOMEN OF MASS DESTRUCTION

Here's an idea for a reality show. Gather up all the female talk show political pundits from the left and the right and put them on *Survivor, Washington D.C.*! Can't you just picture Eleanor Clift and Ann Coulter paddling a canoe across the Potomac? Or how about Susan Estrich and Laura Ingraham lost in the basement of the White House looking for the eighteen minutes of missing tape! Or, how about Katrina vanden Heuvel and Arianna Huffington voting each other out of the tribe on *Meet The Press*! How about Elizabeth Drew and Maureen Dowd standing on a pole in the Tidal Basin until one gives in! Norah O'Donnell with Cokie Roberts trying to light a fire! Margaret Carlson could try and be the first to break into the Watergate!

All of the liberals could be on one tribe and all the conservatives on the other. Or even better, mix the tribes with equal numbers from both sides. What a kick that would be! Think of the teamwork! Think of the bitching! Can't you just picture the tribes in tents and sleeping bags under the Washington Monument? Picture the relay races on the steps of the Capitol and bikinis in the reflecting pool! Spies, traitors, double standards, party loyalty, political snakes, black lists, eating cherry blossoms, bugging phone calls! It would be great! Sneaking into the Watergate! Tribal Council meetings could be in the Supreme Court!

The winner gets one million dollars in campaign funds to run for the Senate and a date with Bill Clinton or Bob Dole!

Best of all, some of the outcasts pose for *Playboy*!

Well, ok, maybe not *Playboy*, but for sure *The Nation* or *The National Review*!

Man, I can't wait for the all-male version!

Paul Begala in a wheelbarrow race with Rush Limbaugh pushing! (Or vice versa!)

Divorce—The Other Regime Change!

My older, wiser sister once told me, "You don't marry the person! You marry the family!" She was right. Why doesn't everyone realize this fact? There would probably be a lot fewer divorces. Think of Elizabeth Taylor and Mickey Rooney—they have had to get to know and suffer through a combined sixteen families. Of course the good news for them is that each family only lasted a couple of years on average!

Ok, so big deal, you get divorced. Get over it! It's not like you're the only one in human history to conclude a marriage! One spouse and the associated regime depart, then, after a while, another one comes along. It's like getting off a streetcar and waiting for the next one. The tough part is it took you two, five, ten or fifteen years to learn and deal with the nuances of the first regime; now you have to spend the same amount of time figuring out the new regime.

It's a lot like the war in Iraq. Everyone thinks it's over when the battle is over and good prevails over evil and the boy gets the girl and the movie ends. But the divorce battle is short compared to the regime change.

Mud Balls

A1, B2 and C3 mud balls. When I was a kid my friends and I would play in the nearby creek. This play time would sometimes evolve into mud ball battles. I'm not kidding! They really sting when they hit you. Back then we used to say snowballs are for girls. Mud balls are for men!

We decided we should classify the quality of the mud into three categories. The categorization usually had to do with water content, compaction and splatter capability. A1 was of course the all-around best-quality mud ball, followed by B2 and C3, respectively.

I think these categories should apply to fights with one's spouse and political talk shows! For the talk shows the audience could vote online for the category of mud that's being slung and combine that with direct hits and the splatter factor to obtain the overall score! The spouse version of the game could be scored by the kids!

Eventually mud ball throwing could be added to Olympic events. Can't you just picture the judging? The French would win every time! Followed by the Russians! Gold, Silver and Brown!

Mud slinging would be competitive! There would really be winners and losers! The hosts of talk shows could literally be voted out of a job if they didn't land enough mud balls! Pundits like James Carville and Mary Matlin could be democratically discarded by the voters on live TV! Wouldn't it be cool if Tim Russert, Chris Matthews and Bill O'Reilly had ejection seats like Dr. Evil? Can't you just picture Carville going over backwards into the fire pit? Too bad everyone comes back to life after being dumped by Dr. Evil!

Just Smile!

Name a few public figures that the vast majority of Americans just love and I'll show you a great, great, genuine ability to smile.

Julia Roberts, Michael Jordan, Tom Cruise, Denzel Washington, Oprah Winfrey, Tiger Woods, Joe Montana, Tim Russert, Bill Cosby, Tea Leone, Bob Hope, Whoopi Goldberg, Eddie Murphy, and Chris Rock are just a few.

Did you notice that politicians do not appear on my little list? Why? It is because our current political leaders have not been able to master the technique of the smile. Maybe they just have never had any laughter in their lives. Our poll-driven politicians today just don't have any charisma. They can't do a genuine smile. And when you can't do a genuine smile with great frequency and sincerity you lose. Al Gore probably lost because he was such a stiff. The first George Bush had this problem. All Jesse Jackson does is scream! What a turn-off! Everyone on both sides of the aisle looks nasty. Lighten up! Ronald Reagan had it! John Kennedy had it! Maybe Teddy Roosevelt had it too. But that's about it. Look at pictures of Lincoln! Man, he never smiled and then he got shot!

Why don't people in politics get this? The public loves smiles regardless of your politics. Give us a sincere, deep, guttural laugh with lots of teeth ten to fifteen times a day, and we'll vote for you. If you decide to run for office, try to smile. Loosen up the audience. It makes us all feel better about our world. You don't have to be a comedian. Just smile. Smile a lot!

I'd vote for me!

Socially Fiscal

When it comes to personal politics, people like to describe their beliefs in snappy little sound bites! They want others to think they've put a lot of thought and careful study into their beliefs. In recent years, I've heard a number of my friends say, "I'm socially liberal and fiscally conservative!" They say it in a snobbish, arrogant way as if it's some brilliant, original statement. When I think about those who have used this line, it's always someone that didn't vote, doesn't read, has no grasp of history and is generally without intellect. This doesn't mean the statement can't be true. It's just an annoying comment.

So the next time you're at a cocktail party and someone says to you, "I'd describe myself as socially liberal and fiscally conservative," just respond by saying, "Oh, really? Then you won't mind if I proposition your wife and ask for a discount on her rate?"

Try this. Describe yourself as "socially conservative and fiscally liberal" and see what happens!

Might make for a very interesting cocktail party!

Everyone In America Has Multiple Comments And Comebacks For Whatever You Say!

We might as well stop talking! Anything anyone says is subject to immediate ridicule, cynical comments, name-calling, race-bashing, political posturing and cultural sarcasm. It doesn't matter who you are, what you do, what you look like, what you wear, what you say or when you say it—somebody out there is saying something as a comeback. It's sad we can't talk seriously about anything or listen respectfully. Everything has to end in a comment as if we're living in some sort of perpetual sitcom.

Here are some examples of what I'm talking about.

"Tick, tick, tick, tick, tick." .... "God, I hate that sound! Get a new theme song you smug bastards!"
"I'm Mike Wallace." .... "Oh, just retire! Give somebody else a chance!"
"I'm Steve Kroft." .... "Get a haircut!"
"I'm Ed Bradley." .... "Nice earring Ed! What's that about?"

"I'm Leslie Stahl." .... "Still looking good, Leslie!"
"All that; Clinton and Dole." ...... "Get them outta here! Enough already!"
"And Andy Rooney." .... "Have you seen his eyebrows? What else is on?"

Ironically Enough, I Once Cooked Hot Dogs for Spiro Agnew!

I was playing golf with a friend one Saturday afternoon when we realized that then-Vice President Spiro Agnew was playing right behind us. This was not a huge surprise because my friend's father was Spiro Agnew's physician. But nevertheless it was a little unnerving to try and hit a good tee shot and get as far ahead down the fairway as possible. Unbeknownst to my friend and me the Vice President had been invited to a very casual barbeque that evening at my friend's home. So was I.

At that time President Richard Nixon and the Vice President were about one year into their second term. The anti-war movement was at its peak. The civil rights movement, gay movement, and women's movement were transcending all things in the U.S. The Watergate investigation was well underway. The criticism of the administration and all things associated with it was overwhelming. Frankly, knowing the Vice President's propensity for bad shots in golf and tennis, and having a juvenile understanding on my part of the extreme pressure he must have felt just to get up in the morning, I felt a sort of compassion for this man. I guess maybe a simple barbeque on a backyard grill at an anonymous suburban home was about all the relaxation a man in that position could obtain.

I was asked to be the chef by my hosts, since they wanted to

Five Potatoes

spend time with and pay attention to the Agnews. I wasn't very comfortable about this, since my culinary talents included only the burning of hot dogs and hamburgers. Notwithstanding, my friend and I lit the charcoal and began the process. As we began to cook it occurred to me that the Vice President might like his hot dog a certain way. You know, well done or lightly heated or something. Maybe he wanted the bun toasted. I didn't know. As we were rolling the hot dogs on the grill I thought I should ask him how he liked his hot dogs. So summoning up some courage, I went inside and waited politely until there was a pause in the conversation. Then it just sort of came out. "Mr. Vice President, would you like your hot dog burned?" Laughter broke out! I didn't realize the crude way I had asked the question, nor the consequences. The Vice President looked at me like I was crazy. He must have been thinking, "Yeah, stupid kid, I want mine too black all over and shriveled up!" Fortunately, he was thoughtful for a moment and must have understood my predicament. So he let me off the hook and said, "Any way you cook them is fine with me."

He treated me well in that stupid, awkward, fleeting moment. For that I respected him. He even took my friend and me aside for an entire hour after dinner and spent time with us talking about some of his least favorite topics: the war, the press, the elitists, the nattering nabobs of nepotism and so forth. That was an incredibly generous gesture given the time constraints he must have been under. Maybe he just wanted to escape for a few minutes or practice articulating his thoughts in front of two kids who would not pressure him.

I often think about that moment. I think about what became of Spiro Agnew only a month later: his indictment for taking payoffs and his subsequent resignation from the second-highest office in the land.

I suppose you could say that symbolically his hot dog got burned anyway. But in that moment, I appreciated his kindness.

FOURTEEN POTATO: JUSTICE

Smart People Don't Go To Court

Have you ever read Donald Trump's book *The Art of the Deal*? I like "The Donald." He does what he says he's going to do. I don't really care if he ends up with ten wives and ten supermodel girlfriends. He seems to live his life to the fullest and it appears that he's having fun and enjoying the good things life has brought him. I've never met him, but I was spending a week in New York, showing my kids the sights, when we saw him in the Plaza. He's really tall!

Anyway, I really appreciate one of the things he writes about in his book. "Smart people don't go to court!" he declares. (Not an exact quote, but close enough.) Every time you think about going to court for any reason, think again. Once you go, the situation is out of your control. There are judges, juries, lawyers, arbitration judges and witnesses. The jury doesn't even want to be there. You are outnumbered. These people don't care about you or your situation. They've heard it all before. You are just filling a chair. These people will decide what happens. You won't. Not to mention that the emotional toll is just too much to pay. Life is short. Have fun; enjoy as much time as you can. The Donald does!

Be like The Donald. Stay in control; be the decision maker. Get and pay for sound advice and understand the legal ramifications. But take responsibility and get it resolved quickly. Even if some minor things don't go your way, in the long run it's cheaper than going to court. Don't give your money to lawyers.

I'm sure everyone understands this concept. But it's likely your spouse doesn't. "Let's fight!" she demands. "I hate those bastards!" she shouts! Draw upon all your persuasive powers and convince her otherwise. There are countless other methods to apply justice in subtle ways over time. Remember, the best revenge is living well!

Isn't it serendipitous that his name is "Trump"?

I like that guy! We could be good buddies!

THE BAD GUYS DO WIN!
GET OVER IT!

The bad guys do win! And they win a lot! We all should accept this, get over it and move on! But it still pisses me off! So, sometimes, I wish I could be more of a bastard! Just to screw over the real bastards a little more frequently! I'd be the double-super-secret bad guy, who's really a good guy in disguise!

If you've watched enough episodes of *The Twilight Zone* you know that when you wish for things and they magically happen, those things usually turn out to be bad. But sometimes I wish I could be more of a bastard and take *The Twilight Zone* challenge, and ultimately the consequences, just for the satisfaction of seeing the bad guys go down for a change!

Sadly, bad guys do win! The screamers, the pencil-throwers, the cell phone psychos, somehow all come out ok. Bad guys get the undeserved promotion! They get the special perk! They make excessive expenditures! And they end up with a bigger bonus! The bad guys get away with outright violations of company policies! Their bad behavior goes unpunished! They get huge recognition for the one thing they did all year! Yes, it's unfair. It's unfair in reality and in perception. Most of the time reality and perception can't be distinguished. Good things happen to undeserving people. We need to get out of our *Ozzie and Harriet, Cosby Show, Cheers*-type, happy ending world and accept this. Television leads us to believe that all things are resolved in a half-hour or an hour. Yet most things aren't resolved even in a lifetime. Sooner or later, I'll take my own advice and get over it.

The business world makes us want to believe that everything is fair and "equitable." But we all realize within a week of working in any business environment that fair and equitable are huge lies! How many times have you heard someone in a leadership position say, "We must create equity in our salary bands"? Or, "We must treat everyone equitably." Or, "Everyone deserves the same treatment." I've heard it hundreds of times and I've come to realize that such philosophies are nonsense! Only people who don't know their people make these kinds of rules. And usually only the bad guys seem to prosper under such ludicrous thinking. We should all recognize that people in our offices are individuals of phenomenal intellectual and physical and social diversity, not to mention diversity in talent, experience and savoir-faire; therefore, different strokes for different folks. Similar titles will make different salaries. Similar salaries will have different responsibilities. Varying talents will have different perks. People don't fit into formulas. It just doesn't work. Get over it!

I think Bill Gates is one of the good guys. But I don't know for sure. I know he recognized his own talent and his non-talents. He summoned up great courage and dropped out of Harvard. I could see dropping out of Glendale Community College, but Harvard? He knew he didn't fit the formula. Then he ends up in the New Mexico desert. His parents must have been flipping out. He took enormous risks and had some fun doing it. Was he a good guy or one of the bad guys? Or did he flip-flop over time? I don't know. Maybe Paul Allen knows. All I know is that I didn't invent Microsoft, so I don't have $60 billion!

I'm almost over it!

WHY ISN'T *GONE WITH THE WIND* GONE WITH THE WIND?

I don't care what anybody says! Clark Gable was ugly! Scarlett was just way over the top! And with the exception of the scene where Atlanta was burning, *Gone with the Wind* was not much more than a semi-historical, well-costumed soap opera.

Yeah, yeah, yeah! Get over it! Move on! You know it's true!

My brother-in-law is from Boston. He doesn't understand why we fought the Civil War. Oh sure, he gets the whole slavery thing. It's not that. He thinks that the South represents the worst of everything. He's never heard of Lewis Grizzard. He thinks the North should have let the South secede. I just laugh and tell him, "Well, so much for the theory that all those elitist Ivy League schools are bastions of liberalism! I guess you Northerners aren't as smart as you thought! Why don't you tell the North to secede now? What's the matter? Oh, you won't be able to keep your horse in Charlottesville! You'd have to give up the house at Hilton Head. No more golf at Myrtle Beach! No more trips to the Homestead! And no more South Beach! Gosh, I guess you'd be stuck with Atlantic City! Well, y'all have fun up there!

"Did I mention Krispy Kreme doughnuts? No more Krispy Kremes for you Yankees! If the North secedes, Krispy Kremes will be gone with the wind! Take that!

It's All Bullshit! (Quid De Utilitate Loquar Stercorandi?)
Cicero, *De Senectute*, Xv, 54

(What shall I say about the usefulness of spreading manure?)

Have you been in a good bookstore lately? Have you watched the cable and network talk shows? Have you paid attention around your workplace? Have you seen the plethora of magazines on the newsstand? How many issues of *Cosmopolitan, People,* and *FHM* can you read before they all just blur together in a brown mess like many different colors of paint being mixed together? How many meaningless, fruitless, waste-of-time efforts have you put in at work that came to nothing? Spreadsheets and reports and manuals that no one reads—they are endless.

How can there be this much bullshit out there?

How many things do you participate in each day that you really care about? How many things really add joy to your life? After all, isn't joy the real treasure to discover in life? The word joy covers everything you could want or desire and surpasses all other emotions for its completeness and fulfillment.

Bullshit is not joy. I looked up the word "joy" in an antonym dictionary and found the word "bullshit." There is no usefulness in spreading manure. There is no achievement, no success, no satisfaction, no advancement, no optimism, no glory, no spirit, no friendship or love when we spend the majority of minutes in a day dwelling on bullshit.

When stopping at the dry cleaners on the way home from work brings you more satisfaction in the completion of this errand than your entire day at work, there is something wrong with what you and your colleagues are doing!

The Justice Of Justification

I was busy justifying my existence the other day, when I realized that everything requires justification, which is when I realized the great injustice of justification. Without justification there would be no appreciation, no enjoyment. There would be no demonstration or proof of good reason. There would be no freedom from guilt.

Every thought and movement, chore and activity requires justification. Of the thousands of justifications we do each day, nearly all of them are conscious, with the exception of breathing and blinking or some other sort of involuntary movement.

Well-founded justification usually absolves or validates one's thought or actions as fair and honorable. Poorly-founded justification usually loudly proclaims stupidity, guilt, selfishness and vanity. This is all pretty obvious. But justification doesn't necessarily result in justice. Justification is only an action. Justice has to do with honor, fairness, equity, merit, honesty and integrity. Justification's only component is rationalization, whether true or not, fair or not.

This is why there is only occasionally justice. Those who believe that justice will somehow be done are misguided. Justification ends up diluting and then ruining the pursuit of justice. And, of course, justice for one is injustice for another, further disillusioning one into even more acts of justifying.

After asking my wife the other day why she had to go out to buy yet another Prada purse and then listening to her response, I read this to my wife. She responded, "Oh! Just shut up!"

In my opinion, that justification didn't do her justice!

THERE IS NO JUSTICE; THERE IS ONLY THE LAW!

Just ask O.J. There is no justice; there is only the law! His lawyers taught him that. The law will set you free! His lawyers knew that from countless other cases they had tried. Anyone associated with the legal profession knows these little clichés. It's just that most people who go to court forget them in what they think is the pursuit of justice. It's not about justice. It's about following the law. Precedent, procedure and the word "reasonable" are the defining guidelines for almost everything legal.

If you go to court, don't expect justice. It's too hard to define for all parties. The laws are the just or unjust guidelines relied upon for the justification of the outcome in defense of one's interest. I guess it makes everybody feel better that there is a system establishing rule.

Can't you just hear Johnnie Cochran?

"I don't care what you saw!
All that matters is the law!

Truth is easily defied!
All you have to do is justify!"

I Was Misinformed!

I'm misinformed about almost everything. When I was a kid I used to think a little "dab will do ya" was one word! You know, a little "dabeldoya." Humphrey Bogart must have said, "I was misinformed," about three or four times in *Casablanca*. I think being misinformed is not about bad information. It's about hearing things incorrectly. Like my sister: when we were growing up in the sixties, she thought the song *I'm Your Venus* was "I'm your penis"! I don't think she was the first to think that. The 60's version of the song really sounds like that. Even today, I don't think there is agreement even by music industry people on all the words to *Louie, Louie*. My son watched *Top Gun* over and over when he was little, about three years old. He learned how to advance the video so he could just watch the flying scenes, then he would jump up and say, "Son of a bit! Break right!" We would laugh hysterically. He didn't know it was "bitch," not "bit," so we understood when his preschool teacher called to say, "Your son is using profanity on the playground!" She was in fact not hearing exactly what he was saying. She was hearing what she thought he was saying.

I can't possibly recall all the things I've heard and then repeated incorrectly over the years. Most of my misinterpretations involve the lyrics to rock music. That's why I really appreciate artists that put the words inside the jackets. No doubt over the years a lot of people have had a good laugh at my expense! But every now and then it happens in normal conversation. It's kind of like acoustic Freudian slips. It's what your brain wants to hear.

Something like this happens in spelling as well. Jay Leno's "Headlines" are great examples. But my personal favorite is when I wrote my girlfriend and addressed her as, "Dear Sweat Pea"! She confronted me with this misspelling and all I could say was, "Apparently I was misinformed!"

HEAVEN

I'VE ONLY SAVED ONE PERSON'S LIFE, BUT HE'S DONE WELL EVER SINCE!

Ronald Reagan is reported to have saved seventy-two people from drowning when he was a young lifeguard. I wonder what became of those rescued people?

I haven't saved seventy-two people. I did save one person, however.

There is no reason to recount the entire episode. Let's just say I pulled a friend out of the way of a speeding streetcar at the very last second. He was standing right on the tracks. You get the idea.

What is really cool, though, is that the person I saved, who was only twenty at the time, went on to do well ever since. We stayed in touch over the years. He got a college degree from Notre Dame. He got a master's degree from Harvard. He became an architect. He works for one of the premier firms in the country. He contributes his designs to the built environment. He takes care of his parents. He contributes to charitable causes. He is spiritually enriched. He is dedicated to his friends, his teachers and his mentors. He has a great yet modest humor. He is not driven by ego or politics or his station in life. He doesn't care that at fifty he is sitting in a cubicle and not a private corner office. He has traveled extensively. He is modest about his spending, yet generous with his time and good nature. He is a teacher and he is a friend to many in the most profound sense.

Maybe the life that is saved is inconsequential in the scheme of things, but I doubt it. Only a life unlived is inconsequential. I realized this little piece of knowledge is the return gift to the lifesaver. I imagine Ronald Reagan received this gift seventy-two times. I received it just once and gratefully so. Just ask my friend. He's done well ever since!

WHO WERE THOSE DEAD GUYS?

Did you ever watch one of those movies like *Braveheart* or *Gladiator*? I like some of the old movies like *Ben-Hur* or *Spartacus*. I always wonder: who were the real guys that got killed in those brutal hand-to-hand battles? What happened to those guys? What were their lives like? We only get attached to the main characters in a movie, but what about all those extras making up the battalions that march on Sparta or Rome or wherever? Obviously, these stories are reasonably true. So in the real battles, who were those guys that got hacked in the stomach or the neck with that big blade thing? What a miserable death. Those dead guys were somebody's sons too. Who went around and picked them up off the battlefield? Did they just rot there or did they get buried in a mass gave dug by the winners? Who was left alive to march a thousand miles back to wherever to inform the village that all the men were dead? Who told their parents or wives or children they were dead? I guess they just never came home and their relatives were left to wonder, "What ever happened to Bob?" Well, ok, maybe not "Bob" but Alexander or Augustus or Moronicus or Stupidicus or some such name. "Yeah, remember, Moronicus, left here about three years ago with his sword and his shield. Haven't seen him since! Well, if he doesn't come home in another two years, I got dibs on his hut! Hey, anyone seen Ignoramus in the past year?"

One has to wonder if the world would be any different today had just one of those battles not taken place. Would there have been a great philosopher, inventor, or ruler among those anonymous soldiers that did not come home? And would the world today be more enlightened because of his survival? Would civilization have progressed further or faster? Who knows?

But maybe we have progressed. Today they know who you are on the battlefield and they come to your family's home thousands of miles away. In a soldier's garb they knock on the door and inform your family that you were among the dead.

Small progression.

Thelma & Mel

One night at dinner in the Century Plaza Hotel in Los Angeles, I mentioned the movie *Thelma & Louise* to my friend Mel. Mel was obsessed with the movie. I like the movie too, but not that much. Anyway, as the evening wore on, we got into a discussion about the last scene of the movie. My friend argued with passion that Thelma and Louise did the right thing by driving off the cliff. I was vehement that they should have stopped and hired a famous attorney and they would have easily gotten off and could go back to line dancing! Anyway, this argument got serious. Mel was raising his voice and admonishing men for existing. I was citing such profound clichés as, "Live to fight another day!" Mel continued to praise the writers for the dramatic ending and offered that the only way out was over the cliff because it would make such a powerful statement! Somehow, he managed to name God and Hitler in the same sentence in some kind of twisted justification for suicide! By now others in the restaurant were looking our way. The empty cognac glasses were collecting! I compared Thelma and Louise to the two killers in *In Cold Blood*. Alone they were insignificant. Together they were a new personality and a deadly one. I asked Mel if he could drive off the cliff. This impassioned him further. Our voices were now overlapping one another. Everyone in the restaurant was looking our way. Then the maitre d' came over and told us we would have to leave if we continued disturbing the other guests.

Then, like typical men, we continued arguing in very loud whispers! Finally, I said, "Look, we're never going to agree on this. So you get in the car and drive over the cliff with Susan Sarandon and I'll take Geena Davis and we'll go line dancing! (After she posts bail!)"

Mel paid for the dinner and drinks. This gesture helped me get over our differences on this issue. But to this day, whenever *Thelma & Louise* comes on cable, I picture Susan Sarandon and my drunk, fat, white, bespectacled, cross-eyed, bald friend Mel going over the cliff holding hands with her! *Thelma & Mel*! I wonder what his last thoughts would be? Probably something like, "Damn, I was wrong!"

Just Spread My Ashes In The End Zone Next To The Student Section!

Alas, all glory is fleeting! All victories and defeats fade from memory. But the feeling doesn't! Most of us don't play the game. We just watch as fans and take on the bias that accompanies our institution, our city, our country or a friend or family member who is participating.

Do you remember the feeling of being with your friends in the student section when your team wins the big game? Maybe your team won in the last minute or maybe they lost but all outside responsibilities were truly vanquished from your mind, even for just a few moments, but sometimes for the entire weekend. It's such a genuinely good, truly human feeling, particularly when your team wins.

It's a feeling over which you have no control. You are not playing the game. You have no responsibility for the outcome and no glory either. You just have that sense of relief, of joy. A shared experience with fifty to ninety thousand people is a good one.

You don't have to like football. Maybe you like soccer or tennis or golf. Maybe you like gymnastics or baseball or rowing. In every sport there are indescribable moments that make your spectatorship moments to remember. You can't escape the feeling of sharing a suspenseful moment when you care about the outcome. To know that others feel the exact same way you do right at that moment is powerful and enriching.

Think of the great places and spaces that are immortalized in sports, like Centre Court at Wimbledon, the 18th green at Augusta, Fenway Park, Madison Square Garden, the LA Coliseum. But what is important to you? Maybe it's your high school track or your college soccer field. Humble though they may be, these are the places where you felt that special feeling of sharing the moment with your friends, the momentary freedom from all responsibility and the joy of victory.

So have at least some of your ashes deposited in that winning spot so that future generations might cheer along with you. And feel secure in knowing that when you're gone your spirit will be there with the team, figuratively and literally.

And watch out for the Zamboni!

To Die In An Attempt To Swim The Hellespont!

"The spirit of everlasting rebellion and Irish wit. If there is a project afloat, be it ever so hazardous, you will always find him at the bottom of it—an instigator of all campaigns that border on the pale. Mention anything under the sun from whippet races in Tia Juana to the outcome of the next election, and he is there with an almost flawless solution, because intelligence happens to be one of his many attributes. Add to this a boundless supply of energy, a wild Celtic temperament that was nurtured and thrived among the progressive atmosphere of the Far West, and you have possibly the most romantic figure portrayed for you.

"Being an inherent daredevil with the prowess of a Napoleon, he causes many to forsake Dame Reason to pursue some fleeting will-o-the-wisp, but usually his foresight and judgment are sufficient to turn defeat into glorious victory in every endeavor. In the near future he expects to follow the lure of the great outside, and someday, perhaps, be presented to the Court of Saint James, or to die in an attempt to swim the Hellespont."

Yearbook biography of Henry Bell Twohy, Class of 1929
United States Naval Academy

The Lucky Bag 1929, Charles Weakley, Biography Editor.

Who was Henry Bell Twohy? Long ago he was just a young man with the attributes noted so eloquently above. But read closely. Doesn't that description depict the vision of glory you sought in your youth? Those words are likely to contain the nobility of what you thought you might accomplish someday. They describe all the possibility and energy of youth and embody what you aspired to be, even if just in your fleeting thoughts. These are words that reference friendships, mischief and chivalry and the making of memories to be retold in old age. But most of all they impart an intelligent foresight of noble accomplishment as one's destiny. If only we could each have our destiny prescribed in something as routine as a yearbook.

Henry Bell Twohy was not presented to the Court of Saint James nor did he attempt to swim the Hellespont. He was killed while piloting a plane in a routine training accident not long after graduating from the Naval Academy. His path to noble accomplishment was so randomly foreshortened. To wit, each of our paths to noble accomplishment is just as random. Alas, while incomplete, for Henry Bell Twohy, his was prescribed. We should all be so fortunate.

I've Never Won A Trophy!

Everyone has a trophy. My kids get trophies in sports just for showing up! They start getting them around three years old in those group play classes. Then it's T-ball, soccer and little league. The whole team gets a trophy! The kid who was sick and never showed up until the awards ceremony gets a trophy! There are so many trophies given out in high school and college that it seems the whole school gets them. Then adults start getting trophies. You know, things like "World's Greatest Dad," "World's Greatest Boss," "World's Greatest Secretary," "Salesman of the Year," "Employee of the Month," "Company XYZ Softball Team," "Bass Fishing Champion," "Fundraising Champion," "ABC Bowling League, 8th Place," "World's Greatest Grandma." You get the idea.

I've never won a trophy or even received a trophy for showing up. I guess I fell through the cracks, a lost soul with no trophies to certify my existence. There are no trophies in my den. There are no trophies on my mantel. I don't even have a cheap plastic trophy stored in a box in the garage.

I don't need a trophy. I don't want a trophy. Why? Because apparently I have not deserved one. Nor was I lucky enough to show up at the right time. So, what is my trophy destiny?

I know I will receive the ultimate trophy one day. I'll be receiving a very large trophy. Yep, my trophy will be so big and heavy I

Williston Lamar

won't be able to lift it! It will have my name on it and even my birthday. I'll have it placed on a small strip of green grass above my head and I'll rest in peace knowing that I finally have a trophy!

Penny's In Heaven

I knew Penny for a year. She was my true friend. She was remarkable. In that time she touched me with a kind of love, compassion, tenderness and joy that I had not experienced in my life. She exasperated me with her passion for raising hell and getting into serious trouble. She knew how to get me mad and yet she was so forgivable. She played me like a fiddle.

Penny was just thirteen years old when I met her. Her energy and enthusiasm disguised her illness and disabilities. I adopted Penny. I saved her from a group home and a prior abusive family.

Yep, I only knew Penny for a year. I chose to adopt her knowing her condition. Knowing the operations she needed would be expensive and knowing that despite the operations the end of her life was near.

Penny was a nut case. She was incorrigible. She was a ball of fire and soft as a pillow all within five minutes. Penny was a hellion and an angel in one body. She helped me understand that friendship is a journey, not a given, and that parenting has more meanings than we can count. She gave me strength. She made me laugh out loud when no one was around and she made me act ridiculously silly. Despite her physical and mental shortcomings she was unconditional and instantaneous in her love for me and in the enthusiasm she had for being alive. I guess it could be called unconditional enthusiasm.

Penny had suffered for most of her life. A genetic eye condition prevented her from seeing very well. An eating disorder made her skinny as a rail. She never complained. She overcame her disabilities. Her hair was always brittle and sparse. Sometimes chunks of her hair would fall out. She didn't mind. She never really seemed to care what she looked like. I would try and help her look nice, but I could tell it was not a priority for her. She suffered from so many things, including extreme joint deterioration. She could not bend her knees, forcing her to walk funny. Even with her discomfort she loved to play hide and seek or keep away. Sometimes people made fun of her awkwardness. But she didn't care. Nothing was awkward to Penny. She was free of all prejudice.

Penny loved to sing. It would seem like she could sing forever. She obviously took great joy in her singing. She didn't know any lyrics but she didn't care. The pleasure of making noise for everyone was enough.

One of her favorite things to do was to answer the doorbell. She wanted to be the first one to the door to see who was there. If she didn't like the person at the door she would huff and look to me to handle the situation. If she knew and liked the person she would visibly shake with pleasure and usually sing a little.

She never took her time getting into bed and would therefore end up just sprawled out in awkward positions; sometimes her head would be off the bed, her legs turned sideways. When she was tired, she was just plain tired and nothing else mattered. I would have to come by, adjust her body and tuck her in.

When we went to the store or around town you would think we were going to the beach. Any occasion to get out of the house was a joyous occasion. Sometimes she would close her eyes and just take in the air or other times she would examine the people in the car next to us.

Penny really liked to watch TV with me. She was particularly fond of shows with animals that make funny noises, and basketball. She didn't understand the game but always watched with great intensity. She loved popcorn. I think it may have been her favorite food. Her sport was swimming. She loved the backyard pool. The water temperature never bothered her. The water would be intolerable for me but for Penny it was always perfect. She would often do a lap or two in the pool and then sunbathe on the steps of the pool to dry off. Then she would get up and walk over to the chaise lounge and lay out like a bikini model.

I used to watch from a distance as she would sit in the backyard, quietly watching any and all activity. She would sun herself as if she needed a tan to help her scrappy appearance.

Penny liked to take the last sip out of my wine glass. She had no particular preference for red or white. She just liked to know that we were sharing something. It made her happy.

Penny was so loving and so happy that I was envious of her zest for life. I was envious of her joy. I didn't have any of her problems, yet the events of my life were conditional. The burden of this was not lost on me, nor was the freedom I saw in her. She was an education for me. I just wanted to squeeze her with big hugs hoping her unconditional enthusiasm would rub off.

I don't know how she got the name Penny. She didn't have copper-colored hair or freckles. I guess it was a family thing or a sibling thing. But it was a good name and seemed to fit her personality. Despite her visible and not-so-visible shortcomings, I would have to say that she was truly a shiny "Penny."

The adoption was so clear to me and it was a simple thing. No sacrifice at all. Over the year, being near her and with her had cured me of so many things that I didn't even realize she was adopting me. Yep, I was the one being adopted. Her very existence helped me define joy in my life and overcome a cloud of unhappiness.

I rescued Penny and she rescued me right back.

Near the end, cancer had taken over. Her spleen was leaking fluid into her body cavity. Her legs stopped working. She refused nourishment. I carried Penny into the hospital for what she and I knew would be the end.

The doctors looked at charts and x-rays and spoke to me about her condition. I knelt on the floor so my head would be next to hers at bed level. I spent a long time with her. She could no longer speak or sing. Her breathing was heavy and forced. Her body was limp. Her eyes were open and staring into mine.

Then in a heavenly gesture her eyebrows raised to look at me once more. This was the moment.

She put her paw on my shoulder and she was gone.

Penny's in heaven.

Arlington

Salute the life, peril has passed
Uniformly at ease in solemn rows
A life, history now has grasped
Leaves fall upon the hollows

Shadowy green, white thy stone
Life's battle lost, others won
For those interred, war is gone
All are gathered in Arlington

Iron gates, who goes there
Rifle through the names engraved
Seek no peace, peace is here
Halt the march, free those saved

Among the terrible swift swords
Stripes of honor address the unknown
The truce is with one's chosen Lord
Across the hill in Arlington

Brass tradition calls upon the bugle
Voice of order, flag to fold
Three shots rifle fired, oh so fragile
Honor the service, in death, truth is told

Williston Lamar

Cowardice, bravery, honor, disgrace
Defeat, victory, five stars, one chevron
My insignia and name will not suffice
I can not take my place in Arlington

The nation's corps has been depleted
A life is gone, all judgment mum
New sentinels for those defeated
White gloves, shoes shined, muffled drum

Hymns of honor so attest the songs
Here are life's paths to march among
Oh, how I miss my Dad and Mom
Please take me to Arlington

Based on an idea by Margaret Swann, U.S. Navy Nurse Corps, Pearl Harbor, December 7, 1941

Inside The Coffin! What Are You Going To Take With You?

For all of recorded time humans have tried to enter the afterlife with a few belongings they might need. From the pharaohs to the peasants, from the Popes to the penitent, from the polished to the poor, everyone wants to leave with something. Even if you choose cremation, I don't think they throw you in there naked! You could at least wear Armani!

So what are you going to take with you? For discussion purposes, let's say you have decided on the traditional coffin thing. Let's also say you can take three things.

My mother wants a handle she can hold on to and a brake pedal near her right foot, both for the journey, which will make her nervous. She would also like a radio so she can listen to the news on the all-news station.

I was thinking I'd like a picture of all the members of my family. This will only count as one thing. Then I'd like a can of Coke. I might need a little caffeine. Finally, I'd put in an autographed copy of this book. Since it's not likely to be a bestseller, the guy who digs me up might like to know what I was thinking at the time.

What would you take? Your class ring? Your teddy bear? Your favorite CD? A good book? Your best report card? Your favorite t-shirt? Your Cuisinart? The St. Christopher medal your mother gave you? Your Black & Decker cordless toolset, in case you want to get out? A lucky penny? You gotta admit it's something to think about and it's something to tell your relatives about before it's too late. You sure don't want them deciding what goes in the coffin! Your brother-in-law would probably toss in a whoopee cushion!

So given this life-and-death dilemma, I took a very unscientific survey of a few people I know to see what they're taking on the last trip. Maybe you can get some ideas from this list. Think about it. If it was good for popes and pharaohs and peasants it's probably good for you.

- Wallet with cash and charge cards
- Favorite pair of sweats
- Memorabilia from favorite team
- Love letter from husband/wife
- Religious item (e.g. rosary, Bible, statue)
- Bottle of a favorite beer
- Porn video
- Aspirin
- Headphones
- Photo of the Golden Gate Bridge
- Copy of *The Catcher in the Rye*
- Photo with famous person
- Roll of toilet paper
- Cellular phone
- iPod
- A great bottle of Shiraz
- Red licorice
- Sunscreen
- Dried flowers from wedding bouquet
- ThighMaster
- Pager
- Ticket to Maui

Five Potatoes

- Laptop
- Voodoo doll of ex-boss and ex-wife
- Passport
- Inflatable sex doll
- Background check to show St. Peter
- Calendar
- Photo of favorite pet
- Mom's recipe book
- Nail clippers
- Best college essay
- *The Best of Eddie Murphy on Saturday Night Live* tape
- Putter
- Traveler's checks
- Favorite pair of Nikes
- Dustbuster
- Remote control
- Wrinkle cream and moisturizer
- Chocolate
- Desk lamp
- Reading glasses
- Bottle of Jack Daniels
- Pack of Camels
- *Charlie's Angels* poster
- Childhood blanket
- *Five Potatoes*
- Last three tax returns
- Death certificate
- Elvis or Sinatra version of "My Way"

Thanks

Many thanks to the following great people (alive or dead):

Agnes Edgerton, Al Nardi, Al Torgerson, Al Vasquez, Alan Turner, Alan Ward, Andy Mandell, Ann Moss, Ann Senechal (Editor of *Five Potatoes*), Anne Sweeney, Ashley Moss, Ashley Smith, Barbara Borders, Bill Hoy, Bill Marriott, Brittany Lynn Dye, Chris Paige, Christine Pureka, Clarence Moss, Conrad Hilton III, David Harder, David Smith, Dean Duplantier, Dick Senechal, Enrico Plati, Frances Ramsey, Frank Antonides, Frank Montana, Frank Rounds, Gary Beggs, George Hincapie, Helen Voss, Henry Bell Twohy, Jack Graves, Jack Synder, Jeff Morosky, Jerry Raeder, Jess Kuncar, Jim Cramer, Jim Fox, Joanna Doyle, Joe Kilanowski, Joe Trovato, Josefina Leon, John Dengler, John Harder, John Nehmer, John Ziegler, Judy Pureka, Kelsey Grammer, Ken Daniel, Ken Wright, Lance Armstrong, Larry Bullis, Lillian Golovin, Lincoln Corbin, Linda Herman, Lydia Thorndike, M. William Voss, Major Bowington, Margaret Dye, Margaret Truitt, Marilyn Smith, Mark Jachec, Mark Schirmer, Mark Sinsky, Mark Zwagerman, Mel Wright, Melissa Counts, Mia Ferrara, Michael Armm, Michael Pureka, Michael Stanton, Mike Godby (graphic designer of Five Potatoes), Odis Corbin, Olivia Rosas, Oscar Liedenfrost, Pam Turner, Pam Schirmer, Pat Camuso, Paul Gaiser, Paul Lamar Chester, Paul Pureka, Penny Dye, Peter Studner, Phil Kiepper, Rahsaan Bahati, Rich Bullene, Rick Ryniak, Robert Barringer, Robert Leader, Sally Voss, Scott Simpson, Skip Niemiec, Stephen Dye, Steve Bradley, Steve Voss, Sudhakar T'Desai, Susan Kary, Susan Voss, Tami Corbin, The Beatles, Thelma Corbin, Trey Dye, Vale Truitt, Vicky Hernandez, Victor Exner, Walt Disney, Walter Wrobleski, Williston Dye, Sr.,

BVG